ALSO BY CHARLIE N. HOLMBERG

The Paper Magician

The Glass Magician

The Master Magician

FOLLOWED by FROST

CHARLIE N. HOLMBERG

47NORTH

Published by 47North, Seattle

www.apub.com

Amazon, the Amazon logo, and 47North are trademarks of Amazon.com, Inc., or its affiliates.

ISBN-13: 9781503946323
ISBN-10: 1503946320

Cover design by Ray Lundgren

Printed in the United States of America

To my daughter, Shiloh,
who warms my heart with her every smile.

PROLOGUE

I have known cold.

I have known the cold that freezes to the bones, to the spirit itself. The cold that stills the heart and crystallizes the blood. The kind of cold that even fire fears, that can turn a woman to glass.

I have seen Death.

The cold lured him to me. I saw him near my home, his dark hair rippling over one shoulder like thick forest smoke as he stooped over the bed of the quarryman's only son. I saw his amber eyes as he tilted the rim of his wide-brimmed hat to greet me. I saw him kneel in the snow before me with his arms wide and heard him whisper, "Come with me."

I have known cold, the chills with which even the deepest winters cannot compare. I have lived it, breathed it, and lost by it. I have known cold, for it dwelled in the deepest hollows of my soul.

And the day I broke Mordan's heart, it devoured me.

CHAPTER 1

The first bite of honey taffy melted in my mouth. I savored its sweetness, spiced lightly with cinnamon imported from the Southlands beyond Zareed—strange, savage lands with strange people and stranger customs, but nothing in the Northlands could compare to their intense, exotic spices. Merchants only delivered the candies in the early spring, and their first shipment had arrived that morning. Together, Ashlen and I had bought nearly half a case. My satchel bulged with paper-wrapped taffies to the point where I had to switch the strap from shoulder to shoulder every quarter mile, the bag weighed on me so.

"My pa will be so angry if he finds out!" Ashlen laughed, covering her mouth to hide half-chewed taffy. Her plain, mouse-brown hair bobbed about her shoulders as she spoke. "I'm supposed to be saving for that writing desk."

"This is a once-, maybe twice-a-year opportunity," I insisted, resting my hand on the satchel. "We could hardly let it pass us by." I didn't tell her that I had more than enough in my allowance to cover her share. If Ashlen needed a writing desk, her father could put in more hours at the mill.

Ashlen unwrapped another candy. "I could die eating these."

I poked her in the stomach. "And you would die fat, too!"

We laughed, and I hooked my arm through hers as we followed the dirt path ahead of us. It wound from the mercantile on the west edge of Euwan, past the mill and my father's turnery, clear to Heaven's Tear—the great crystal lake that hugged the town's east side, and the only thing that put us on Iyoden's map.

My world was so small then. Euwan was an ordinary town full of ordinary people, and I believed myself an oyster pearl among them. But I was about to spark a chain of events that would shatter the perfectly ordinary shell I lived in—events that would undoubtedly change my life, in its entirety, forever.

My father's turnery came into view, the tar between its shingles glimmering in the afternoon sun. At two stories, it was the second largest building in Euwan, though still the most impressive, in my opinion. The sounds of saws and sandpaper echoed from beyond its door, left open to encourage a breeze. My father had been a wainwright for some twenty years, and his wagons were the sturdiest and most reliable that could be found anywhere within two days' distance, and likely even farther. For a moment I considered saying hello, but spying my father's single employee outside, I instantly thought better of it.

Mordan was bent over a barrel of water, washing sawdust from his face and hands. Unlike most, Mordan hadn't been raised in Euwan—he had merely walked in during fall harvest, on foot, carrying a filthy cloth bag of his immediate necessities. His sudden appearance had been the talk of the town for weeks, making him something of an outcast. Much to my dismay, my father was a charitable sort, and he hadn't hesitated to hire the newcomer. The community mostly accepted him after that.

Mordan, twenty-five years in age, was a slender man, though broad in the shoulders, with sandy hair that wavered somewhere between chestnut and wheat. He had a narrow, almost feminine face, with a long nose and pale blue eyes. I didn't notice much about him beyond that. At that time I only noticed that he existed and that he was a problem. I quickly stepped to Ashlen's other side, using her body as a shield.

"What?" she asked.

"Shh! Talk to me," I said, quickening my pace. I kept my head down, letting my blond hair act as a curtain between myself and the turnery. It was natural for a man to take notice of his employer's family, perhaps, but Mordan's interests toward me had grown more ardent over the last year, to the point where I could hardly stand on the same side of town as him without some attempt at conversation on his part. Even my blatant regard for other boys in his presence—whether real or feigned—hadn't discouraged him.

I thought I had escaped unseen when he called out my name, his chin still dripping with water: "Smitha!"

My stomach soured. I pretended not to hear and jerked Ashlen forward when she started to turn her head, but Mordan persisted in his calls. Begrudgingly I slowed my walk and glanced back at him, but I didn't offer a smile.

He wiped himself with a towel, which he tucked into the back pocket of his slacks, and jogged toward us.

"I'm surprised to see you out so late," he said, nodding to Ashlen. "I thought school ended at the fifteenth hour."

"Yes, but lessons cease at age sixteen," I said. Only a dunce wouldn't know that. "I finished last year. I only go now to pursue my personal endeavors and to tutor Ashlen." My personal endeavors included theatre and the study of language, the latter of which I found fascinating, especially older tongues. I planned to use my knowledge to become a playwright, translating ancient tales and peculiar Southlander fables into performances that would charm the most elite of audiences. My tutoring of Ashlen was more a chance for chatter and games than actual studying, but so long as she pulled passing grades, none would be the wiser.

"Of course." Mordan nodded with a smile. "You're at that age now."

There was a glint in his eye that made me recoil. *That* age? I struggled to mask my reaction. Surely he didn't mean engagement. As far as Mordan was concerned, I would never be *that* age.

Glancing nervously to Ashlen, Mordan continued, "I've been meaning to talk—"

"In fact," I blurted out, "Ashlen is being tested on geography tomorrow morning, and I promised I'd help her study before dinner. Her family eats especially early, so if you'll excuse us . . ."

Ashlen had a dumbfounded look on her face, but I tugged her along before she could question me in front of him. "Good evening to you," I called. Mordan quickly returned the sentiment, and he may have even waved, but I didn't look back over my shoulder until the next bend in the road hid the turnery from sight.

"You're loony!" Ashlen exclaimed, pulling her arm free from mine. A grin spread on her face before her mouth formed a large O. "Goodness, Smitha, don't tell me Mordan is *still* at it."

"Absurd, isn't it?" I rolled my eyes and switched my candy-laden bag to my other shoulder. "He has to be the most stubborn man I've ever met."

"Maybe you should give him a chance, if he's trying so hard."

"Absolutely not. He's too ridiculous."

She merely shrugged. "People can change for those they care about."

"Ha!" I snorted. "People don't change; they are what they are. Did you know he actually pressed the first blooms of spring and left them on my doorstep? He would have given them to me in person, but I didn't answer the door when I saw it was him. No one else was home."

"How do you know they were the first blooms?"

"Because he *told* me. In a *poem*. And Ashlen, the man is as slow as he looks. It was the most wretched thing I've ever read in my life, and that includes Mrs. Thornes's lecture notes on the water cycle!"

"Oh, Smitha," she said, touching her lips. "How harsh. He seems nice enough."

"But not so nice to *look* at," I quipped before glancing at the sun. "I'd best head home before Mother throws a fit. I'll see you tomorrow. Don't eat all your candies tonight; I won't share mine!"

Ashlen stuck out her tongue at me and trotted off the road into the wild grass. Her home lay over the hill, and that was the fastest way to reach it.

She grinned back at me as she went and waved a hand, her fingers fluttering the words *Don't get fat* over her shoulder. The signs were part of the handtalk I had invented at fourteen, when I first learned of a silent language that had once been spoken in the Aluna Islands in the far north, beyond the lands where wizards were said to dwell. That would not be the last time Ashlen spoke to me in our secret signs, but it would be the last time she looked at me with any semblance of a smile.

My family lived in a modest home, though large by Euwan standards. My little sister, Marrine, and I had our own bedrooms. After bidding Ashlen farewell, I retired to my room and stashed my share of the honey taffies in the back of my bottom dresser drawer, where I hoped Marrine wouldn't find them if she came snooping, which she often did. My sister begged for punishment, and I had a variety of penalties waiting for her if she crossed me.

A small oval mirror sat atop my dresser, and I studied myself in it, appreciating the rosiness my walk had put in my cheeks. I retrieved my boar-bristle hairbrush and ran it through my waist-long hair several times from root to tip. I knew I was pretty, with a heart-shaped face free of blemishes, a small nose, and big green eyes. The doctor himself had told me they were big, and I had learned batting them just so often helped persuade the boys—and often grown men—in town to see things my way.

At seventy-six of one hundred strokes I heard my mother's voice in the hallway.

"Smitha! Could you fetch some firewood?"

I groaned in my throat. I wasn't the one who had dwindled the supply, and the last thing I wanted to do was dirty my dress gathering firewood. I cringe to remember my behavior then, but it is part of the story, and so I will tell it honestly.

Hearing Mother's steps, I set down my brush and crouched against the side of my dresser. The door opened. I held my breath. Mother sighed before closing it and retreating.

I smiled to myself and picked up my hairbrush to finish my one hundred strokes. After taking a moment to admire my reflection, I braided my hair loosely over my shoulder, savored one more honey taffy, and quietly stepped into the hall.

My mother didn't notice me until I reached our kitchen, large given that we were a family of only four. My mother, still in good years, spooned drippings over the large breasts of a pheasant in the oven. It was from her that I got my blond hair, though I hoped my hips wouldn't grow so wide. Across the room, a pot boiled on the hearth. Someone else had fetched the firewood, I noticed.

Straightening, Mother wiped her forehead and glanced at me. "I called for you."

"Oh," I said, fingering my braid, "I was at the latrine. Sorry."

Mother rolled her eyes and turned to a bowl of cornbread batter on the counter. "Well, you're here now, so would you wash and butter that pan for me?" She jerked her head toward a square pan resting beside the washbasin.

Frowning, and knowing I didn't have an excuse, I dragged my feet to the icebox for the butter.

After the cornbread baked, the pheasant browned, and I had grudgingly mashed the potatoes from the cook pot, I stepped out of the kitchen to cool off. I had not yet reached my room when I heard the front door open and my father exclaim, "Smells good! Room for one more?"

"Always." I could hear my mother's smile. "It's good to see you, Mordan. How was work?"

Cursing to myself, I hurried down the hall, almost crashing into Marrine. With her plain brown hair pulled into a messy ponytail, her narrow-set eyes, and a cleft to her chin, I was obviously the better-looking sister, so much so that a stranger would never guess that Marrine and I were related.

"Where are you going?" she asked. "Is Pa home?"

"Shh!" I hissed at her, but rather than explain, I ducked into my room and shut the door. I rushed to my window and opened the pane, wincing at how boldly it creaked. Ashlen would be more than happy to have me for dinner, and with an extra mouth in the kitchen, surely my parents wouldn't miss me.

This was not the first time Mordan had come to eat, of course, but I had a bad feeling about it. He was getting bolder in his attentions. Besides, the best way to tell a man he had less chance with you than a fair hog was to ignore him so completely that even *he* forgot he existed.

Balling my skirt between my legs, I lifted myself over the sill and dropped a few feet to the ground below. I had only made it halfway across the yard when I heard my name called out from behind me. Mordan's voice raked over my bones like the teeth of a dull plow.

He walked toward me, waving a hand. Why had he stepped outside *now*? Perhaps he needed to use the latrine, or he might have spied me in my escape. Regardless, I had been caught, and no amount of talking would see me to Ashlen's house now without sure embarrassment.

I released my hair. "Oh, Mordan, I didn't notice you."

He stopped about four paces ahead of me. "Your father graciously invited me over to dinner."

"Is it time already?"

He nodded, then suddenly became bashful, staring at the ground and slouching in the shoulders. "I've actually been meaning to talk to you, but I haven't gotten the chance."

My belly clenched. "Oh?"

"But . . ." He hesitated, scanning the yard. "Not here. And I've got a delivery in about an hour . . . Smitha, would you mind meeting me? The dock, around sunset?"

His eyes finally found mine, hopeful as a child's.

At that moment I truly appreciated my study of theatre, for I know I masked my horror perfectly. For Mordan to want to speak to me alone—and at so intimate a spot!—could only mean one thing: his interest in me had come to a head, and no amount of feigned ignorance would dissuade him.

Mordan wanted to marry me. I almost retched on his shoes at the prospect.

"All right," I lied, and a mixture of relief and warmth spread over his delicate features.

Before he could say more, I touched his arm and added, "We'd best hurry, or dinner will be served cold!"

I walked past him, but he caught up quickly, staying by my side until we sat at the table, where I had the forethought to wedge Marrine between us. I remained silent as my father told our family, in great detail, of the work he had done that day. While not one for exaggeration, my father always told every last corner of a story, explaining even mundane things so accurately that I often felt I wore his eyes. Tonight, however, halfway through his tale of broken spokes, he interrupted himself for gossip—something for which he rarely spared a moment's thought.

"Magler said there's a fire up north, near Trent," he said, carefully wiping gravy from his lips before it could drizzle into his thick, brown beard. "Already burned through two silos and a horse run."

"A fire?" asked Mother. "It's too early in the year for that. Did they have a dry winter?"

"Rumor says it was the craft."

That interested me. "Wizards? Really?"

"Chard, Smitha, I'll not take that talk in here," Mother said.

Let me take a moment to say that wizards were unseen in these parts, and supposedly rare even in the Unclaimed Lands far north, where they trained in magics beyond even my imagination, and none of them for good. A traveling bard once whispered that they have an academy there, though to this day I'm not sure where. I certainly never thought I'd one day search for it myself.

Mordan's eyes left me to meet my father's. "What's the rumor?"

"Some political war or some such, which led to two of them fighting one another. Perhaps even a chase. I have a hard time believing any man could throw fire, but that's what Magler claimed. He heard it from a foods merchant passing by this morning."

Marrine, mouth half-full of cornbread, said, "I'd like to meet a wizard."

Mordan smiled. "They can be a dangerous sort. Tales often fantasize them, for better or for worse."

"So long as they don't come down here," Mother said, roughly heaping a second helping of potatoes onto her plate, spoon clinking against the china. I hoped she wouldn't butter them. Mother gained weight in the most unsightly of places. "Mordan, how is your sister? I recall you mentioning her a little while ago."

Mordan's blue eyes glanced back to me, as they had already done several times during the meal, smiling even when his mouth was not. I did not smile back. Returning his focus to Mother, he described a sister of his who lived somewhere in the west, but I paid little attention to what he said. Instead I wolfed down my food and excused myself to my room. If either parent disapproved, they did not voice it in front of a guest.

Inside my little sanctuary, I stretched out on my bed and selected one of three books I had borrowed from Mrs. Thornes, my teacher, which she had borrowed from a scholar in a neighboring village. To me old tongues seemed like secrets—secrets very few people in the world knew, let alone knew well. The book in my hands was written in Hraric, the language of Zareed and the Southlands, where I believed the sun never set, men built their homes on heaps of golden sand, and children ran about naked to escape the heat—with their parents hardly clothed more than that. I had studied some Hraric two years earlier. I didn't consider myself fluent, but as I browsed through this particular book of plays, I could understand the main points of the stories. Southlander tales were far darker and more grotesque than the ones we studied in school, and I soon found myself so absorbed that I hardly heard the scooting of chairs in the kitchen and Mordan's good-byes as he went to complete his deliveries. I did, however, take special note of the time, and as the sun sank lower and lower in the sky, casting violet and carmine light over Euwan, I smiled smartly to myself, imagining Mordan standing alone on that dock long into the night, his only company the proposal I would never allow him to utter.

While I wish I could say otherwise, my conscience did not bother me that night, and I had no trouble sleeping. Had I known the consequence of my actions, I would never have closed my eyes. I slept late, as there were no requests upon my responsibility on sixth days. I woke to bright morning sun, dressed, and brushed one hundred strokes into my hair before deciding I ought to have a bath. Spying Marrine in the front room, I asked her to fill the tub for me.

She looked up from her sketch paper and frowned. "No!"

"Why not?"

"I don't want to carry the water."

"I'll give you a taffy. Honey taffy, with cinnamon."

She considered this for a moment but ultimately shook her head and returned to refining her mediocre talents as an artist. With a sigh I stepped outside into the warming spring air and trudged to the barn to retrieve the washbasin myself. There was an empty stall on the far end of the barn where we took our baths, which was mostly free of horse smell. Despite my best efforts, I could not convince my father to let me bathe in my room, so it was an inconvenience I had learned to endure.

I set the tub in the stall and retrieved the pail for carrying water. As I turned to exit the barn, I shrieked and dropped the bucket, my heart lodging into the base of my throat. Mordan stood in the open doorway, a vision of a ghost, his eyes trained on me. I had hoped his shame would keep him at bay for at least a month. Why couldn't he bow in his tail like any other dog and leave me be?

"Mordan!" I exclaimed, seizing the pail from the hay-littered floor. I gritted my teeth to still my face. "What are you doing here? And with me about to bathe!"

"I apologize," he said, somewhat genuinely, but there was an unusual hardness to his eyes and his voice. "I need to speak with you."

"I'm a little—"

"Please," he said, firm.

I let out a loud sigh for his benefit, letting him know my displeasure at his interruption, but I hung up the pail and followed him out into the yard. I folded my arms tightly to show my disapproval of his actions, all while hiding my surprise that he had come to see me so soon after my blatant disregard for him and his intentions. He had not been the first man I had left waiting for me—I suppose it gave me a sense of power, even amusement, to push would-be lovers about as though they were nothing more than checkers on a board. But Mordan *was* the first who had dared confront me afterward. Still, his backbone shocked me.

He didn't stop in the yard but rather led me across a back road and into the sparse willow-wacks behind my house, on the other side of which sat the Hutcheses' home. He stopped somewhere in the center, where there were enough trees that I couldn't quite see my house or the Hutcheses'.

He eyed me sternly, though a glint of hope still lingered in his gaze.

"I waited for you at the dock until midnight, Smitha," he said. "What happened?"

I kept my arms firmly folded. I preferred subtlety when breaking people, but if this was what it took to sever whatever obligation Mordan thought I had to him, then so be it. "Nothing happened," I said. "I didn't want to go."

He jerked back, a wounded animal, but then his expression darkened. "Then why agree? I don't understand. I had—"

"You're dense as unbaked bread, Mordan!" I exclaimed, flinging my hands into the air. "Do you think me stupid enough not to read your intentions? Not to notice that pathetic way you look at me when you think my back is turned?"

His eyes widened, and his face flushed, though from anger or embarrassment, I couldn't be sure.

"I don't know if my father has given you the wrong impression," I continued, the words spilling from my lips, "but I do not give you the slightest thought."

Mordan turned from red to white, and his eyebrows shifted in such a way that he resembled a starving hound. I should have left it at that, but my knack for the dramatic and my fury at the situation fueled me.

"Surely a toad could hold my interest longer, and be more pleasant to look at!" My cheeks burned. "We live on different levels of life, Mordan Alteraz, mine far higher than yours. The sooner you realize that, the better off you will be. I do not care one ounce for you, and I never will. *That* is why I didn't go to the dock, and why no sensible woman ever would!"

I found myself oddly breathless. Mordan had gone to stone before me, and I admit that a twinge of fear vibrated through me rather than the sense of sweet victory I had expected. Never had someone looked at me so grimly.

He laughed—no, growled. The noise that escaped his lips sounded more animal than human. He stepped forward, and I stepped back, my back hitting the trunk of a green-needle pine.

"And to think I felt anything for a woman like you," he whispered, his face contorting into a snarl. "How blind I have been. Your heart is ice."

I opened my mouth for a retort, but his hand came down hard on the trunk beside my head. I winced. He leaned in close, a malicious smile on his face.

"If only you knew who I was," he said, even quieter now. Gooseflesh rose on my arms unbidden. "Now I can see the soul that lies hidden behind your beauty. You are a horrid, selfish woman, Smitha."

I slapped him hard across his cheek, putting my full weight into the blow. It turned his head, but his hand did not budge from its place on the tree beside me.

He licked his lips, smearing blood along the corner of his mouth. Straightening, he studied me up and down, his expression covered in shadow.

"I came here to get away from it, to leave it all behind," he growled. "But I have enough left for you."

"Enough *what*?" I asked, but his other hand came down on my throat, cutting off my last word. I clung to his wrist and dug my nails into his skin, but he didn't so much as flinch. He stared hard into my eyes, and my fear ignited so abruptly I felt I would turn to ash in his hold.

"*Vladanium curso, en nadia tren'al*," he murmured. "I curse you, Smitha Ronson, to be as cold as your heart."

His fingers turned to ice around my neck, and I shivered as the cold traced its way down my skin and beneath my clothes, branching out to my arms and legs, my fingers, and the tips of each toe. It rushed up my neck and over my head. The chill gushed into my mouth and nostrils, washed down my throat, and crept into my stomach and bowels. It opened my insides like a newly sharpened knife, cutting down to my very bones.

"May winter follow you wherever you go," he said, "and with the cold, death."

Mordan did not move, but some force punched me, and my entire body caved in on itself. The breath left my lungs, and a chill colder than any I had ever experienced filled my core and shot through my veins. My arms and legs went rigid, and every hair on my body stood on end. My very heart slowed. The sun vanished from my face, hidden by a thick, white sheet of clouds. A bitter wind blew over me, tousling my hair.

Mordan released me with a sneer and vanished, the air behind him opening its mouth and swallowing him whole.

CHAPTER 2

I stood there in the willow-wacks for several moments, staring at the place where Mordan had just stood, the only sign of his presence the flattened grass where he had stood. I shivered, a trembling that engulfed my whole body. The gooseflesh that had spread across every inch of my skin could not be soothed. A frozen vise clamped down on my chest, making it hard to breathe. My eyes felt like packed snow, my tongue wet leather.

I dropped to the earth and hugged myself and rubbed my arms, but it did nothing to alleviate the chill. I blew into my hands, my knuckles stiff, but my breath was a cold wind that did nothing to warm them. I gaped at the sight of my hands—the skin had turned near white, my fingernails violet. They ached with cold. All of me ached. Frost even crusted my clothes. It was as if I had jumped into the depths of Heaven's Tear midwinter and had only just been pulled from the ice.

My mind folded over itself like bread dough with too much flour as I tried to sort my scattered thoughts. Mordan, here. His hard eyes. His hand around my neck. Cursing me. Cursing me?

"They can be a dangerous sort. Tales often fantasize them, for better or for worse."

I gasped, the air shuddering as it passed through my frozen throat. Surely Mordan didn't know the craft. Surely he couldn't—

All strength left me, and I bowled over, hunching over my knees. My ears rang.

But I had heard his words, the strange language he had uttered, a tongue even I didn't recognize. He had come to Euwan to get away . . . from what? Magic?

"I curse you, Smitha Ronson, to be as cold as your heart." Those were his words, and I had *felt* them pierce me, my body a flimsy, unraveling cloth beneath their power. I had seen him disappear before my eyes, into the very wind itself.

A faint pattern of frost ebbed out over the soil beneath my knees. I watched it wide-eyed as it crept slowly outwards, a web woven by an unseen spider. I reached a trembling hand forward and touched it, and the ice bloomed beneath my fingertips, thickening and spreading like a ripple in water.

I screamed through chattering teeth.

I yanked my hand back and forced myself to stand on shaky legs. Though spring had settled in its fullness in Euwan, tiny snowflakes began to fall from the sky. They started as dust, but when I peered up at the sky, I saw the clouds above me expand rapidly, devouring the blue. The snowflakes grew larger and larger, until I stood at the heart of a full cascade of winter. The icy crystals landed on my hair, shoulders, and hands. I waited for them to melt, but they held their frosty designs against my flesh. As though I were no more than ice itself. I jerked back from them but could not escape the swarm.

I pressed a hand to my mouth and sobbed. A single tear escaped the corner of my eye, but even that held no warmth. Trailing down my cheek, it slowed and hardened, becoming a droplet of salty ice. No. This wasn't real. None of it was. A dream. A nightmare. I had to wake up.

I ran.

Forcing my rigid legs over tree roots, I ran through the willow-wacks and into my yard, where soft snow settled lazily on rooftop and road alike. My father and mother stood on the front porch, marveling at the swift storm, pointing to the rigid line in the sky where the snow clouds met clear blue—beyond the borders of Euwan but before the ground rose to meet the mountains.

"Pa!" I shouted, running toward him. "Pa!"

He turned and saw me with startled eyes. "Smitha! What on earth happened to you?"

Mother ran out to meet me. She looked at me in blanched horror. "You look frozen half to death! What—"

She reached forward to cradle my face, but her words cut off as soon as her skin made contact with mine. Her hand snapped back on reflex, her palm covered in frost. Both of us stared at it, gaping.

Father ran out to join us. "What's going on?" he asked, taking my mother's hand. He reached for mine as well, but the moment our fingers touched, he hissed and jerked away, his fingertips frozen to the first knuckle.

I pressed both my palms to my lips and sobbed, the chilling tears flowing freely now, turning hard on my cheeks and sticking to my eye-lashes. Father sucked on his fingertips to warm them, his face flushed red.

"What happened?" he demanded, snow melting in the curls of his dark hair.

"Mordan!" I cried, shuddering, shivering. My voice came out in a cloud, too slow to dissipate. "He did this to me . . . He's one of them! A wizard!"

My father reeled back as though struck, his eyes wide and red-rimmed. Mother swayed on her feet, her slender fingers touching her parted lips.

Shaking his head, my father muttered, "They're . . . real? And . . . Mordan?"

"God save us," my mother whispered.

Two slow heartbeats, and my father flew back into the house, throwing the door open as he went. It banged loudly against the wall behind it.

My mother had paled significantly, and with stiff movements guided me into the house, careful not to touch me again. Marrine, who had been standing by the window, ogled me.

I screamed again, clawing at my hair. Why was this happening to *me*? Why not Ashlen or some other girl in the town? I glared at my scrambling family and wailed. Why not *them*?

Father returned to the front room with his shotgun.

"Chard, no!" Mother cried.

But Father said nothing, only shook his head and rushed outside, not bothering to close the door behind him.

Mother's lips pursed to a point. "Marrine, stoke the fire! Quickly!" Then, to me, "I'll make you some tea, hmm? That will warm you right up."

Even I could hear the doubt in her voice, but she darted into the kitchen to busy herself.

"You look dead," Marrine whispered, rubbing her hands together. She shivered from the cold and quickly went to the hearth to build the fire. Or, perhaps, to get away from me.

Sobbing, I ran to my room and slammed the door, the knob frosting beneath my touch. Grabbing either end of my dresser, I stared into the mirror and screamed once more, the sound ripping painfully through my frozen throat.

My skin had gone pallid, and purple rings lined my eyes. My lips had turned nearly blue, and my hair, at the roots, had changed to a grandmotherly white. My sister was right; I looked like a corpse.

Another icy tear dropped from my chin and shattered against the floorboards.

My mother boiled water over the fire and made me a large cup of tea. I grasped it and drank deep, but the tea ran cold down my throat. I swallowed only twice before it froze within its cup. I sat by the fire, closer, closer, until I dared to thrust my frigid hands into the embers. Even with my hands among the flames, I could not feel the slightest sensation of warmth; the red-hot coals hissed from the chill. When I removed my hands, my skin remained pale and stiff and as glacial as it had been before.

My mother began crying in the kitchen, as though the torment were hers and not mine. Marrine merely watched me the way one watches a circus performer, her lips parted, her gaze unblinking. I stayed by the hearth, watching the angry flames dance. This cold was potent enough to have killed the strongest of men. An hour passed, and then two. I trembled with bitterness, my heart beating slow, lethargic beats within my wintry chest. Marrine stared out the window at the swirling storm, occasionally passing a glance my way. Only when I glared and threw a coal at her did she skitter back into the kitchen.

My father returned hours later, almost blue in the lips himself, his clothes wet from the snow. "He's gone," he said between panting breaths. "Mordan is gone, his house ransacked. There's no sign of him. I have men searching, but . . ." He shook his head, eyes watery.

I stared at him, the words striking me like a hammer to a nail, each syllable piercing down to my frozen core. No Mordan. No hope of being restored.

Balling my hands into fists, I slammed them into the hearth's coals.

"I hate you!" I screamed, tears freezing in the corners of my eyes, blurring my vision. I lifted my hands and smashed them into the coals again, sending embers and charcoal flying all around me. "I hate you, Mordan! Damn you! I hate you!" Ashy smoke assaulted my face, and I coughed and gasped for air, pounding the heatless fire until the heavy soot forced me back.

All the while careful tendrils of frost grew out from my person, climbing over the floor and walls until my family's breaths hung as clouds in the air, and the blanket of snow grew thicker and thicker over the ground and rooftops outside.

⁂

Mother unpacked our winter clothes, our cloaks and coats, blankets and boots, and we dressed warmly. My own layers did nothing to keep me warm. They added only weight, and they grew stiff as soon as I put them on, the fabric freezing over my icy form. Father kept the hearth roaring to combat the cold that flowed from me, fire that consumed what little wood we had collected during the first month of spring. Arctic wind howled outside, and the snow fell unceasingly. The same men who had searched high and low for Mordan now broke out their shovels to clear roads and porches. My curse had created the heaviest snowfall in Euwan's history, and in the early months of spring, no less.

I withdrew from the fire and took to my room for the next two days, huddled and shivering on my bed, thinking of how the world—and how Mordan—had so cruelly wronged me, and wishing death would take me. I realize now how ironic such a plea was, but at that point I had truly meant it, for each moment was a misery.

The snows hardened the ground and killed the weak sprouts that had pushed through the soil—flowers and vegetables alike. Many tried to unbury their gardens and cover them, but my snow would not relent. Our own food stores had grown weak over the true winter, and we had not yet purchased or harvested enough produce to last through another. Men started to slog through the snow to my home to either complain or to brainstorm a solution to the problem. However, my home was the coldest in Euwan, so my father began to meet with them elsewhere. What they discussed, I didn't know, but I wanted to.

On the third day I left my house of my own volition, ignoring my mother's pleas for me to stay. I stepped into the storm shoeless and coatless, for the cold could not possibly affect me more than it already did. The storm seemed to follow me wherever I went. When I walked far enough, the snow lessened for a time, but as soon as I stopped, it brewed around me anew, icy winds whipping through my hair and whistling in my ears.

I walked from home to home, aching and sore, searching for my father. It wasn't until I gave up the search and walked to Ashlen's house that I found the village men. They had rendezvoused in my friend's home. I wondered if they'd kept Ashlen from seeing me or if she'd been too cowardly to brave the snow.

I stopped outside the front-room window and watched as the eight or nine men inside stood in a circle and argued. The wind and the glass hid their words from me, but I could tell they were angry, worried. My own father stared hard at the floor, his mouth twisted into a perpetual frown. It was through this window Ashlen saw me in passing. Her face, uncharacteristically gaunt, was almost unrecognizable. Then again, so was mine.

The wind blew over me. I made the signs for *What is happening?* with my hand, my frozen fingers barely nimble enough to form the words.

She signed back, *My brother is sick.*

No, the men. What is happening?

She shook her head. *He's sick from the cold.* Gesturing to the circle, she added, *Worried.*

So am I! I motioned with both hands, struggling to bend my knuckles. *Cold! Cold! Why am I not dead?*

But Ashlen only shook her head, solemn, and signed, *The Hutcheses' boy is dying.*

I threw my hands in the air and turned away from her, heading back into the storm. Even my best friend had no sympathy for me.

But as I climbed over the snowy hill toward my house, I thought of what she had said. The Hutcheses' boy, dying. That family only had one son, a six-year-old boy with big ears but a charming smile. All the children in Euwan shared a classroom, and Bennion Hutches always sat so attentively in the front row. He had once picked flowers for me, not knowing they were weeds.

I could not believe Ashlen's claim—surely my storm was no worse than a bad winter night, and no one could grow ill so quickly. I decided I needed to see Bennion for myself. I passed through my yard and cut through the snow-laden willow-wacks—several branches had fallen from the trees, unable to bear winter's weight—and over to the Hutcheses' small cottage.

I knocked on the door, the wood frosting beneath my touch.

It took a long moment before Antrid opened the door, a short, plump woman with stubby fingers. She didn't recognize me at first— I could tell from the way she squinted over her glasses, frames I had always thought too thick for her face. When she knew me, she seemed afraid, but common hospitality kept her from slamming the door shut.

"Bennion," I said, snow blowing over me. "I heard he's sick."

She nodded, shivering. "Caught in the storm . . . The cold is too much. Please . . . go home. It's too cold."

"I want to see him."

She hesitated. Antrid was a mousy woman, but she still managed to say, "I don't want your curse in this house."

I shivered and folded my arms, some small part of me still thinking the gesture would warm me. "Please," I added.

She frowned, but the moment she relaxed in consideration I shoved the door open and stepped aside, barging into her home. A fire blazed in the hearth on the far side of the front room, heating a pot of water. Lines of frost spread from my feet across the floor, but the fire drove them back. It must have been very warm inside the house, though I could feel none of it.

"Please don't hurt him!" Antrid begged. I did not see her husband, Toren, and wondered if he was with the others at Ashlen's house.

I followed Antrid down the hallway and into her bedroom, where Bennion lay in the middle of her large bed, blankets pulled up to his chin. His cheeks were flushed and his breaths strained with each small heave of his chest. Sweat beaded against his temples.

Antrid took a rag from atop his forehead and turned it over, then frowned. Ignoring me for the moment, she hurried from the room, perhaps for water.

I stared at Bennion's tiny body and listened to his labored breaths. Sick from the cold. Sick because of me, though I blamed Mordan for it. Mordan had made this child ill. Mordan had killed the crops in Euwan. Mordan had frozen me through, causing me such unrelenting pain that even sleep was nearly unachievable.

Mordan had caused this twisting guilt in my chest.

Suddenly a man stooped over Bennion. I blinked, certain it was a phantom, but he was still there, and my sluggish heartbeat quickened. The man looked ethereal at first, but he appeared more and more solid the longer I stared. And stared I did, for I had never seen this man before, and there were only two ways into the bedroom: through the door beside me or through the window, locked and curtained. That, and I had watched him materialize, a ghost turned flesh. Though I had not thought it possible, an even colder chill ran through my body.

The man was tall. *Very* tall. He had pale, white skin lined with bold, violet veins. A soft, wide-brimmed black hat rested on his head, from which fell a cascade of dark auburn hair, spilling over his shoulders like thick forest smoke. He wore fine clothing: a maroon coat, black velvet cloak, and high black boots with large gold buckles. A gold necklace hung from his neck, and a ruby the size of a duck egg shone from the amulet at its end.

My bones grew all the colder at the sight of this strange, richly dressed apparition. I wondered if I had finally lost my wits.

As if feeling my gaze, he turned his head and looked at me with bright amber eyes. My back hit the wall; I had not realized until then that I was retreating. He reached up with a veiny hand and tipped his hat to me just as Antrid shuffled through the door with a freshly moistened rag and bowl of broth.

She gave me a hard stare before sitting on the mattress beside her son, completely oblivious to the towering, shadowed man across from her. I realized she could not see him. This man was not an ordinary person, but he did not seem like one of the craft.

"His time has come," the dark figure said, and I realized he spoke Angrean, a dead language recorded in only the most scholarly works, the language that had first inspired my fascination with old tongues. I had heard it spoken only once, by a scholar passing through Euwan two summers ago, but this creature's tongue uttered it in a darkly musical way that no human could ever hope to imitate. Had my mind not been so warped with fear, I would have been shocked by my ability to understand the language's nuances. I held my middle tightly as though ready to sick up, and clenched my jaw tightly to keep my teeth from chattering.

He placed his hand on Bennion's forehead, over the new cloth Antrid had set upon it, and lifted it skyward. Ethereal smoke rose from the small boy, swirling in tan and cerulean flames. It vanished just as quickly.

The man turned from the bed and smiled at me. "Until we meet again, Smitha."

He left the same way he came—not suddenly, as Mordan had, but by slowly fading: flesh, to ghost, to gone.

I gasped, cold air flooding my lungs, for I knew then that I had seen Death himself, that he had *spoken* to me, and that he knew my name. Death, a being so reviled that few dared speak of him, even in fairy tales. A force that could only be named by the finality of his purpose. No sooner had he disappeared than Antrid wailed, a horrid sound that echoed between the wooden walls.

"No! No, Bennion!" she cried, throwing herself over the boy's body. "God in heaven, don't take him!"

I shook my head, my own cold forgotten for the moment, and darted from the bedroom and out the front door. I stumbled through the willow-wacks and collapsed outside my barn. I retched, spilling the few contents of my stomach into the snow, then retched again, droplets of acid freezing to my lips.

Had I known Death then as I do now, I would have pleaded with him over the Hutcheses' boy. Bartered with him, perhaps even attempted to reason with him. But I had not, and so he had come, taking the soul of little Bennion in his wake.

The death of the Hutcheses' only son was "the last water in the well," as Imad would later say. For the following morning, I could not convince even my own father to keep me.

CHAPTER 3

"She must go."

The words echoed between my ears. I looked away from the villagers who had gathered around the hearth in my own house and locked my cold eyes on to the window, where the gap between the curtains provided yet another reminder of my suffering. The dawn sun peered over the mountains to the east, in the one sliver of sky untouched by my snow cloud. It cast a reddish glow on the storm that ravaged Euwan, almost making the snowflakes look like raining blood. I sat on the kitchen floor, massaging frozen fingers with frozen fingers, wincing as cramps tore at my muscles. It took all of my strength not to curl in on myself and disappear into a single, frozen knot, but I would not cower before these people who believed they had the right to decide my fate. People who, I believed, would have proclaimed to love me only days earlier. Ice crystals veined the floor around me, stretching as far as the fire's heat would allow. And now these men—Toren Hutches, my neighbor and Bennion's father; Jacks Wineer, Ashlen's father; Cuper Tode, who ran the mercantile; and even *my own father* stood discussing my fate in front of me as though I were a pestilence. As though I weren't sitting right there, hearing everything from their mouths.

"It's killed my boy!" Toren shouted, tears in his blue eyes. "And look at your other child!"

My father glanced at Marrine, who lay curled in blankets by the hearth, her head resting on Mother's lap. Mother stroked her hair. Marrine had fallen sick like the others, the continuous cold too strong for her to bear. Still, her fever had broken during the night.

"She's a disease, Chard," Cuper said, not bothering to lower his voice. Wrinkles etched his forehead in tight arches, emphasizing his receding hairline, and he trembled with the chill of my aura. "You've seen how it follows her. I wouldn't wish this curse on anyone, let alone on her and your family, but we will all die in our very beds if she doesn't go. There's no hope of catching Mordan, not now. We don't even know which direction he went. And you'd be a fool to seek out another wizard's aid! You'll curse the whole town, you will."

I slammed my fist against the cupboard door beside me, sending frost cascading across it. A sharp pain ran up my arm, magnified by the cold. "This is my home!" I cried, my tears freezing on my lashes. "I have every right—"

"You lost that right when you brought the wrath of a wizard upon us," Toren interrupted.

"I'm not the one who let him stay here in the first place," I quipped.

All eyes went to my father. He had been the one to open his heart to Mordan when Mordan was only a weary traveler. But no one could blame him for it. My father hadn't known any better, and Mordan had seemed to be a perfect citizen until that day in the willow-wacks. The day he couldn't take no for an answer.

Jacks, Ashlen's father, met my eyes, and I saw some sadness in his gaze. I had spent so much time at his home over the years, I was nearly family. "Will you really stay here and watch your family die? Watch them starve away or freeze to death? What will it take, Smitha? Marrine's passing? Ashlen's?" His words were harsh, yet his tone was soft, pleading.

"That isn't fair!" I cried, panic seizing my frozen heart. Not only did I have to be cursed, but cast out as well? I'd die! "You don't even know how it feels. You don't even know! I feel dead already, so cold . . . You don't even know!"

I covered my face with my hands, tears slowly freezing against my palms. I would die next, anyway. I had seen Death, and he had known my name. A human body wasn't meant to survive such a curse. I shivered.

The men were silent for a long moment, or perhaps they spoke in whispers—I could not hear over my own sobs. Finally, though, I caught my father's words: "Give me one day. One more day, and she'll be gone."

For a moment I was truly frozen, immobile in my prison of ice. I had always expected to leave home someday, when I was wed. Not like this. Not with my own father betraying me.

I pushed myself to my feet, frost webbing about my footsteps. I stared at my father, unable to summon the words to defend myself. I looked to my mother, but she avoided my gaze. I had been cast out by my own family, my own flesh and blood. For the first time in my life I was unwanted, cast aside like sawdust.

I had nothing to say, nothing that could soothe the indignity that clung to me like candle wax. I turned from the kitchen and ran down the wintry hallway to my room, slamming the door behind me. The wood had chilled so thoroughly over the days of my cursed residency that it splintered. I didn't care. If they wanted me to leave, I *would* leave. They would have the rest of their lives to marinate in the regret of their choice.

I dropped to the floor, followed by frost, and rummaged through the boxes under my bed. I pulled out my schoolbag, threw it on the bed, and began searching through my dresser drawers for clothes. I expected a knock on my door, an apology, but it never came. No one, not even Father, sought to make amends.

Even my anger felt cold.

I cried, icy teardrops pattering unevenly on the floor as I wadded up a chemise and shoved it into the corner of my bag, the fabric already stiffening from my touch. My bag was not large, so I took my two favorite dresses and folded them tightly inside, then pulled a third over the one I wore. I packed my hairbrush, chalk for my teeth, and three of my books, one of which included the Hraric volume I had borrowed from Mrs. Thornes. She would get her spring back, but she'd never see this book again.

Crouching, I pulled out the last drawer of my dresser and grabbed my hoard of honey taffies. I took one in my hands, and my rigid fingers struggled with the wrapper. Before I had fully removed it, the taffy had turned rock hard. I let it fall from my hands. It hit the floorboards and cracked into three uneven pieces.

I trembled but not from the cold. Not entirely. My curse gripped me like a noose, expanding as far as Euwan's borders and stealing from me even the small joy I would get from something as small as a cherished candy. I realized then, staring at the broken taffy, that I was truly on my own—for if my own family could cast me out, surely no stranger would show pity on me. The very cold that had destroyed my life was my closest and only companion.

I resumed packing, moving much slower now, wanting to savor what little time I had left in my room. When I finally emerged, the men had gone. Father and Mother sat silently in the front room, and Marrine dozed by the fire. I went to the icebox to collect what food I could carry—how I would manage to find food after leaving Euwan and its surrounding villages, I did not know—and rummaged through the cupboards for extra supplies without a word. At least I would not have to worry about the food spoiling, only how I would be able to chew it.

My father came into my room as I was cramming my rations into what little space remained in my bag. He stood at the doorway. I heard his teeth chatter from being even that close to me.

"We have a day, Smitha," he said, sounding hoarse. Was it from emotion, or was he, too, catching sick? "You won't have to leave until tomorrow. We agreed on a day."

"I will not stay where I am unwanted," I said, truly feeling the role of a martyr. "I'll leave now."

I wanted him to argue with me, to insist—no, demand—that I stay until morning, to tell me I was still part of the family, no matter what had happened to me. No matter that my eyes appeared sunken and my skin sickly, no matter that my very breath froze the air around me. No matter that I could not so much as hug my family good-bye without hurting them.

But he did not. At that time, my father had resigned himself to what must be, and I did not care to see the pain that ate him up inside, a pain that surely must have surpassed my own, for his had come by choice, and with choice came guilt. My father had always been my greatest supporter—he drove me to the city for plays and tutoring in theatre despite my mother's objections to it, he thinned out his money to ensure I had all my needs and most of my wants, and he even, I'm ashamed to say, believed every false account I offered him, including those that maligned Marrine. The decision to cast me out must have hurt him more than anyone.

"We love you," he said as I fastened the buttons along the mouth of my bag. His words croaked in his throat. Ready to cry again, I bit the inside of my cheek to contain myself.

I turned to him and saw pools in his eyes, one tear escaping to be lost in the forest of his beard. I stepped toward him but stopped myself. Though I wanted to hug him badly—for his comfort and my own—I knew I could not touch him. I had seen how quickly my skin had frozen my parents' hands. The layers of his shirt would not be enough to protect him. I was angry, I was forlorn, but I did not want to hurt my family.

I did not want another Bennion on my shoulders.

I thought of Ashlen's brother. Yes, I would leave now, before I hurt anyone else.

Swallowing, my icy throat barely able to pull the spit down, I pulled my schoolbag over my shoulder, braided my hair, and left my room. I waited for my father to step aside before I walked out of the room. My mother stood from the worn sofa as I entered the front room and tried to speak to me, but sobs bouncing in her throat made her words unclear. Again I bit my cheek, hard enough to taste cold blood. I had to leave quickly, before I could think too much on the matter. For whatever reason, I was determined not to let my family see me cry.

I glanced to Marrine, who watched me with a pout. My pest of a sister had no respect for my privacy and shared none of my interests, yet she somehow tolerated me to the point of loving me, most days. Strangely enough, I would miss her most of all.

"Remember me," I said, a whisper, for my own throat had swollen with emotion. "How I was."

My mother cried, her choked breaths fogging in the cold air—*my* cold air—as I walked to the front door of the only home I had ever known. I opened it to the torrent outside, a blizzard of purest white, and heard Marrine call out my name just as I shut the door behind me. A tear formed in the corner of my eye; I whisked it away before it could freeze.

I marched into the whiteness—blinded by whiteness—and did not look back.

Even with the constant shoveling from the snow harvesters, the snow on the road reached my knees, and I trudged through it as one might wallow through mud. It clung to my skin, though its touch was no colder. Still, it sucked me down and slowed my progress. I was panting before I even reached the turnery, but the exertion brought no flush to my face, no sweat to my body. My heart, at least, beat a little quicker, though it still felt like a cold and leaden weight within my chest.

I passed the mercantile and a few more homes, shutters closed and chimneys smoking, before the road stretched into the forests. My feet already ached, but I pushed forward, this time not wanting anyone to find me or chase after me. I gripped my skirt in hard fists and marched away from my home, the shield of opaque clouds following. I did not know where I would go, only that my route needed to be away. Away from Euwan.

The snowfall began to lighten one mile outside of Euwan and stopped completely after another. The storm seemed content to rest as it floated over me, tracing my path with a strange exactness, always keeping me at the center of its shadow. As the forest thinned and the ground sloped, I looked back at Euwan, mostly hidden beneath its layers of snow, and saw the sun shining on it so brightly it hurt my eyes. I determined that the storm Mordan had bestowed upon me reached about a mile beyond me in any given direction. The snow would stay off my hometown if I stayed where I was, but surely the cold winds would still haunt it in the summer, and I was unwanted besides, so I kept moving, my frozen feet throbbing with every step.

I occupied my thoughts with Mordan as I plodded onward, trying to distract myself from my walk and from the cold by thinking of what I would do to him should we ever meet again. I imagined my hands around *his* neck, squeezing until he couldn't breathe, the bitterness of my touch freezing the blood in his veins. How ironic it would be for him to die by the very thing he had created. It reminded me of a Hraric play.

I went over what I would say to him until I had a full speech memorized, and I muttered it again and again as I passed over a stream too quickly for the water to freeze. Each time I added to it—another insult, another observation, another plea. I recited it so many times that, to this day, I still remember every word.

I don't know how far I had gone by the time the sun began to set, sinking into the distant horizon where my winter did not reach. Fifteen miles, at least. I realized that the land around me was completely unfamiliar. I could no longer be sure in which direction Euwan lay.

Shivering, I sat amidst the roots of an old oak tree and removed my bag from my aching shoulder. I rubbed the muscles at the base of my neck, but it did little good. My schoolbag retained the shape of my shoulders, the fabric having frozen in place. My stomach growled, for I had not eaten all day. I carefully wrapped a piece of cheese in my skirts in the hopes of keeping it warm, and I devoured it quickly, swallowing half-chewed bites before they could freeze in my mouth.

I saw no reason to build a fire, as I needed it neither to cook nor for warmth, but when a lone wolf's hungry howl sounded in the mountains behind me, I scrambled for the flint I had taken from my kitchen and began gathering what wood I could find. Each stick and twig froze in my fingers. I quickly realized I could not touch the wood with my skin, for surely my fire would never light. I pulled gloves from my schoolbag and hastily tugged them on and built a fire the way Danner had once shown me—Danner, the last boy I had allowed to kiss me, one year my junior. I wondered, briefly, what he thought of me now, and felt some relief that he had not seen me in my cursed state, ugly as I was.

I paused before my unlit fire. Did I really want the light? Any passersby would be able to see all I had lost—the paleness of my skin, the age in my hair, and the dark circles around my eyes . . . I would win no hearts with my face, and my body had lost its softness and flexibility. Even my dresses hung awkwardly from my frame, the stitches too rigid to fall as intended.

Ultimately my fear of the dark overpowered my vanity, and I returned to my fire. It took several tries, and I nearly lit my left glove on fire, but I managed a spark to get my kindling going. As soon as the flames started, snow began to fall around me, dainty flakes I couldn't even feel. Fortunately the thick boughs of my oak tree protected my little camp enough that my fire did not go out. Still, I kept my distance from it, not wanting my surrounding chill to weaken its blaze.

Searching the darkness around me for wolves, I comforted myself with the fact that any predator that dared to enter my prison of winter would only get one bite of me before the cold overtook it. But animals have a keen sense humans do not. Perhaps they sensed the wrongness of my storm, for no wolf ever trespassed my camp, not then nor in the years to come.

However, as I tried to forget the cold long enough to sleep, I realized there was one predator who would not be frightened off by my curse. On the contrary—it seemed to draw him to me like a trout to a fly.

He appeared on the edge of the firelight, his grin spreading from cheek to cheek, his velvet cloak stirring in the winter wind. I recognized him immediately.

Death tipped his hat to me.

CHAPTER 4

"We meet again," he said, speaking in old Angrean. His voice sounded like warmed molasses.

My body grew so cold—so *terribly* cold—that every breath raked burning trails down my throat and lungs. My knees and elbows locked. It was as if the very sight of him had turned me into an ice statue, half-carved and immobile in the heavy block of my foundation.

The light seemed to bend around him as he stepped to the side of the fire. The black of his cloak appeared never ending: a deep pit with no floor, or dark sky with no moon or stars. His amber eyes glowed almost the way a cat's would.

They were narrow, searching eyes set above a long nose and wide mouth, which curved at the ends in the hint of a smile. His face looked ageless and smooth—a carving of alabaster.

"Have you . . . come to kill me?" I asked in flawed Angrean. My voice quavered with my question.

To my surprise, he threw back his head and laughed. I jumped, horrified by the idea of Death finding the prospect of my demise amusing.

He collected himself and answered, "I see I can pass on the introductions."

Somehow I found the strength to crawl away from him, backwards, until the thick trunk of the oak tree blocked my escape. Its roots glimmered with frost under my hands. "You are Death."

He smiled. "Ofttimes those close to the brink can see me, or parts of me. But you, Smitha, you are special."

I shivered uncontrollably, my teeth chattering. The snow started to thicken around my camp, the small flakes falling with a greater purpose. "Because I see all of you?" I whispered.

"Because I have not come to collect," he replied, taking a seat beside the fire. The ruby amulet around his neck glinted orange. The light, at least, touched that much of him.

I stared wide-eyed. "Collect?"

"Not in the way you suppose," he said coolly, tilting his head slightly to the right. The wide brim of his hat hid his eyes, but I knew he still watched me. I *felt* his gaze the way one feels the pelting of hail or the slip of a hammer. My chilled heart raced. Still a slow drum, but quicker than it had beaten in days.

"You will live another day," he said, more amused than anything else. "I can hardly kill someone who speaks my tongue so adequately."

I swallowed but found no moisture in my mouth. "Then why can I see you? And how do you know my name?"

"I know the names of all who are born," he said, leaning forward and revealing those penetrating eyes. "For all of them will eventually die. As for you . . . you've drawn my attention, Smitha. It is a deathly curse you carry, if you'll excuse the joke."

"I didn't ask for it."

He grinned. "Does any man or woman ask for a curse? But yours carries death with you. Is it any wonder that I would take an . . . interest?"

"No!" I shouted, my violet fingernails digging into the oak's root. "I did not kill that boy. Mordan did. He did everything!"

Chilly tears brimmed in my eyes. I quickly blinked them away.

"I see how it is," Death replied, rubbing his smooth chin.

I pushed a stray hair behind my ear. "Why are you here?"

"I told you," he said, smile unfading. "You interest me. However you may see it, Smitha—however you wish to lay the blame—you and I are a lot alike. We are neither dead nor living—entities who exist between worlds. There are few of our kind, but we tend to make good company."

I scoffed.

"And we're both cold, in our own way," he finished, those glowing eyes studying me from foot to forehead. "Your curse doesn't bother me."

He stood and walked toward me, his long legs carrying him faster than they should. I leapt to my feet, but before I could run, he appeared before me, leaning down, the brim of his hat almost touching the top of my head.

He took my wrist in his hand, a loose grip, and held it before my nose, his skin almost as pale as my own. He wore no gloves, not even a ring, but touching me directly did not so much as raise goose bumps on his skin, and surely the heat of the fire—heat I still could not feel—was not strong enough to banish the cold.

I realized I still trembled, even more so in his grip. He released me after a moment and stepped back. I craned my neck to see his shadowed face.

"No one will help you, Smitha," he said, his voice deep and honey-like, quiet. The fire cracked behind him. "No one will take you in. But I will."

The shock of his words ceased my trembling. "What?"

He smiled. "The realm beyond this one is grander than you could imagine."

I shuddered, imagining my body still and unmoving, buried deep in the frozen tundra beneath my feet. I imagined a world of blackness and mourning, the cries of the dead forever echoing around me. And though I had often considered death a preferable fate to life with my curse, I was suddenly desperate to survive.

I hugged myself. "No. No!"

He closed the small space between us so quickly I did not see him move. He took my chin in his long fingers.

"Come now," he said with a smirk. "Do you fear Death?"

And with no warning, he faded before my eyes just as he had in the Hutcheses' home.

I half wondered if so many days in the unyielding cold had begun to warp my mind, for surely Death had not just stood before me, *touched* me, and offered to take me away to the unknown world beyond. Surely I had imagined all of it, for Death himself could not have taken an interest—an *interest!*—in me, whatever that entailed. Surely Death did not lust after women the way mortal men did. He had talked to me more like one talks to a pet than a person.

But glancing to my wrist, I could still feel the press of his fingers. An insignificant gesture, but no one had dared touch me since Mordan had laid this godforsaken curse upon my head. No one had touched me since my father had reached for my hand and drawn his back, burned.

I touched my cold wrist with cold fingers and knew that Death had come for me.

It was the first visit of many.

CHAPTER 5

I woke the next morning encased in snow. Without a roof over my head and a fire burning in the hearth, there was nothing to protect me from the elements of my own curse. A biting chill flowed through me, and I wished to fall asleep again, if only to escape it.

I dug my way out, only to be greeted by whipping winter winds. Everything around me shimmered white, and the oak's great branches sagged under the weight of snow. The winds had scattered the wood of my fire for several paces, the flames long since extinguished.

I grabbed a handful of snow and ate it slowly as I walked. My father had once told me, if caught in a storm, not to eat straight snow for refreshment, for it would lower my body temperature and cause me to freeze. Now that I was already frozen, that wisdom no longer applied to me. The snow didn't even melt on my tongue.

The winds slowed as I loped through the snow, and gradually the clouds rested from their mystical downpour. It seemed so strange to walk over green grass and past flowering trees when I felt so bitterly cold. As long as I kept walking, my storm could not build enough strength to harm any of it. As long as I kept walking.

My feet quickly remembered the previous day's trek and began to ache before midmorning. Euwan was a small village, and I was not accustomed to walking very far for anything. The cold that encased my feet made every step that much more painful. There was no relief, for the skin never numbed. I cursed Mordan's name for the thousandth time, but there was no one around to hear me.

But thoughts of Mordan reminded me of the last dinner I had shared with my family, the one Mordan had so selfishly intruded on. Father had spoken of wizards up north—something about throwing fire and a political war.

Save for early morning and dusk, my storm cloud hid the sun from me, but I was not so far from Euwan that I could not determine which way was north. I hoped, a spark amidst cinders, that perhaps the rumors were true, that other wizards had come as far south as Iyoden. A wizard had cursed me; perhaps a wizard could cure me as well.

Fear clawed at me as I began my slow slog north. My knees stiffened with it. If I could even *find* a wizard, who was to say he would not laugh at my plight, worsen it, or even kill me?

A new layer of gooseflesh ran up my back and down my arms, each bump burning with cold. What if Mordan had fled north, to his own kind? How much more pain would he rain down upon me should we reunite?

But Mordan had come to Euwan for a reason. I concluded he had run from the wizards the same way he had run from me, so onward I trekked.

Yet I had not forgotten the previous night's visitor. Several times in my journey I glanced over my shoulder, searching for that tall, cloaked silhouette, but Death did not follow me. There was, in that, some sense of relief. The cold that afflicted me was unbearable, but I feared death, and determined then that, even alone, I would survive. I didn't know how, but I would live.

I ate my breakfast as I climbed hill after wooded hill, careful to wrap the dried meat in my spare chemise before lifting it to my lips, trying to keep it as soft as possible. Somewhere in the shadow of the storm clouds that followed me, an owl hooted and took flight, the cold having awoken it from its slumber.

During a rest I pulled off my shoes with inflexible fingers to study my frozen feet. The skin over my heels had begun to crack. I wept as I traced my fingertips over the splits. I had no oils or salves to rub into the flesh. I had not thought to bring any. Again I recited the harsh words I had prepared for Mordan, and when that failed to offer me comfort, I scripted a speech for all those in Euwan who had abandoned me. Not even Ashlen had come to say good-bye.

The cracks in my feet marked only the beginning of my ailments. I learned quickly enough that, were I not careful, my own urine would freeze to me when I relieved myself. I could not bathe without the water—no matter how swift the river's current—hardening around me. And, no matter where I fled, Death was never far behind.

He appeared on the opposite bank of the river two days after his last visit, strolling as casually as if he were within the walls of his own home. I did not notice him at first, but when I did, I startled. Acting on instinct, I ran in the opposite direction, darting through forest and thicket. Thorns caught on the skirt of my dress and tore it, but I did not slow. The clouds above me shifted, always keeping me in their shadow, and a chilled wind pushed at my back.

I didn't stop until I reached a small glade, a flock of blackbirds springing skyward at my arrival. As I leaned against a birch tree, gasping for air, the trunk quickly frosted beneath my touch.

Death appeared before me, smiling as though the chase had never happened. Then again, I doubted Death had chased me at all, only waited for me to stop.

"I assume that's a yes," he said, lifting the rim of his broad hat.

I held my stomach, sucking in gulps of air. "T-To what?" I couldn't be sure if the stutter came from the constant chattering of my teeth or from the fear that roiled in my gut like bubbling iron.

He tilted his head. "That you are afraid of me."

"Of course I am!" I shouted, turning back the way I had come. I moved as quickly as my sore feet could carry me, trying to keep the trees between us. "Everyone is afraid of death!"

He materialized before me again, effortless. I stopped so suddenly I fell backward, landing hard on my tailbone. I winced at the impact but picked myself up, gripping the strap of my schoolbag.

"Not everyone," he said, for once appearing more thoughtful than amused. He studied me once more. "Sadriel."

I backed away from him, my eyes wide.

He took a step forward, but only one, allowing me my space. "My name," he clarified. "Sadriel."

I laughed, a single, mirthless expelling of air. "Death has a name?"

"He has many," he said, those vibrant, amber eyes glinting.

I took a moment to catch my breath before asking, "What do you want? Why are you here again?"

That smile returned. "To pay my respects, of course."

He took the hat off his head and bowed deeply, flourishing his cloak. His long, dark auburn hair fell in thick waves over each shoulder.

I backed away another step.

Death—Sadriel—straightened and replaced the hat atop his head. "You are queen of the forest now, empress of the wild." He grinned. "You have been at it for days!"

"So you've come to mock me," I spat.

"Has no one else?" he asked, glancing about the glade. "But that's right—there is no one else."

Those few words crushed my anger to crumbs, and a wintry breeze stole them away from me, leaving me with nothing but my emptiness. But I refused to cry again.

Sadriel stepped forward. This time I did not move.

"My offer stands," he said. "I can help you."

The smile returned to his lips, and he got down on one knee and opened his arms to me. "Come with me, Smitha."

My hands began to throb from their tight grip on my bag, but I didn't loosen them. "To be queen of hell?"

He barked a laugh. "I'd have none to rule beside me, Smitha. Certainly not a mortal, however obscured your mortality might be. But I could make you free."

I frowned and forced half-frozen spit down my throat. "Would I have to die?" I whispered, shocked to hear the question pass my lips. Still, I pressed on. "I would, wouldn't I?"

He lowered his arms. "Not in the way you know death. You would merely . . . change. No sickness, no aging, and very little pain." He snapped his fingers. "You would hardly notice. I'd even make it fun, just for you."

The glade around us darkened, the storm overhead thickening as it always did when I stayed stationary too long. I almost laughed, but instead quipped, "No one can 'merely change.'"

I gazed at him for a long moment, feeling the chills shoot up my arm and legs. Then I asked, "Could you make me warm again?"

"Smitha," he said, folding his arms, "with or without me, you will *never* be warm again."

A single snowflake fell between us as his words—his proposition—floated over me.

Never. The finality of the word was unacceptable to me.

I shook my head. "No. *No.*"

The faintest frown touched Sadriel's lips, but a grin quickly hid it. After bowing one last time, he dissipated, leaving me alone in the forest once more.

I hesitated for a moment before walking to the spot where he had stood and waving my hand through the air, half expecting to find some remnant of him. Nothing. I was alone. As Sadriel had said, there was no one else.

My rejection did not deter Sadriel from visiting me as I continued my march north—he sometimes called when the noon sun shone beyond the congested sky above me, or I would awaken in the middle of the night to see him watching the burning embers of my fire. The heavy snow and bitter winds never once touched him.

On none of his visits did he help me. He would neither stoke the fire nor help me gather wood. When attempts to wash my clothes in ever-freezing water left me in tears, he never offered a hand, not even when I begged it of him. He only came to chat or silently observe, rarely staying for more than a quarter hour. But every time he appeared— *every* time, even when they were the only words he spoke—he presented his offer to me, and I refused. His promises meant nothing to me if they could not make me change. Still, part of me was comforted by his visits, for as I struggled to survive the cruel restrictions of my curse, Sadriel was the only company I had, however fleeting. I confess there were times when I craved his company so badly, when I felt so utterly alone, that I convinced myself to accept his offer, to join him in the realm beyond—as a servant, as a lover, as anything he would allow me to be, for what Sadriel wanted seemed to change by the day, and he never spoke directly. Fortunately, Sadriel never appeared during those moments of despair, only in times of clarity.

He finally asked me, after nearly two months in the wilderness, "Why do you go north?" He grinned, following a pace behind me, watching my worn shoes pick their way through a rocky mountain pass. "You're not seeking wizards, are you?"

I glanced back at him. "What do you know of wizards?"

He laughed. "I *love* wizards. They're always killing one another in the most fascinating ways."

My steps slowed, but I kept moving forward.

"Do you know how their magic works?" he asked, clasping his hands behind his back. "They harvest manna from the bowels of the earth, scraping it out of the bodies of beasts that died long before your kind ever took form. They covet it, kill for it, then eat it until their eyes glass over and their brains fill the realms adjacent to yours. Sometimes they die from it, but they take the risk in the name of 'magic.'" He chuckled again. "Good luck getting one to use his manna on you. Then again, you already have, once."

A fresh chill ran down the back of my head and zigzagged over my spine. I did not entirely understand Sadriel's description, and I still don't, but I did not press for further explanation. "They're my only hope."

Before Sadriel could dispel the claim and repeat his monotonous offer to me, I asked, "Where are they? Where can I find them?"

He glanced ahead, over narrow valleys, to where the mountains grew thin, spiky, and white. "You know where they are, Smitha. So far north even *you* could blend in."

He vanished and I, my mouth dry, moved onward. And I did blend in—the snowcaps on the mountain peaks gradually moved down until they filled the valleys with seas of white. I assumed I'd passed into Yorkishan, a small, sparsely populated country ruled by a regent rather than a prime minister, as was the custom in Iyoden. Beyond the fact that it exported coal and people spoke Northlander, I knew little about it.

I found new, bizarre villages of men and women so pale they almost looked blue beneath their furs. Avoiding the main roads that would lead to larger cities, I trekked through the mountains until I reached Yorkishan's northern border, where the people lived in tiny, weather-beaten houses. I passed near one or two villages when I could find no other route northward. Though travelers had to be rare in this part of the world—and I, the rarest of all—those who saw me said nothing, only kept their heads down and went about their work. One man caught me stealing a few pathetic, half-filled sausage casings from his smokehouse and didn't even bother to stop me. In my haste to flee back into the scant wood, I overheard one shivering woman telling another, "—screeching again. The initiation. If they involve us, I'll kill myself. I won't lose another baby."

It didn't take me long to learn why. These were people who knew better than to dabble in enchantments or the enchanted.

I continued my northward trek through mountains so high I would never see their peaks, even without my storm. The air about them smelled strange, something like spoiled wine: sweet, tangy, and nause-ating. Between these mountains stretched a passage so tall and narrow no sunlight could reach its floor, and I knew without explanation that beyond it lay the territory I sought—the land where the wizards lived.

But around this pass hung horrors upon horrors—men, women, even children and animals strung up by their ankles or necks, cut up in the most terrible ways or mutilated to look like demons and fairy-tale chimera. Magicked in ways that made me retch those precious sausages onto the snow. If this was the working of wizards, I wanted none of it.

I ran from that place, never stopped by the locals who seemed to fear me as much as they did the wizards. Taking advantage of their humility, I stole provisions from them so I wouldn't have to forage on my way back. So I could put as much space between myself and that unknown world as possible.

"How do you stand it?" I asked Sadriel when he appeared to me again, weeks later, somewhere near Iyoden. I sat before a fire, smashing walnuts between rocks and harvesting what little meat fell from their centers. My hair—now white to my chin, the blond quickly fading—fell in a braid down my back. "What the wizards do . . . How does it not bother you?"

"I see such things every day," he answered, nonchalant, pacing about my fire. "But if you came with me, I would hide it from you."

I scoffed. "Why do you care?" It had been roughly three months since my village cast me away. Three months without the slightest waiver in my predicament, either for good or for ill. "Why do you persist, after so long?"

"Because you're fascinating," Sadriel answered, leaning against the trunk of a pine tree some six paces away. "The living do not see me, and the dead do not hear, but you can do both. You are special, Smitha. And you are beautiful, even with your aged hair and gnarled hands."

I frowned and focused on my walnuts. Though I had prided myself on my looks for most of my life, I hardly thought myself beautiful now. We lingered somewhere in northern Iyoden, though where precisely, I could not be sure. There was a village some five miles south of me, and I admit to having considered entering its confines to steal as I had done in the far north. I needed clean clothes and better food than what I could forage. I still had not dismissed the idea, but I did not have the courage to approach the town after what I had witnessed at that pass.

"And think," Sadriel continued, staring off into the valley beneath us, "how much more beautiful you'll be when mortality no longer drags on you, and without these dismal clouds hovering over you day in and day out."

He made a weak, skyward gesture with his hand.

I cracked another walnut and struggled to collect the pieces with the limited dexterity of my fingers.

Grabbing another nut, I placed it before me and lifted my rock, but Sadriel stopped my hand. Whether he had walked over to me or merely flashed himself closer, I had not seen.

"You *need* me, Smitha," he said, taking the stone from my grasp. "Think of it this way, if you will. A wizard's magic—your curse—is held by the laws of the mortal realm. Leave the mortal realm, and the curse loses its power."

The gooseflesh that covered me stiffened, like a pheasant newly plucked. I met his gaze, his amber eyes penetrating me, and for a moment I felt naked, the worn fibers of my dress stripped away.

I forced my eyes from his and took back my stone. "You told me I would always be cold, didn't you?" I asked, smashing the walnut. "That I couldn't change? No, Sadriel. Please don't ask me again. You know my answer."

Why I managed to so readily reject his offer, I'm not sure, even today. Leaving with him would have been a simple matter. I know I wished to see my family again, for the memory of my fleeting farewell to them had come to pain me. Maybe, deep inside, I was unwilling to believe the curse would last forever.

Perhaps I said no simply because I did not trust Sadriel. His words were too careful, his eyes too sly. His being extended so far beyond the scope of my own that I could not begin to fathom what accepting him would have meant for me.

"Think on it," he said, standing. "If nothing else, I can offer you a real bed and better food."

I crushed my last walnut, and when I looked up again Sadriel had disappeared. Slowly chewing the nut, I gazed out into the valley and noticed that snow was falling beyond the force field that followed me. A cool autumn had settled on the outside world. For a brief moment, I reflected on Sadriel's words.

Change. Could I change? Could I possibly break the curse myself? I did not see how such a thing could be possible, but I clung to the idea. I had no resources, no contacts, and my heart beat as cold as it had that first day in the willow-wacks. Surely Mordan had not built me a curse fragile enough to break.

I gathered my harvest, left the broken shells behind, and followed the line of the mountains west, away from the unnamed village below. I had no idea how to begin the task I had laid out for myself, and in my desperation for survival, I put little effort into the venture.

CHAPTER 6

I never adapted to the cold.

Even the most stubborn of pains can be forgotten when one is distracted by a good book or song, or when chores demand the mind's full attention. My curse worked differently. Even after a full year under Mordan's spell, the cold still bit down to my bones. I never grew accustomed to it, and not once did I forget its presence. Sleep provided my only respite from the insufferable chill, yet even in the bliss of slumber my body shuddered with winter. Dreams where I was myself—my old self—became less and less frequent, but I clung to the few I had despite the sting of awakening from them. Memories of warmth, of home, of family. How desperately I missed my family—my mother's home cooking, my father's laugh, Marrine's candor. I no longer held any ill feelings for them, for a year spent alone had opened my eyes to my own shortcomings.

I spent most of true winter in the valleys, for the natural snows in the mountains grew too steep for me to ascend. I ran out of food quickly, no longer able to forage. It took a toll on my frostbitten body, making me gaunt and doll-like. More than once I snuck into nearby villages or townships at night, when the natural snow blew hard and masked my curse. I stole whatever I could find—eggs, oats, even chickens, though the relentless weather made fires nearly impossible and forced me to eat most of my meat raw. Sadriel found this especially amusing, though I saw less of him in those months. More men died in winter than any other time of year. At least, I assumed that was what kept Death away.

I tried not to steal too much from any one village, for I feared being seen. I knew the distaste my own village held for wizards and the craft; I could only imagine the disdain others had for those cursed by it.

As soon as the earth began to warm and the snow melted, I climbed back into the mountains somewhere on the west edge of Iyoden, and there I remained, moving between camps when my snow grew too deep. I carefully built a fire to dry my newly snow-scrubbed clothes. They all needed mending, but I had not thought to bring a sewing kit with me, all those months ago. I doubted my inflexible fingers could manage a needle, besides.

I sat near the fire, my skirt pulled up to midthigh so it wouldn't burn, the worn volume of *Ancient Phonetics of Larcott* sitting beside me on the earth. I watched the flames caress my frozen hands and taste the tiny cuts along my knuckles and the icy calluses of my fingers. No matter how long I kept them in the pit, the fire's heat never touched me.

I kept my long, white hair tucked into the back of my dress, for it *would* burn, and I still fancied it after spending a year in the wild, despite knowing the atrocity of my appearance. I had not seen a mirror since I left Euwan, fortunately.

My braid slipped from my collar and I started. Looking back, I saw Sadriel behind me, deftly unbraiding the strands. I made no effort to pull down my skirt and make myself modest—after so long on my own, I hardly thought of such things anymore.

"No old men to escort today?" I asked, turning back to the fire. "No sick children? Birthing mothers? Soldiers?"

He didn't answer me. He simply finished unbraiding my hair and ran his fingers through it. I bit down hard to keep my teeth from chattering as he worked through a snag. Finally he picked himself up and found a seat across the fire. The flames' heat didn't bother him any more than the brisk cold of the mountain morning did. They didn't bother either of us.

He leaned his cheek on his fist and watched me for a long moment.

"You could turn over that chemise," I said, jutting my chin toward my drying laundry.

He made no move to do so. "Have you reconsidered my offer?"

"Do I ever?" I picked up a coal and turned it over in my fingers.

"You've been in these mountains a long time," he said. "It's not like you to remain stationary. The cold must have reached the nearby village by now. How sad, after such a harsh winter."

I frowned, thinking of Euwàn. I had lived as a cursed woman for only three days within its borders, yet because of me Bennion had died, and many others had sickened. I may have killed livestock, too, and ruined countless crops. That guilt weighed heavily on me, pushing against my slow, cold heart. I never had apologized, not even to the Hutcheses for killing their little boy.

"I don't need you to remind me," I whispered, not sure if he could hear my words over the crackling of the fire.

Mordan still haunted my thoughts every day—it was impossible not to think of him. The anger I held for that man, the contempt, was often the only fuel that got me up in the mornings. I would brush off my blankets of snow and live another day, if only to spite him. Still, I realized I could have—*should* have—dealt with him more gently.

Despite what he had done to me, the horrors he had unleashed on my life, I believed his feelings for me had been sincere.

"Oh, but you do," Sadriel said, grinning as usual. He reached across the fire—the flames bent away from him—and stroked my jaw. "Because I'm the one who can make you forget. It's been too long, Smitha. Come with me. The dead make poor companions."

I jerked away.

He didn't quite frown, but his lips pressed into a thin line for a fleeting moment. He stood, adjusted his hat, and said, "By the way, there are hunters with dogs heading up the mountain. You may want to run, or you'll be in my domain sooner than expected, and not in the manner I would prefer."

He grinned and tipped his hat.

I stiffened at his words and pulled my hands from the fire. "There can't be," I protested. "I've stayed far enough away from the villages. My curse doesn't reach them!" I stabbed my finger upwards, toward my eternal storm, to illustrate my point.

"Ah," said Sadriel as he faded away, "but it reaches the springs."

My breath caught in my throat. I leapt to my feet and peered higher up the mountain. Springs ran down from the snowcaps up there; I had passed them often between camps.

Wadding my skirts in my hands, I jogged up the mountain, its jagged surface jabbing my feet through wearing soles. I wound around a steep cliff and navigated over thick pine roots before the first spring came into view—a small river formed from mountain runoff.

It clung to the brae like a sheet of glass, netted like lace around the rocks interrupting its path. The entirety of it was frozen. Sadriel was right. I had stayed here too long.

I heard a howl further down the slope—not the call of a wolf, but of a hound, much like the red-haired basset Ashlen's father took with him on hunting trips.

My cold heart leapt into my throat. I could barely breathe. But why would they have sent out hunters rather than assume the winter had hit harder than usual? Did these unknown villages know of me? Had my curse become a rumor left in my frozen wake across the land?

I thought of all the malicious rumors I had spread in school to diminish or get revenge on my fellow classmates. The irony almost made me sick up.

The springs had frozen, which meant the towns at the base of the mountain had no water to their newly planted crops. I had a feeling these hunters had not brought their dogs along for the mere purpose of asking me to leave.

I bolted back down the mountain, slipping on frost and patches of snow, tumbling over loose rocks. I skidded and fell, skinning my knee. I winced as cold blood trickled down my leg and froze, but I pushed myself up and sprinted to the fire. I collected my cold, damp clothes, pulled on my coat and gloves, and shoved the rest of my things into my bag before throwing it over my shoulder. I scooped up as much dirt and debris as I could and put out the fire, patting down the flames with my hands. I ran back to a patch of snow and scooped up an arm-ful of it, dropping it onto the coals. They hissed, sizzled, and smoked. I dashed away.

The hounds brayed behind me—three of them—as I hurried across the mountain, running until my path dropped into a steep incline, forc-ing me to climb rather than hike. I slid and caught myself on the rough trunk of a fir, then carefully picked my footing until I could run again. My narrow, rocky path opened up into a wide, tree-rimmed clearing, its muddy soil dotted with grass and clover.

Men's voices sounded beyond the excited dogs, though I could not make out their words. I pushed my stiff legs faster, willing my frozen joints to bend, begging them to carry me. My right foot sunk into mud. I wrenched it free, leaving my shoe behind.

The dogs' barks hung in the air. Glancing behind me, I saw two harriers and a basset—just as my clearing ended in a steep landslip, free of trees. I struggled to climb the loose rocks, but for every two steps up I slid one back. I didn't realize the dogs had reached me until a harrier snapped its jaws onto the hem of my skirt and yanked me down.

"Whoa, whoa!" a man called, and the other two hounds waited beneath me, growling. I fought off the harrier, slapping my hand across its muzzle. It yipped and released me. Flinging myself against the landslip, I started to climb again, feeling tiny rocks dig into my hands and my one bare foot. I heard one of the men behind me curse. The other bellowed something about an ice witch.

"You've caused us trouble for too long!" the first shouted as he grabbed my shod foot and yanked me off the steep incline. I fell hard onto my hip and cried out. The same harrier who'd snapped at my skirt grabbed my coat sleeve and tossed its head back and forth. I clawed at it until its master called it off. I couldn't breathe.

I met the master's eyes—a man in his thirties, perhaps, a short hat strapped to his head around his chin. An axe in his hands. He and his companion were bundled against the mountain chill with boots, long pants, coats, and gloves, only their faces and necks exposed.

"Leave me alone!" I screamed, kicking with my back against the landslip. The other man—much older—managed to get an arm around my thighs, clamping my legs shut.

"If you wanted to be left alone, you shouldn't have brought your spell to Mayshaven," the younger spat, adjusting his grip on his axe. The hounds yipped so loudly around me I could barely hear him say, "Let's do this quick and get gone."

I shrieked and writhed in the older man's grip, his arms like a bench vise, as the younger shooed the dogs. I screamed for help, cried out for Sadriel, but no one answered. I was alone. I had been alone since the day Mordan took me to the willow-wacks and set this curse upon me.

My curse.

As the axman neared my shoulder, I bit the middle finger of my glove and ripped it off. I could not reach the axman, but I could grab the hunter who held me.

Clenching the muscles in my stomach, I bolted upright and grabbed my captor's exposed neck with both hands. He immediately released my legs, but I clung to him, my nails digging into his flesh as frost stemmed from my right hand, tracing up his jaw and down his neck, beneath his layers of clothing. He screamed, but I did not let go, even as he fell backwards with me on top of him, even as his hands tore at my back and shoulders. One of the dogs bit my calf, and the animal yipped loudly as ice shot into its teeth.

A hand grabbed a fistful of my hair and yanked me back, but the axman was too late. His comrade already lay as a statue in the mud, his arms bent at the elbow and frozen in place, his eyes wide and mouth agape. His skin shimmered with frost, his skin pale, lips blue.

The axman released me and ran to the frozen man's side, then turned to ogle me with wide, quivering eyes. I backed away, limping, but instead of coming after me, the axman ran back across the clearing, his hounds fast at his heels. The dog that had bitten me—the basset—limbered behind slowly, shaking its head, its tongue dragging across the earth.

It happened so quickly I could barely register it, even with the frozen man lying before me, even with blood caking over my knee and oozing from the puncture wounds the hound had left on my leg.

I sat there, soft snow falling around me, panting, cold air passing in and out of my lungs. Angry moths flew circles in my gut. I shivered and held myself, trembling at the sight of the frozen man. A man who had come to kill me. I had no doubts about that.

The air to my left darkened and took shape. Sadriel stood beside me, though I did not look at him. I only stared at the frozen man, still rigid in his desperate form.

"I had to," I whispered between chattering teeth, my heart folding around itself. How very cold I felt. The blood from the bite wound had already frozen to my skin in forking trails, stopping just above my heel. "I-I had to."

Sadriel walked around the man, inspecting him like he were an entry to the town fair. "He's not dead," he said, tapping his fingers against his lips, "just dying." He grinned and looked at me. "See? You already have a taste for me."

Crouching down, Sadriel touched the man's forehead and then lifted his hand, tan and cerulean smoke following his fingertips. I recalled the day I first met Death in the Hutcheses' home, when Sadriel had done the same to Bennion. Even with the hunter truly dead, his body remained unchanged. Still frozen, still screaming, still gaping. His frosted eyes peered into the world of Death and feared what they beheld.

He looked like me.

A tear ran down my cheek, freezing before it reached my chin. "I called for you!" I shouted, rising to my feet. My leg throbbed and the mountain teetered, but I ignored both. "They wanted to kill me! I called for you, but you didn't . . . you didn't . . ."

I shook my head, wiping away a second tear that froze to the side of my hand.

"You handled it well enough, hmm?" Sadriel said with a grin. "And I warned you, didn't I?"

I didn't answer, only continued to shake my head as I limped past the corpse and into the clearing. By the time I found my lost shoe and jerked it from the mud, Sadriel had, once again, disappeared.

I did not look back at the hunter. I did not need to, for his pained face had carved itself into my memory. I have never forgotten it, though my dreams of him have subsided, thankfully. My fear of dogs, however, lingers with me to this day.

I had to keep moving, and I had to stay far away from any village, far enough that I could not so much as see one, for I deeply feared a repeat of that day. If stories of the "ice witch" had reached this far, I did not think I could be safe anywhere. I could not settle down, and I dared not stay in any single place more than one night. I didn't even dare steal from another town again, even when true winter hid my presence.

I had never been a good hunter—my father had never taught me because I was a girl—but I learned to catch frogs by freezing their ponds and chipping them from the ice. The ice did not melt in my hands, and as long as I kept it away from my infrequent fires, the meat stayed fresh. I built several caches for myself for the following winter, places I could return to when I grew desperate for food. Nuts, apples, tubers, and any eggs I could find, whether robin or snake. I focused on survival, and my early preparations pulled me through the next year relatively unscathed.

But my third year in the wilderness, the third year of my unrelenting curse, would bring one of the darkest times of my life. I would stand on the very brink of death, wanting only to be welcomed into the black abyss beyond.

CHAPTER 7

In late spring I traveled east, away from the mountains and closer to the coast. I had no specific destination in mind; I only knew that I had to keep moving. If I lingered in one place too long, I feared the storm that followed me would form a pillar of snow towering to the heavens themselves, with me crushed into its foundation. The mountain crests of inland Iyoden often hid my storm. They also gave me a wide view of my surroundings, so abandoning them invoked anxiety in me, but I trekked east anyway, hoping to outrun the rumors that had sprung up along my trail. Hoping to stumble upon some sort of technology or magic that could relieve my curse. I had once pondered on traveling this way once I became an established playwright—but such fancies had long been buried.

In my journey I passed very close, uncomfortably close, to Heaven's Tear Lake, but Euwan resided on its southwest side and I passed over its north. The lake is large enough that even the best eyes would not be able to see my crawling storm as I passed by. I took comfort in that, even though my heart ached for home.

Other than Sadriel's infrequent visits, I continued to travel alone, which gave me a great deal of time to spend with my thoughts. Mordan still weighed heavily on my mind, but I began to think beyond the moment he'd wrapped his fingers around my neck and used his last magic to thrust me into an eternal winter. I realized I had never truly known him. Yes, he had cursed me, and I hated him for it, but perhaps he was not entirely evil. Everyone in Euwan had seemed to like him, my father especially. I imagined myself in his stockings, as the saying goes, a lone stranger hoping for a fresh start in a small village where no one knew him, trying to break away from the horrors he had witnessed at the gate to magicked territory. It must have been hard for him. I realized I might have misjudged him. Admitting that to myself helped eased the weight of hatred in my heart.

Unfortunately, my journey did not remain entirely in its solitude, for as the warmer months settled in Iyoden, the reach of my cold alerted new men, and though I distanced myself, I was a cursed being, an "ice witch," and a party far larger than the two men with dogs began to pursue me. Whether in anger or perhaps in sport, I do not know, for I dared not linger long enough to ask. But they came for me, and I turned back for the mountains, running when my body could run, crawling when it could not. I wore through the soles of my shoes and had to discard them. But even with bleeding feet, I could not stop moving.

Once I feared my pursuers had obtained horses, I began to travel into the night, running until my chilled body could not run anymore, and then only sleeping until dawn awoke me. I had to move constantly and quickly, for I could not hide, not with ever-present storm clouds flagging me. I barely had time to forage, and I grew too thin. My clothes—old and in need of mending—became tattered with my constant movement. During that time I rarely saw my own snow, for it only fell when I stayed in one place too long.

It took me three months to finally lose the hunting party, and by then the peak of summer made the world blossom green around me. But those three months had fatigued me to my bones, and the persistent fear had torn my heart open. I had lost myself somewhere between the end of Iyoden's mountain ranges and where the wide rivers cut through the land, perhaps not too far from the Unclaimed Lands that walled the Southlands from the north. I recognized nothing; I was hungry, and I was alone. My heart and my resolve had broken, and I could not find the strength to start a new day, to forage, even to read my beloved books, which had become memorized bricks in my faded schoolbag. A darkness seeped into the cold that flowed through my veins, and it gradually consumed me.

One day I sat on summer grass white with frost, delicate snowflakes dropping in silence around me, my legs curled up to my chest. My skirt fell in tattered strips around me, and my unbound hair curtained me from the world. I had folded my arms against my knees and leaned my forehead against them, sobbing, crying as I had never cried before. I cried every ounce of my misery until I could barely breathe, but even breath did not cease my despair, nor the endless, frozen tears that clung to my dress and sleeves, neck and breast.

I knew Sadriel had come—even through my own darkness, I could feel his presence, but I could not stop the tears. I felt only the shards of what I once was and the bitter chill that tortured me.

"I can't do it anymore!" I managed through choppy sobs. I shivered, gasped for air. "I can't . . ."

Sadriel did not smile at me, nor did he frown. His lips held a flat line, and his brow knit over bright amber eyes. He seemed almost sympathetic in his silence, almost . . . sad. He sat on the frosty grass with his legs folded before him, untouched by the dust of my snow, wordless, mirthless.

"I just want to die," I whispered through trembling lips. "It hurts . . . It hurts so much."

Even without tears I wept. When I finally spoke again, my voice sounded hoarse and aged. "I c-can't touch anything without . . . I can't touch anything, anyone. I'm . . . I'm a monster. I just w-want it to end . . ."

And then Death knelt before me, his eyes like molten fire. He reached out his long fingers and touched the side of my face.

I gazed at him, his ageless features, those bright amber eyes.

"Come with me," he whispered.

I didn't answer. His fingers lingered on my face, and I was filled with the wonder of feeling someone, anyone, touch me. Beneath that I felt empty, void of emotion, void of thought, void of spirit. I watched him, frozen tears on my eyelashes.

And I nodded.

The brim of his wide hat brushed the top of my head, and his lips pressed against mine, strong and indelicate. His hands slid over my jaw and entangled themselves into my hair. I opened my mouth to him. He kissed me fervently, breathlessly, his teeth grazing my lips, his tongue tracing my tongue.

I fell back onto the earth with him on top of me, his hair falling against my cheeks, his mouth on my lips, my neck, my lips. His hands caressed my sides and flowed down my thighs, moving under my ragged skirt. In that moment I lost myself to him, savoring him, the one man in the world whom I could touch and who could touch me.

But then a draining sensation engulfed me as his arm snaked behind my back. My life slipped away in smoky wisps with each kiss, with each touch of his hand. I was dying, and though it scared me, I almost let it happen, let him take away the pain and the darkness, let him pull me into the realm beyond this one.

Almost.

Mordan had taken away the life I had known, but even his curse had not taken my *life*. Without that, I would be truly frozen, unable to change. Unable to save myself. My life, albeit a hard one, was the only thing I had left.

And no one—*no one*—could take that from me.

I found the last dregs of my strength and pushed Sadriel away from me. "No!" I cried. Screamed. "No! You cannot take it from me! I will never go with you!"

He gazed at me in shock, his eyes as wide and mouth as open as the hunter I had left frozen in the mountains, but the surprise receded and his eyes blazed with fury. One moment he sat on the ground beside me, and the next he stood, a raging shadow. He cursed me in his old tongue—"*Shiksha, Obiden, Tyar!*"—and vanished in a swirl of maroon and black.

The setting sun colored the horizon a bloody red, and I found enough strength to pick myself up and crawl to my schoolbag. I changed my chemise and my dress, took a bite of a half-frozen apricot, and slowly, hazily, began collecting wood. For the first time in three months, I lit a fire, and though I could not feel its warmth, I savored its light.

By the time the true snows of winter came once more, I had restored my old routines and returned to the mountains. More importantly, I had learned to recognize the mercies Mordan had allotted me, even in his rash anger. I still had my mind, my memories. I could still move, even if my frozen muscles made my limbs sluggish. Most importantly, I still had my life.

Staring up at the wisps of silent, falling snow, I forgave Mordan. It was that resolve—a strange sort of hope that I *could* change for the better, one way or another—that fueled me through the years to come.

CHAPTER 8

Sadriel, whose company I both craved and despised, did not visit me that winter, and I had come to believe I would never see him again, save on my own deathbed. But our confrontation had ignited within me a new will to live. Where once I had gripped on to life with white knuckles for fear of death, I now cherished life for the love of it.

I reflected often on my life before the curse. Rather than bestowing me with comfort or joy, the memories often made my heart heavy with remorse. Even the smallest things, like the time I had eaten both brownies Ashlen's mother had sent home with me, when I was meant to share one with Marrine. Or when I had mercilessly teased a young woman at school for her ill-fitting dress. I pondered on every chore I had skipped or completed haphazardly, on every piece of misleading advice I had shared with friends, on every boy I had ever made empty promises to and then discarded like an empty flour sack.

I considered all these things and made confessions and apologies I could only utter to myself. I traced the empty words in ice and sculpted my old home, the turnery, and poor renditions of my loved ones' faces in the snow. Then I left my sad artwork behind to be buried by the next storm, always moving forward on cold and bare—but determined—feet.

When spring settled, I followed the runoff past the mountains and soon found myself on the northeastern border of Iyoden, which I recognized only from school maps and my own speculation. I spent a day determining whether or not to cross, and at the following dawn I did, dragging my storm with me. Less than one week into my travels I discovered what appeared to be an army camped in the distance: clean, uniformed rows of beige tents and fires, men whose livery I dared not get close enough to identify. I thought of circumventing them, but I decided not to chance it and turned back.

I had crossed to the other side of the first mountains, perhaps six days outside Euwan and Heaven's Tear Lake, when I stumbled upon a black-cloaked figure with a broad hat, garbed in maroon, his long tresses stirring calmly in the cool breeze.

I paused and adjusted the schoolbag on my shoulder, its handle held together only by knots.

"I didn't think I'd see you again," I said. Thoughts of our last meeting would have flushed my skin had such a thing been possible.

Sadriel laughed heartily, his broad hat almost falling from his head. He seemed taller, or perhaps I had grown smaller in his absence. "You interest me, Smitha," he said once he had controlled himself. "You amuse me. And I can hardly stay away from good amusement for long."

I pinched my collar and tugged it up—all my dresses were near rags, hardly able to pass for modesty. "I didn't mean to . . . When I saw you last, I—"

He appeared before me in an instant, a blur solidified. His long fingers grabbed my hair and jerked my head back, forcing me to look at him. His amber eyes blazed, and his mouth curled into a sneer.

"What will you say to me, Smitha?" he asked, and I winced in his grip. "Do you think you broke my heart?"

He tugged my hair back further until I was sure my neck would snap. His lips almost touching my ear, he whispered, "I am Death. I don't *have* a heart to break."

I peered into his face, forcing myself to look into those fire-hot eyes. "I'm sorry," I murmured, choked. As loud as I could say it, throat bent as it was.

He released me and stepped back. I coughed and rubbed my frozen neck.

"I am part of you, Smitha," Sadriel said, his slender brows knit tightly together. "I have waited longer than a few years for men to fall to me."

He vanished. I shivered at his words. Indeed it had been a few years; I had already entered my third since leaving Euwan. I did not know the exact day, but I imagined my twentieth birthday would be upon me soon enough.

CHAPTER 9

They came in the spring.

If Sadriel knew, he chose not to warn me. I had finished my breakfast of wrinkled apples and was sculpting a fox out of snow when I saw them, a band of about thirty riding along the overgrown trail in the valley below—an uninhabited valley, narrow, with young trees, a crisscrossing of brooks, and dark soil that made me believe a fire had passed through some time ago. They rode in a snakelike formation, pushing their horses. With nothing but nature around us for miles, the only thing they could be looking for was me.

I ran.

I had the advantage of higher ground, and I knew horses did not handle steep inclines easily, but as I had learned when the hunting party from the eastern beach was pursuing me, the clouds that followed me would not allow me to hide. I climbed the steepest paths of the mountains and ran across rocks and roots to hide my prints, hoping the remnants of my frost would melt before they could be used to track me. I avoided streams and other runoff, which flowed at their fullest, for if I lingered too long in the water, it would freeze and snare me like a deer in a trap.

I ran until my frozen throat could barely pull in enough air to keep me breathing. I stopped only to pull burrs from my aching feet. Switching my schoolbag to the other shoulder, I continued on, a little slower but no less determined.

I wandered up and down the slopes, winding around the mountain until the narrow valley disappeared behind me, my storm trailing me all the while. I needed to forage for food, and soon, but I'd rather be hungry than dead. I ate my last apple and tuber as I walked, my jaw aching as it worked the frozen bites.

I walked until the sun had sunk so far below the mountains I could barely see two paces in front of me. I could have lit a torch—if I wrapped my hand before touching the wood, the far end would not grow too cold to burn, and if I kept moving, the winds would not whip too strongly—but I feared being seen. Instead, I settled down at the base of a pine tree, winter-hardened needles poking through my tattered clothes. I stayed awake for a long time, listening and shivering, too aware of my own burning cold. Hours passed before I fell asleep, and I doubt I remained unconscious for even an hour. Snow fell around me. The moment the first blue lights of dawn illuminated the mountainside, I hurried down the slope and into the next, narrow valley. I pushed myself when the earth flattened, desperately trying to gain some distance on my pursuers. I walked through the entire day, carefully picking a path through the forest and hills.

But the third day I saw the riders again, still in formation, and close enough that I could make out each individual person. Clad in indigo, they looked exotic and far different from anyone I had ever encountered. Some had large feathers protruding from their shoulders, while others were wearing strange, lizard-like armor. Their horses were large, dark, and sleek—larger than any plow horse or pony back home.

Warhorses.

My heart hammered. I ran, urging my frozen limbs faster, willing my cold blood to warm up enough to fuel my escape. My feet throbbed first, then my thighs, my chest, my shins. My throat ached with a fierce chill, dry and raw. I wove through a forest of white-trunked aspens, the cliffs above the tree line too steep for me to scale. I heard the thunder of hooves in the distance and stifled a cry. A thick root tripped me and I fell hard, a web of frost shooting out from where my hands planted themselves in the moist earth. I forced myself to my feet and ran, gasping for air. Praying to anyone or anything that could help me.

The cacophony of hooves grew louder. I heard shouting. My muscles seized and my head lightened.

Run! I urged myself, my weary, frozen limbs slacking. *I have to run!*

A blur of black sped past my left—a dark rider on a dark horse. He passed me, expertly weaving through the trees. He turned suddenly, wheeling his warhorse into my path.

I tried to evade him, bolt to the right, but my heavy limbs slid in the dirt. I toppled hard on my side, the impact flinging my flint and one of my books from my schoolbag. My ankle blazed with a new pain, pounded with an old chill.

I looked up, hair in my face, my chest heaving with every sparse breath. The warhorse danced uneasily in my presence, as most animals did. Its rider was a tall man in loose clothing, deep indigo sleeves and a strange black vest that crossed over his chest, lined with some sort of ringed mail. He wore dark leather riding gloves and loose beige slacks that bowed where they tucked into tall black boots. A helmet, ridged on either side to look like horns, covered most of his head, but dark, almost black eyes peered out from beneath it. Dark eyes set in dark skin on an expressionless face.

I would have stopped breathing had my body not been so desperate for air.

Southlanders.

As a child, I had often heard stories of Zareedian mercenaries who stormed towns in the night searching for disobedient children. Only stories, but it was still common knowledge that the Southlanders—men who lived in the scorching deserts beyond the Unclaimed Lands—were merciless warriors.

The thunder of hooves behind me slowed. I turned and watched as the band of warriors approached me from behind, led by a man dressed similarly to the one who had felled me, albeit in shades of deep scarlet and copper, the body of a large spider carved into his helmet, which revealed the entirety of his face. He held out an arm, urging his men to slow.

I grabbed my bag—willing to leave the flint and books behind if only I could escape—and leapt to my feet. My ankle cried out in protest, but I ran best I could. I did not get five paces before the first man in indigo charged my path, once more cutting me off.

"Please, Svara Idyah, do not run!"

I whirled around and nearly tripped myself. The words, spoken in my own northern tongue, carried a heavy accent that elongated the vowels and softened the consonants. But Svara Idyah—those were Hraric words, and ones I recognized from my studies. They meant *bearer of cold*.

The man in the spider helmet had spoken them.

Panting, I said in my own tongue, "I have meant no harm! Please forgive any trespasses I have caused and let me go. Please!"

The man rode closer without the rest of his entourage. I pulled up the collar of my dress, feeling exposed beneath the eyes of so many.

The man dismounted and removed his helmet. I sensed the indigo-clad rider behind me tense.

He was young, perhaps only a few years older than myself, with deep brown skin and bright gray eyes, a startling contrast. His black hair was cut short, save for two thin braids woven close to the skin over and behind each ear. A golden rod was pierced through the center of the cartilage of his right ear, and two small gold loops curved through the lobe of his left. He was a handsome man, narrow at the waist and broad shouldered, his face smooth and clean shaven, his nose straight. About Mordan's height, though perhaps a little shorter.

I stepped back as he neared, and he immediately halted his approach, leaving five paces between us. He raised empty hands.

"My name is Imad," he said, his accent smooth as cream. Close enough that his breath clouded beneath his nose. "I have sought you for a long time. When my men were unsuccessful in locating you last year, I could not accept defeat. I came myself, and now I have found you. Please, I mean no harm. Be at peace."

I shivered and hugged my bag close to myself.

"Forgive me for scaring you. I need your help," he continued. For a moment, I didn't think I had heard right. He requested *my* help? Me, who had caused so much devastation, who could kill with a touch? "I come from Zareed, far south of here. My land and my people are suffering from a long drought; the mountains no longer give us water. Our food is low. Many people and animals have died.

"But I heard tales of you, Svara Idyah, from a merchant. A woman in the Northlands followed by the cold. A woman who is followed by snow." He glanced up, ready for snow to fall from the opaque clouds overhead. Our chase had been fast paced, so they remained dry. "This snow can save my country. If you will only come back with me, I will offer anything you wish. Only for a time, on my honor."

I stared, wide-eyed, my thoughts as frozen as the ground beneath my feet.

"Anything, anything," he repeated, enunciating each syllable as though I had not understood. He clasped his hands together and went down on one knee. Many of the riders behind him murmured. "Please. We have traveled long and hard to ask you this."

I swallowed, no moisture on my tongue. I asked, "Your country?" The words came out raspy. "Y-You are a king?" My mind searched its memory of my Hraric book. "A *sheikh*?"

The latter term surprised him, but he answered, "My full name is Prince Imad Al'Hraith of the Fourth Generation."

I felt faint and not solely from my exhausting run. For years I had only inspired fear and hatred in those who learned of me, and I had not spoken to a soul outside of Sadriel for so long my throat felt unaccustomed to speech. Now a prince of Zareed knew the truth about who and what I was and he *knelt* before me, unalarmed by my curse. Inspired by it!

I felt something spark inside my chest that felt distantly familiar.

Imad stood again, bits of decomposed leaves clinging to his knee. He made no effort to brush them away. He stepped forward. I held my ground.

"We are down to the last water in the well," the prince said, stifling a shiver. "Please accompany us. We have brought a horse, and we will provide you with whatever comforts you need."

I shook my head no, and his face fell. I quickly explained. "I cannot ride. I . . . Whatever I touch freezes." I stepped back and gestured to the frostbitten ground where my feet had been and the new tendrils of ice that snaked from my feet even as I spoke. "I will hurt your animal."

Imad smiled, a grin far different from the one Sadriel so often bore. His seemed hopeful, and it lit his entire face. "We have blankets, many blankets, for it is cold for us in the Northlands." He glanced at the indigo rider behind me—I had forgotten he was there, barring my exit. "And we can switch horses as necessary. Please, you will consider?"

It seemed unreal, standing there in the sloping aspen forest at the base of a mountain I had no name for, surrounded by Zareedian soldiers garbed in terrifying armor. It was like something out of one of my books. Their dark eyes watched my every movement, some hopeful, others skeptical, many wary. These men had chased me for three days, causing the utmost terror to course through my frozen veins, but they *wanted* me. A prince—a prince!—was begging for my aid, presenting me with a way to use my deathly curse for good.

I loathed to leave Iyoden and the safety of its mountains. Despite my adoration for their plays, I had heard terrifying tales of the Southlands and of Zareed. Yet Prince Imad had addressed me civilly, and if he did not fear my curse, I knew I should not fear him. Had he wanted me dead, I would not have been standing there debating his offer. How long I stood, studying him, I do not know, but he waited patiently.

I nodded.

Imad raised both his hands and turned toward his soldiers, who cheered, a cluster of low and high noises that echoed among the trees.

To me, he said, "Come, come," and motioned for me to follow him. Uncertainty still rooted me to the ground, and I did not budge. After rummaging through his own saddlebags, Imad pulled free a folded piece of cloth—a yellow weave that looked almost gold. When he unfurled it, I saw it was a shirt similar to the one he wore, with thick seams and long, baggy sleeves.

The soldier who stood sentry behind me as I spoke with Imad finally rode his gelding forward. I flinched away from him. His dark eyes disregarded me, and in Hraric he said, "She can wear one of the soldiers' extra uniforms."

I admit I impressed myself by understanding his words.

Imad shook his head and replied, again in Hraric. I did not catch every word, but I understood enough. "A woman who will save our country deserves finer. Relax, Lo. What damage can this do?"

Lo was one of the words I did not recognize, but from context, I assumed it to be the soldier's name. He cast a dark glare at me, as if to blame me for the disposal of this finery, and I looked away, shivering.

Imad offered me the shirt. I refused at first, but he insisted. "I will not have you ride with us in rags. Please." He smiled.

I took the shirt from him, and though he wore long sleeves and gloves, I was careful not to touch him. I pulled the smooth fabric over my own dress and tied it around my waist. Big enough that it billowed around me, it was nevertheless the finest thing I had worn in three years, perhaps longer. It seemed to be made of cotton, but I had never touched cotton so soft.

To Lo, Imad said, "See her to one of the spares and give her our best rations. She is terribly thin; after a Northland winter, she must be famished."

"I'm not hungry," I said in my own tongue. In truth, I did not think I could keep anything down; my stomach twisted in cold, tight knots. "But thank you."

Imad stared at me, blinking, before a grin warmed his face. "You speak Hraric," he said in Hraric.

"Very little," I answered in Northlander, though I spoke more than that. Actually *hearing* the words, though, had made me realize I had gotten several pronunciations wrong. I did not try to speak it for fear of butchering it.

Imad nodded and gestured to Lo, who still sat tall and overbearing on his black warhorse, uncaring for this added shred of my intelligence. "This is Lo, captain of my guard. He will take you to a horse, and we will set out immediately unless you object, Svara Idyah."

"My name is Smitha," I said. I managed a smile—it was hard not to smile in the presence of one who exuded so much sincerity. "And now is fine. Thank you, for your kindness."

"Smitha," Imad repeated, though in his heavy accent it sounded like "Smeesa." "My never-ending thanks goes to you, Smeesa."

He clapped his hands, and the guards at his back straightened and retook their formation. Lo strode up beside me as Imad returned to his horse.

The captain of the guard said nothing; he only glanced at me with those dark eyes before walking his mount forward. I quickly retrieved my flint and books from the ground and followed him at a safe distance. The man scared me, to be frank, and I had no desire to linger near him. He paused by a brown dun mare in the middle of the company. The animal had already been heavily blanketed from rump to ears. But while Lo intimidated me, I seemed to have the same effect on the animal. The horse shied away from me, blowing out a breath through her nostrils that fogged in the chilly air. I hesitated.

Turning his mount around, Lo grabbed the mare's reins to hold her still. She whinnied, but did not shift too much as I approached her. Lo did not offer me a hand in mounting, but I could hardly blame him. Fortunately, I knew how to ride, and though gripping the reins proved an effort with my chilly fingers, I managed to seat myself and turn the mare about. Lo left without a word, and the other soldiers hesitantly gathered around me, unabashed with their stares.

I heard the word *devil* behind me and frowned. More whispers followed, most of which I couldn't hear or couldn't understand. I slumped my shoulders, wishing to be smaller, invisible.

Within moments, however, Lo turned his warhorse about and glowered at the soldiers. "The prince has said she will save our people!" he barked in Hraric. "Do you dare mock your sheikh?"

His bellows snuffed the murmurs. Lo didn't so much as glance at me before turning back and whispering something to the prince. Still, I appreciated his intervention. No one had stood up for me in a long while.

"Thank you," I heard behind me, the words muted but undeniable.

I turned to look at the man beside me. Like the others, he was dressed in indigo. His helmet rested on his pommel, etched with the shape of a horrifying insect with great pincers and a long, arching tail—what I would later learn was a scorpion. An older man, perhaps in his forties, he had black eyes and his head was shaved bald.

He nodded to me. "Thank you, coming," he said, his accent heavier than Imad's.

I nodded back, the spark inside me burning a little brighter—almost enough for me to imagine it being warm. How strange it was to see a genuine smile directed toward me. He grinned, but the front of the line began to move, cutting off any further conversation. My mare started on her own, following the line of horses in an arch through the aspens until the party pointed south, toward Zareed.

Soft snow began to fall around us as we continued onward. The soldiers marveled, eyes darting between me and the sky. A few laughed.

Prince Imad glanced back from the front of the line. Our eyes met, and he smiled.

CHAPTER 10

The first two days of riding passed in almost complete silence, save for the occasional whisper or murmur among the soldiers. I had to change horses three times a day to prevent the animals from growing too cold through the thick coating of blankets. It would have been more, but the exertion from the long days of walking and trotting was enough to save the animals from frostbite, even with me as a load.

Lo was usually the one who would direct one of the soldiers to switch mounts with me. He often rode without wearing his helmet, though the absence of the horned metal did little to ease the sternness of his features. Lo's hair wound in tight spirals to his chin, and his hard, humorless expression looked like it had been carved from dark granite. His face was covered in heavy stubble, making him look even more intimidating. He seemed to be the exact opposite of the stately and cheerful prince.

Each time we stopped, whether to change a mount, eat lunch, or camp for the night, Imad would check on me. I appreciated his attention, and even more so the tent I was given to sleep in at night—my first real shelter in such a long time.

After the first night, the Zareedians learned to keep their fires going until dawn, and they wore multiple layers to bed, often waking up in thick layers of snow. My presence among them created a source of discomfort and tension. Later, however, as we passed through the flatlands south of Iyoden—farther south than I had ever traveled—the soldiers began to relax somewhat, returning to what I presumed to be their normal camaraderie. They put on a more dignified show when Prince Imad or Lo came nearby, but left to their own devices, they laughed and joked and made fun of one another. I enjoyed listening to them talk, if only for the opportunity to decode their quick words and heavy accents. I pulled out my Hraric book of plays often to reread the passages now that I had a better idea of the genuine cadence of the language. One night, while gently scraping frost from the brittle pages as I turned them, I realized I felt genuinely happy. Here I was around other, *real* people, teaching myself about their language. Yes, they still shied away from me and whispered when they believed I did not hear, but I was once again part of a group.

One night, a day outside the Unclaimed Lands, Imad brought me a bowl of stew. I did not know what meat floated in its dark orange waters, but I recognized the leeks. Southlanders, apparently, liked their food spicy. When I asked Imad why, the older soldier with the scorpion helmet, named Eyan, jested in Hraric, "To kill anything living in it!"

I couldn't help but laugh, and was forced to set down my half-frozen bowl to prevent the food from sloshing onto my hands. I couldn't remember the last time I'd laughed, and it felt both strange and revitalizing.

Others chuckled and regarded me with a curious eye. In Hraric, I responded, "I think I've already killed anything within a mile."

They laughed—either from my joke or from my slaughtering of their language, I couldn't be sure. Imad grinned from beside me, if two paces away could be called "beside." Any closer than that was too close for most people. Even Lo's mouth seemed to twitch with the threat of a smile. But perhaps that was only a trick of the light.

The soldiers watched what they said around me, and I no longer heard whispers of "devil" or "bewitched"—at least not from that group. The men spoke to me more freely as well. To my relief, Lo did not stop them.

The trees thinned the farther south we traveled, and the soil dried until it looked more gray than brown, and cracked in a jagged disarray comparable to branches of frost. Lo and a few others rode ahead of the party, removing their extra coats once they escaped the range of my storm.

Eyan must have seen my confusion, for he said, "They're scouting. Sometimes bandits roam the borders. If they steal any of our horses, we won't get all our camels back at the way station, even with the prince."

I nodded and looked ahead to Imad, who was laughing at something a soldier had said. I noticed then how tightly the men rode around him, Lo at the front.

"His safety is paramount," Eyan said. "When it comes to Prince Imad, the captain is all seriousness."

I wanted to say the captain was all seriousness anyway, but refrained.

The cracks in the dry earth became longer and wider the farther south we traveled, and soon the parched ground was all I could see in any given direction. No trees, no mountains. A few shriveled, thorny plants struggled from the ground, and occasionally a sand-colored hawk passed overhead, but there were no other signs of life.

The hard, splintered ground gradually transformed to a more grainy terrain shortly before we reached the way station: a long, single-storied building made from pale mud bricks and splintered wood, run by men who claimed only the unclaimed deserts as their homeland, though their complexions—ranging from fawn to umber—and the slurry of their accents told me they were of a worldwide heritage.

Sure enough, the stables were filled with camels—animals I only recognized from pictures and references in books. Perhaps a camel could be said to resemble a horse, if someone were to comb a horse's coat into long, uneven patches and stretch out its neck and legs. The absurd beasts grunted and spat, not a friendly one among the bunch. They were the sort of animals that challenged you with their eyes. I would have preferred to ride Lo's imposing warhorse than to so much as pet one of them.

I did not dismount at the way station when the others did. Men in loose shirts as long as dresses and baggy hoods darted out to collect the animals, many of them gawking at both myself and Imad. Me, because of the curse, and Imad, because, well, he was a prince. When Imad came back to check on me, I asked him if I could keep my horse.

He laughed. "Surely you are not scared of the camels!"

I chewed my cold, trembling lip, trying not to let my teeth chatter. I hated to ask anything of Imad, who had already done so much for me, but the long-necked beasts frightened me enough to risk it.

"You said I could have anything, yes?" I asked, rubbing my mount's reins between my fingers. "Please forgive my asking, but let me ride the horse a little longer."

Imad looked sympathetic. Patting my horse's nose, he said, "Smeesa, beyond this point the earth is too soft for a horse. You have not been to Zareed; let me explain." He gestured south. "My men have enjoyed the trip back, since it is so cool in your presence," he smiled, "but outside of your presence, it is very hot here, and it will only grow hotter. Not far from here the ground is thick with sand. A horse's feet cannot take it, nor can they tolerate the heat. That is why Northlanders ride horses, and we ride *fapar*."

I swallowed, nodded.

"I will give you the tamest," he promised, offering me a gloved hand.

I shook my head and dismounted on my own. "Thank you," I said. "I have seen plenty of wild creatures in my travels. I . . . think I can manage a camel."

"Those bears of yours?" Imad asked, escorting me toward the camels, his braids swinging behind his ears. "I have not seen any, but I hear they are . . ." He struggled with the Northlander word, but instead of speaking in Hraric, he settled on "big."

I nodded, though in truth, I had been thinking of Sadriel. He had not appeared to me since I joined the Southlanders.

I masked my uncertainty as best as I could when one of the stable hands brought out my camel. The beast stood so tall it had to lie down before I could board it, but it encouraged me that its saddle—sitting atop a massive hump—seemed secure. It was fashioned almost like a baby crib, with a rounded pommel in the front and back. Still, even with several layers of protective blankets, the camel shied away from me. The beast even swung its head to bite me when I got too close. Though Imad had claimed he was the tamest animal of the bunch, and I believed him, most animals sensed something *wrong* about me, and this one proved no different. The stable hands tried to calm the animal, brushing their hands over its neck and distracting it with food, but each time one of them guided me close, the animal snapped, scooted, or stood. I stepped out of the way as the stable hands brought out a different camel. Embarrassed at the fuss, I was thankful my cold skin forbade flushing or perspiration. I shivered.

As soon as the next camel spied me, it threw a similar tantrum, shaking its head back and forth, sawing its teeth from side to side. It flicked its tail and locked its knees. Imad watched its antics with a frown, twisting one of his braids around his finger. The rest of his men had already been saddled and were waiting for us. Some chuckled at the spectacle. I wanted to bury myself in the sand.

To my surprise, Lo dismounted and walked over to the fretting animal, pushing past the shorter stable hands. Without pausing, he grabbed the reins just under the camel's mouth—I was sure it would bite him or charge—and yanked them downward so sharply the camel mewed and stumbled before folding its legs and lying down. Lo took a large scarf from around his neck and bound it around the camel's eyes. He grabbed the beast's large muzzle, turned its head away from me, and waited expectantly.

"*Taishar*," Imad said with a grin, thanking him. "Best get on before it changes its mind."

I wanted to ask what would happen if the camel changed its mind while I was on its back nine feet in the air, but I didn't want to cause a bigger scene, so I hurried over the saddle—eyeing Lo—and took my seat, ensuring the blankets protected the unwilling creature as much as possible from the cold of my touch. Once I was secure, Lo released the animal and let it stand. It mewed again and shook itself, but it seemed mostly content with—or at least accepting of—the situation.

"*Taishar*," I said, but Lo merely glanced at me with that stony expression of his before returning to his own mount.

Imad, at least, laughed at the spectacle, if not at me, lightening the mood somewhat. I rode next to Eyan on our trek across the Unclaimed Lands, and he offered me the occasional jab, saying things such as "The desert has never seen snow, and that camel sure didn't want to see you!" or "I've always liked graceful women."

I couldn't help but smile, despite knowing it encouraged him. "Be grateful you have me to keep you cool," I said in Hraric, "or the Unclaimed Lands would claim you."

The Unclaimed Lands stretched for miles, barren and unending. The camels' feet kicked up dust, coating their legs as well as ours. We moved swiftly enough for my storm to withhold its snow, save for when we camped for the night in the middle of the large, dry expanse. I knew the Unclaimed Lands must have been scorching, for not a quarter mile after we set out each morning, I would look over my shoulder and the night's snow would be gone, sucked into the thirsty cracks of the infertile ground.

As Imad had warned me, the sand thickened underfoot, brown at first, then more and more golden where the sun touched it beyond the reach of my cold. In the afternoon the sun shined so brightly off the sand I could hardly stand to look beyond the storm's shadows. The ground formed dips and hills, each larger than the last. Imad led us over their crests, and I marveled at the wavelike patterns that decorated their sides, like a cascade of long hair. I saw, tumbling down one of these hills, the largest spider I had ever laid eyes on. So large it had fur—white fur—and long, spindly legs much like the ones etched onto Imad's helmet. Disregarding my situation with the camels, I couldn't help but be glad creatures like that spider stayed away from me.

We traveled for three days before Imad announced, for my benefit, that we had entered Zareed. How he knew, I couldn't be sure—I spied no signs or markers, and the rolling hills of sand looked identical to the ones we had just passed. By the end of the third day, I could see rough, jagged mountains in the distance, and by the fourth day, the endless golden sand opened up to the most magnificent city I had ever beheld.

The capital of Zareed, Mac'Hliah, was enormous—Euwan could have fit into it thirty times. It nestled into the crook of that jagged mountain range: tall, knifelike mountains that rose like ochre flames, twisted and knotted and proud, from the dust-packed ground. They seemed, from the distance, to be coated in dead moss, and I could only wonder what the incredible range had looked like before the drought had stripped it of life. The sun cast the peaks' toothy shadows over the city, making Mac'Hliah appear to sit in the mouth of a great desert beast.

Homes both large and small stippled the scooping valley like scales on a fish: white, bronze, beige, and flax. They had flat roofs and rectangular doors and windows. No chimneys that I could see. Built of mud brick, most of the houses appeared to be only one story, and the smallest dwellings were no larger than a single room. There seemed little design to their layout, other than clustering close to the mountains, where there would have been water runoff before the drought. Between the brick buildings I caught glimpses of circular tents with vaulted roofs. I later learned the larger ones were homes of nomadic merchants, and the smaller ones housed the very poor. I marveled at the sight. My own home in Euwan would have stood out like a fish in a tree in this city, and would have been considered a grand home indeed.

But what really stole my breath away was the palace on the far end of the city, nestled into the mountains—*carved* from them—presiding over the land. Three tall tiers of smooth stone composed the magnificent structure—the top and bottom floors were striped with grand columns, and the center was cut with wide circle-top windows. It shimmered almost ivory against the mountains, though whether it had been whitewashed or the stone was particularly pale, I could not tell. Each floor featured a curving balcony, and a large stone path extended outward from the bottom story and into the village, as though the foundation had melted, partway, back into the earth. Magnificent carvings of people and strange creatures animated those pale walls as well, but I could not see the details from such a distance.

Imad reined in his mount outside the capital and guided it back toward me. He pointed, as though I might have missed the grand city in the expanse of sandy desert hills. "This land has always been a dry land, but in the winter the mountains used to collect enough rain to sustain us. For three years, however, the rain has not come, and the wells grow more and more shallow."

He grinned and faced his camel forward. "Come, Smeesa, and bring them water."

I nodded, oddly nervous. Imad raised his hand and the soldiers cheered. We raced down the sandy slopes, the camels' hooves raising a cloud of dust. My own anxiety left me dizzy, but I tried my best to mask it as we entered the place that would become my home.

Guards on camelback greeted us before we entered the city, speaking to both Imad and Lo, too far ahead for me to hear what was said. We began moving again, and I almost kneeled in my saddle, straining to see what lay ahead of us.

The sheer size of the population astounded me.

People filled the streets from gutter to gutter. Men wore wide scarves—*mashadah*—wrapped around their heads and under their chins, and long, loose shirts and slacks in all sorts of pastel colors: honeydew and cyan and tan. Women sported long dresses with woven belts to emphasize their waists. They, too, wore the long scarves, but many let them drape around their necks or wrapped them around dark, thick braids of hair. Thick black braids fell to hips, knees, calves. Despite the desert heat, women in Zareed clearly believed long hair to be a sign of beauty. Nearly everyone, even the children, had their ears pierced multiple times, and the more richly dressed members of the crowd wore so many studs and rings their ears sagged. A common fashion was to weave one or two fine chains through the rings—something I had noticed Lo wore on his left ear, when his hair didn't cover it. I later learned that the piercings were a sign of wealth, though I found it interesting that Imad, the wealthiest man in Zareed save for his ill father, wore very few.

All these people bustled down and over the roads, carrying tweed-woven packs on their backs and heads, guiding bizarre-looking deer by ropes, bartering for sales, chasing after stray children. But they all paused for long enough to look up at the hefty cloud that spread over their city, strange and heavy and white. They paused, stared, and pointed, confused. Some cheered when they recognized Imad among our ranks. Others noticed me, my white skin and hair, my blue lips, the tattered pieces of my skirt that hung below my borrowed shirt. And wherever we went, a foreign wave of cold followed. They gawked, whispered, disappeared into tents and doorways or pulled their mashadah over their faces.

Imad directed Lo forward, then fell back to ride beside me. He said nothing, but his presence beside me—and therefore his acceptance of me—spoke volumes to the people of his city. I knew I was not a surprise, for I heard the murmurs of "Svara Idyah" more than once. I saw a few women cross their hands over their chests and pat their shoulders, which I later learned was a gesture to ward off demons. I'm glad I did not know that when I first came to Mac'Hliah, for my nerves were already frayed at the ends, and my own anxious trembling in addition to the shivering from my cold had already threatened to throw me off my camel.

We moved deeper and deeper into the city, and I could not help but marvel at the scene that lay before me. Goats, sheep, and camels pushed through the crowds without any reaction from the people. We passed by a bazaar dyed every color imaginable, carmine and chartreuse and aquamarine, tall stands swathed in fabric, merchants selling chunky metallic jewelry and beautifully embroidered dresses. Women draped in pinks and oranges examined the merchandise.

But though the city was a feast for the senses, I noticed the underlying want. Large bins holding dates, cashews, beans, and rice sat half- or nearly empty. Racks meant to hold plucked chickens and lamb legs stood without meat, even without flies. I did not know the exchange rate of Zareedian coin, but the price tags I saw in passing seemed very high. When I looked closer, I noticed the thinness of the children beneath their loose clothes and the weariness in their mothers' eyes. We passed a well—I would not have noticed if Imad had not told me, for many people crowded around it, hiding it from view. These were a people in famine, men and women desperate for relief. They cast expectant glances at me—no, at Imad—hoping their prince had finally found a way to save them.

"Our granaries are empty," Imad murmured beside me, swaying back and forth with the stride of his camel. "That is why I came to you personally. We need your help, Smeesa."

I looked over the bronze-skinned strangers who surrounded me and nodded. "I will. As soon as we stop moving, the snow will come."

He nodded but did not smile. I could tell the sight of his people's suffering weighed heavily on him.

We reached the palace—that grand, three-tiered work of art in the mountains, even more beautiful close up—and dismounted. Imad helped guide my camel down, and I fled its saddle, not wanting to scare it. Lo barked orders to the soldiers, directing some to take positions in the palace, others to go home and report back in the morning. He rubbed his chin, which was now lined with a full but short beard, and waited for Imad and me to move ahead of him before following after us, keeping his quiet distance.

The grandeur inside the palace overshadowed that of the exterior. Great scarlet curtains draped from ceiling to floor; tiles embedded with what appeared to be mother-of-pearl lined the floors. A great stone staircase spiraled up from the center of that main room, its banisters matted with gold leaf. A giant wind chime, at least the height of a camel, hung from one corner—its chimes made from some sort of aged, hollow wood, its clapper a round disc of sandstone. It would take two men to ring such a thing. I could not fathom what its song sounded like, for we had nothing of its like in Euwan. In Iyoden! Everything about this palace—this country—was so unlike the world I had grown up in it took my breath away. And I had once thought my father's turn-ery so grand . . .

Servants surrounded Imad, and he brushed most of them away, murmuring yes and no, shaking his head or offering thanks. He led the way up those great winding stairs—I ached to touch the railing but dared not for fear it would be damaged by my frost—and into a great throne room, larger than the last, its south and east sides letting in the bright sun through circle-top windows. I peered out of one of them and spied my white cloud hovering above us, shading half the city.

"Smeesa, would you like something to eat?"

I turned and noticed a servant carrying a tray of food had joined Imad. She was a middle-aged woman in a long violet dress and salmon head scarf, and she was regarding me with curious eyes. Lo had left, but two new guards stood at attention at the entrance to the throne room, wearing indigo garb that looked to have chain mail sewn right into the fabric. The serving woman's tray was weighted down with quiche, flatbreads with hummus, raisins, and a strange-smelling wine.

I didn't enjoy eating in front of the others, especially Imad, for it required me to chew and swallow swiftly in order to keep the food from freezing in my mouth. But I was hungry, and besides, I did not want to embarrass the prince by turning down his kind offer.

"Thank you," I said, pulling my sleeve over my right hand. I took a piece of flatbread and, turning away, ate it as slowly as I dared. The simple bread tasted good on my tongue, even when it hardened and turned chewy in my mouth. I accepted a few raisins, which Imad placed directly in my covered hands, understanding the precautions I had to take.

"We need to fit you for some real clothes," he said with a smile, accepting a glass of wine before dismissing the serving woman with a nod. "And some gloves and shoes."

I looked down. My feet were still bare, as there had been no shoes to fit them among Imad's traveling party. The tiles beneath me shimmered with frost. I feared I had made them rather slippery as well, for the serving woman stumbled on her way out.

Imad clapped his hands and called out to one of his guards. As I had already realized on our voyage, he made an effort to know the names of all who served him. "Aghid, would you find Kitora and ask her to take Smeesa's measurements?" He spoke in Hraric and gestured to me when he said my name. "And provide any spare clothes she can wear in the meantime."

The guard nodded and vanished from the doorway. A moment later Lo appeared to take his place. I was amazed at how Imad and Lo seemed unwearied from days of travel, for my own frozen body ached for rest.

Imad noticed and personally showed me to a room larger than my entire home in Euwan, with a bed fit for five women and draped with mustard-colored curtains. A chest of wood, which must have been expensive considering how few trees grew near Mac'Hliah, sat at its foot. A table holding water and a bowl for washing rested on the far side of the room. I even had my own bathroom, complete with a chamber pot and a porcelain tub. A round mirror hung on the wall. I turned away from it, pulled off my gloves, and touched its surface until it frosted over.

I could not sleep right away, however. Kitora, a serving woman about fifty years old with a slight hunch in her back, came to measure me. Either the cold didn't bother her or she ignored it with great skill, for she went about her work without hesitation save for my countless warnings that she must not touch my bare skin. Taking in the sight of my dusty, ruined clothes, she insisted on drawing me a bath. I asked if it would be too much trouble for her to boil the water.

I bathed myself. Baths were a hard thing for me, and over the years I had started washing myself less and less often. Living in the wilderness, I didn't bother to maintain much of a hygienic standard. I wrapped my hands, crouched beside the tub of steaming water, and dipped a rag in it, then scrubbed one part of my body at a time, starting with my face and working my way down. I worked with haste, wiping up as much dirt as I could. Once I was finished, I carefully worked my nails over the tiny flakes of ice that kissed my skin, shedding them one by one. They scattered over the floor like dandelion seeds.

When I stepped back into the bedroom, Kitora had laid out a pale blue *wiptoa* dress and matching head scarf on the bed, along with a pair of tan sandals, long pants, and gloves. I dressed slowly, marveling at the quality and beauty of the clothing. The fabric stiffened beneath my touch, but it fit well enough. I pulled on the gloves and wrapped the scarf around my neck, covering as much of my skin as I could. After braiding my hair over my shoulder, I lay down on the bed, instantly cradled by its softness. Even with my aching muscles, almost-numb fingers, and shuddering shoulders, I managed to fall asleep quickly and ignore my coldness for a little while.

When I awoke my room was dark, illuminated by a single half-melted candle at my bedside. The soft mattress of my bed had grown hard underneath me, and it held my shape when I sat up, the surfaces sparkling with ice crystals. Leaving the candle where it was—I did not want to put it out on accident—I walked to the first circle-top window and peered outside.

Soft, starlit feathers of snow fell in silence from my storm, crowning Mac'Hliah in silver and white.

CHAPTER 11

By morning my snows had cooled the sandy earth enough to stick to the streets, roofs, and mountains in clusters, making Mac'Hliah a white city in the midst of the burning gold that surrounded it. The contrast amazed me. I gripped the balcony of the palace's third story with my gloved hands and leaned out as far as I could, marveling at the wonder of it all, thinking for the first time that the snow around me looked beautiful in its cascading silence. I marveled that my curse, created by one wizard, could so thoroughly disturb Mother Nature, one of the most powerful forces known to man.

Below I spied men and women scurrying about in coats that looked brand new. They must have been warned to prepare for the cold, but the snow may have outwitted them. They shoveled the streets with whatever they had on hand, including buckets, cooking sheets, and garden hoes. Others twirled and marveled at the never-before-seen snow; children laughed as they slid and danced and played. I smiled, feeling more peaceful than I had in years. My curse had become another's blessing. How wonderful, to give this to them.

"Incredible," Imad said, walking across the snow-strewn balcony to join me. His breath clouded in the air, and soft snow melted into his hair. He laughed. "Look at this, Smeesa! Already I feel we've collected enough to return fertility to our ground."

"It is no effort on my part," I admitted.

"But it is incredible nonetheless," Imad said, rubbing his arms. "And it is terribly cold!"

I grinned. For a moment, I had almost forgotten.

Imad clasped me by the shoulders, startling me. "Smeesa, you must go to the other villages and do the same." He pulled his hands away, my dress providing too little protection between my skin and his, but he hid the wince. "You must go to Kittat and Ir and Shi'wanara and bring them water as you have done for us. And then return! Smeesa, with you around, my people will never go thirsty. Please say you'll do it."

He asked me so earnestly, and the thought of spreading more laughter through the streets of this beautiful city and providing more relief to the weary made me nod without the slightest hesitation. Imad clapped his hands.

"I will send my best guard with you. You are the jewel of this desert, Smeesa. I will see to it that you are well protected."

I hesitated, combing through his accented words. "You will not come with me?"

He shook his head and peered out over his city. "I have been away a season already. My people need leadership, and with my father confined to his bed, I must be the one to give it to them. It will be hard to start up the farms again, to feed the . . . *rhatar*, how you say . . ."

"Economy," I said, surprised I had the answer.

He nodded. "Economy. But you will be taken care of; I will see to it. I will send Lo with you; he knows these mountains well."

A fortunate shiver hid my disdain for the idea. Lo, with his cold eyes and silent disposition, was not a companion I desired, but I would not express such ill feeling to Imad, who had done so much for me.

"Will Eyan come along? And others from our journey?" At least that way I would have friends.

Friends. How sweet that word tasted to me.

"I will tell Lo to include them," Imad said with a firm nod. "And you will stay here for the day and night, yes? Until I cannot see the houses for the snow!" He laughed, exuberant.

"Of course. Anything you need."

I returned to the rooms Imad had lent to me, surprised to find two new sets of clothes on the bed. Kitora must have stayed awake all night to make them. They looked much like the belted dresses I had seen the women in the city wearing, one fuchsia and the other mustard. I had two braided belts, both brown but with different weaves. Instead of sandals, I found two pairs of soft slippers with hard soles, one gray and one brown, both with high cloth legs that reached just below my knee. I had two scarves as well, one white with maroon stripes, the other orange with a scarlet fringe. I picked up the fuchsia dress to wear and discovered three pairs of gloves beneath it, two pairs to match the dresses and a third made of the same striped fabric as the first scarf. I touched them and bowed my head, so grateful for the kindness I had found in this place I thought I could burst. After changing—I wore the fuchsia gloves, gray slippers, and orange scarf draped softly over my head, as I had seen other women wear it—I took my old, stained, and tattered clothes from my schoolbag and threw them in the tweed basket near the bathroom, meant for garbage. I almost felt like a new woman, and though my beautiful clothes offered me no warmth and stiffened around my icy form, I cherished them.

"Don't you look thoroughly foreign."

My slow-beating heart quickened at the voice. I spied Sadriel near the window, pulling aside the curtain to look down at the falling snow.

He grinned, that sly, wide grin that rarely left his face. He looked me up and down. "At least someone's found a use for you, hmm?"

I smoothed my stiff dress, urging myself to calm. "They have. It seems such a small thing, but I can help these people."

"But what," he asked, pacing the length of the room, his black cloak fluttering behind him, "will you do when they no longer need your help?"

"I'll leave."

"Back to our old home in Iyoden." Sadriel almost sung the words. "But I don't think my queen of the wilderness will be so willing to be dethroned now that she's found a place in a palace."

I kneaded my fingers out of habit, trying to soften their knuckles. How the cold seemed to claw at me then, with Sadriel so close.

Straightening, I sucked in a deep, cold breath. "Do you need something?"

"You know what I need," he said.

A knock sounded on the door, and a new serving woman poked her head into the room. She averted her eyes from me, but I knew she could not see Sadriel.

"A meal for you," she said, setting the tray on the floor. I tried to thank her, but she left too quickly, closing the door behind her.

Sadriel crossed his arms and patted his shoulders. "Too soon dethroned," he repeated. "But when you are, I'll be waiting. My palace is far grander than anything mere mortals can devise."

He faded to nothing. I tried to ignore his words, but they gnawed at me as I crouched by the tray, too heavily clothed to frost the floor. The wine froze in my mouth after one swallow, and I had to peel its frozen petals from my lips. The grains of rice were small enough that I could swallow them with little chewing: little drops of ice washing down my throat. Even through the bite of the cold I tasted the strong spices, and though they made me cough, I didn't mind.

It tasted so much better than frog.

CHAPTER 12

My storm clouds made dawn seem early. The first serving woman I
met in the palace—Aamina—woke me, dressed in several layers and
multiple scarves. She had more clothes for me from Kitora, meant to
keep me warm, she explained. I thanked her without correcting her.

Outside, my personal troop of soldiers also wore multiple layers.
Coats had been unheard of in Zareed before my arrival, at least ones
thick enough for a Northland winter. All of the men wore indigo as
their top layer, and their peculiar animal helmets were either held under
arms or fastened to saddles, their scales and feathers unseen. I noted
that the camel prepared for me—the one with the most blankets—was
the same beast I had ridden in on. Imad no doubt hoped the animal
would not shy from me a second time.

I spied Lo near the head of the animal line, his goat-horned helmet—Imad had mentioned it portrayed a beast called an ibex—nestled
in the crook of his elbow. He had shaved his beard, save for the dark

hair around his mouth. Besides one other soldier, he was the only one in the group with any facial hair. Most Zareedian men, I noticed, wore their faces clean shaven.

Lo shook snow from his hair and noticed me from the corner of his eye. He pointed to Eyan and directed him to the front of the line before approaching me, his strides heavy as he waded through snow.

He looked especially tall and dark, a shadow, and it took all my willpower not to cower in front of him.

"We will ride in a diamond formation, with you in the center," he said, and my mouth parted in surprise. He spoke to me in fluent North-lander, his accent crisper even than Imad's, his voice deeper. "First we will go north, to Kittat, then around the range to Ir and Shi'wanara. Are you prepared to leave?"

I nodded, dumbfounded and shivering.

He said nothing more, only turned from me and jogged to the front of the line, pulling his helmet over his long coils of hair as he went. I bit my lip. I couldn't imagine surviving a long journey with him at the helm, and I had no idea how far these strange-named cities were.

"Don't let him frighten you too badly," Eyan said in Hraric from his camel as he rode up beside me. The scorpion on his helmet watched me from his pommel. "He can be hard, but he's fair. We'll be back before you know it."

I swallowed against my cold throat and approached my camel, my old, tattered schoolbag slung over my shoulder. A serving woman had offered to replace it, but threadbare as the bag was, I couldn't bear to part with it. The animal shifted uneasily as I approached, but she let me board, and with a little encouragement from Eyan, who was quick to help with some gesturing and tongue clicking, the camel stood without throwing me off her saddle.

Soon after we left Mac'Hliah, the snowfall lightened, and our camels once again trod upon sand. The storm subsided, content to hover above us as we made our journey north to Kittat.

Eyan pulled up beside me and gestured to the mountains. Speaking in Hraric, he said, "Even if we get separated, you won't get lost. We'll follow this range to each city and back again."

My breath fogged against the hot air as I asked, "They're all so close?"

"The cities are clustered against the mountains. That's where the water comes . . . or used to."

Three men from the party broke off the formation and galloped their camels toward the mountains. I watched them, curious, but they continued onward without slowing.

"Is something wrong?" I asked.

Eyan didn't watch the riders, but the mountains. "Captain must have seen something." He shrugged. "Doesn't matter. Our sheikh isn't here."

When I didn't respond, he said, "There's never been a reign in Zareed where a king has been safe."

This alarmed me, but I tried to ignore the sensation, as Eyan showed no interest in further discussing the topic. And he was right: Even if there were men in the mountains, I shouldn't worry about Imad. He was safe in the palace.

I scanned the horizon for Sadriel but did not see him. No one would die here today.

We reached Kittat after two days in the desert. It did not surprise me to learn the people were expecting us. Clouds were a rare thing in Zareed, especially large ones, and the white sheet of my snow cloud was as impossible as it was real. The *sheila*, a sort of governor, welcomed us eagerly. Apparently word of my "snow miracles," as the translation went, had already reached Kittat, and the people were eager for my relief. The men and women, dressed in their loose and colorful clothing, greeted me with smiles and bows, of all things, and then the sheila's men began passing out coats. If any crossed their arms and patted their shoulders, they did it where my eyes could not see. Though I had brought upon them the cold, they could not have offered me a warmer reception.

The sheila took our party to an orange-painted inn made of small mud bricks. It stood two stories in height and had tightly woven sinew screens over the narrow rectangular windows. The inn had been cleared out just to accommodate me and the soldiers. The innkeeper and his wife seemed eager to serve us, and eager to please me, as if the slightest disappointment would prevent my snow from falling. One hour after we reached the inn, snow began to fall, whisking through the city on bitter winds that drove families indoors to light fires for warmth—a rarity in these lands. Our inn had a hearth for cooking purposes, but the innkeeper kept it stoked with black rocks and the twisted, thorny brush that grew in patches along the mountains.

Most of the soldiers, some wrapped in blankets, chose to take their dinner in the front room at my table. The hearth drove back a good deal of my chill, so I imagined, for I only heard the occasional chattering of teeth other than my own. I kept my gloves on as I ate my spicy stew, spooning it into my mouth as neatly as I could manage. Others, including Eyan, ate more like ravenous dogs, which eased my mind concerning my own strange dinner habits.

Halfway through the meal, Eyan chuckled. "Smeesa, you have a curry icicle on your face!" He reached for my cheek.

I jolted back from his fingers hard enough to shake the bench, causing the soldier next to me, Qisam, to slosh a spoonful of stew onto the stone tabletop. A few others glanced at me, including Lo, who sat at the far end of the long table.

I touched my cheek, grateful once more that I didn't flush, and found the droplet of broth frozen there. I peeled it off and let it fall to the floor.

"Careful," I said, trying to sound lighthearted. "I don't wear these gloves for fashion." I didn't know all the niceties of Hraric, so I spoke directly. "My touch is colder than a man can bear. I do not wish to harm you."

The fleeting thought of Sadriel entered my mind.

Eyan looked startled for a moment, but then he laughed and pounded his palm on the table. "She is like a cobra!" he said to the others. "Quick and fascinating, but one kiss and you're a dead man!"

The table laughed at the comparison, and I smiled, glad for Eyan's good humor. When the noise died down, I said, "I will have to have a helmet made."

To my surprise, Lo chuckled from the end of the table, though he did not look my way. It was the first sign that the man of steel was not quite metal all the way through.

The second night, as the snow collected on the streets and the winds whistled through the sinew screens, Lo addressed me from the end of the table—the first time he had spoken to me when the situation did not require it.

"I find it interesting," he began, swirling his spoon over the bed of rice before him, "that a Northlander would speak Hraric, especially as well as you do."

He said it in Northlander, which I found interesting, for only a few of our party knew my native tongue. Most would not be able to understand the conversation, let alone interject their own thoughts.

I glanced at him, wondering at his motives.

"In Zareed, learning the northern tongue is a necessity for any businessman, diplomat, or traveler," he continued, setting down his spoon and staring at me with those dark, near-black eyes. "The earth is fertile north of the Unclaimed Lands, and trade with those farmers and merchants is essential for us. But the Northlanders care little for our own goods, outside of spices and jewelry, which they can obtain with little speech."

Eyan whispered to the soldier beside him, perhaps trying to decipher Lo's words.

"I admit," I answered in Hraric, if only for the others' benefit, "that I did not learn Hraric for love of the Southlands. Since I was a child I have found languages fascinating, especially old or forgotten ones. To me, they are like secrets."

Lo watched me with an unreadable expression. I hesitated but went on.

"The study of Hraric was available to me, and so I learned what I could. Listening to the talk of your men is very helpful, though I fear I now know more slang than actual words."

A few soldiers snickered. Lo smirked.

Folding my hands in my lap, I said, "It's very interesting, really, the provenance of a language. I believe a creole derived from an old Northlander tongue, Angrean, must have made its way down to the Southlands, because many of your root words are similar."

Lo raised an eyebrow but nodded.

"For example," I went on, slow with my Hraric, "the word *ha* means 'man,' and *tar* means 'summer,' which is not so different from the Hraric word for camel: *fapar*. And if a camel is derived from men and heat, that deftly explains why I cannot ride one."

The men laughed around us, Eyan especially, for those who had ridden with me from Iyoden to Mac'Hliah still found my awkwardness with camels a good joke. I smiled at their reaction, then dared to chance a look at Lo.

He smirked, a glint in his eye. Shaking his head, he returned to his meal and did not speak to me again that night.

Lo's silence did not last long, for the day we left Kittat to relish in the wake of my blizzard, Eyan took the front of our traveling formation and Lo rode farther back, his eyes constantly searching the mountains as we passed over them to make our way to Ir. I did spy a few people amidst the cliffs, but if Lo did not feel threatened by them, I knew I need not worry.

I was grateful when he finally spoke to me. Aside from the soreness of riding a camel for so long, my coldness felt especially brisk to me at that moment, and with nothing to distract me from it, I focused on its chill—the way it seemed to chew on me from the inside, like falling through ice and the shock of hitting the cold water, except that lightning-like sensation never subsided or calmed, only ached and throbbed.

Lo was the distraction I needed.

"You say you study languages," he said in Northlander, twisting his camel's reins around his bronze fingers. "How many do you know?"

"Fluently? Only three, not including my native," I admitted. "Four, if you count my own handtalk."

He raised a brow. "Handtalk?"

"A signed code that I made with a friend back home," I said, thinking of Ashlen. I wondered how her last year of schooling had gone, and whether or not she had married by now. "Most of the words are done with one hand, and there is a signal for each letter of the alphabet, so we can spell out words we don't have signs for. It drops things like articles and auxiliary verbs, which really are more modern inventions. It's all present tense, unless past is specified."

I waved my hand down without thought, the signal for past tense.

Lo steered his mount around a hole in the ground before saying, "And this handtalk, you communicated efficiently with it?"

"It was as efficient as two schoolgirls needed it to be," I said with a smile, remembering long-ago days in the schoolyard together. One time, when Ashlen took the blame for something I had done, the teacher forced her to sit on the stairs during recess while the rest of us played. We used handtalk to chat about the boy she liked—Alvin Modder—the largest boy in class and perhaps the slowest. I signed to her each small thing he did, and she signed back how they were obviously signs of his unknown affection for her.

Lo shouted an order behind him to Qisam, telling him to ride ahead and scout.

"I-I could show you, if you'd like."

He regarded me for a moment, almost in that amused way Sadriel so often affected, and I shivered at the comparison.

"How would you say," he began, staring ahead, "'a bandit stands fifty paces to the left'?"

"I don't have a word for *bandit*," I said, "so I would have to spell it out"—I moved my fingers to form the letters, many of which looked nothing like their scripted forms, to make it hard for others to guess the meaning—"or create a new sign for it. Bandits . . . They wear masks even here, yes? So perhaps . . ."

I split my fingers in the middle and laid my hand over one eye, forming half a mask. I then signed the rest of the sentence slowly: "stands fifty paces left."

"That is useful," Lo said, winding and unwinding the reins around his fingers. "To communicate in silence, assuming there is light to see. Simple enough for a soldier."

"Even one with only one arm."

The corner of his mouth formed a half smile. "That it can be done one handed makes it even more clandestine."

His vocabulary—and astuteness—amazed me. I had thought my handtalk rather clever, but already the captain of Imad's guard saw the roots of its fashion.

I nodded.

"And the subject comes first, as in Northlander?"

"Yes, but it can be changed for Hraric."

"No," he said. "It is clearer this way. How do you show geography or distance?"

I began the symbol for mountain, but from the corner of my eye I caught a spot of maroon. I turned my head and spied Sadriel atop one of the steep cliffs lining our path. Though the shadow of his broad-rimmed hat hid his eyes, I felt him watching me.

"Smeesa?"

I shook my head and turned back to Lo, who scanned the area that had captured my attention.

"I'm sorry. Just . . . cold."

I cleared my throat, arched my hand, and pointed my fingers and thumb toward the ground. "Mountain," I said. "To indicate a direction in regards to the mountain, you move the sign itself. Over," I explained, moving my hand in a half circle, up and down, "or under"—I again drew a half circle, down and up.

Lo mimicked my signs. I glanced back to the mountain, but Sadriel had already disappeared.

CHAPTER 13

My mother always said that God made the world in perfect balance, an idea she used to explain the smallest fortunes and mishaps in our lives. I recall a time when she dropped a plate—a piece of my grandmother's china, which we only used at winter solstice and on my father's birthday—onto the kitchen floor. It shattered into hundreds of sharp porcelain pieces, some scattering as far as the hearth. Instead of crying or stomping her foot, as I was wont to do, she merely pressed her fists to her hips and said, "I knew that would happen. I found two extra eggs in the henhouse this morning."

I thought of her and my grandmother's china often in Ir.

Where men and women had been cheering in the streets of Kittat as we rode into town, we were only greeted in Ir by scowls. The townsfolk crossed their arms and patted their shoulders to ward off my evil spirits, though nothing they did could ward off my cold. Where Kittat's sheila had welcomed us with open arms and appointed us an inn, the one in Ir questioned Lo roughly, only offering us shelter after he was provided with a written edict from Imad himself. My snow fell heavily that first night, and while some found relief from the water, I heard rumors of many falling ill, which terrified me. I told Lo of Bennion Hutches, and though he did not seem to take my warnings seriously, we left before nightfall on the second day rather than staying the designated three. I prayed earnestly that the ill would recover, hoping that the prayers of a coldhearted woman would be enough to help them.

I had little time to worry, for as soon as we departed from Ir for our southbound trek to Shi'wanara, Lo had me instructing him again on my handtalk, which was how we spent the majority of the journey. He learned quickly, and only occasionally tweaked signs to motions he found more efficient. I knew his changes would have bothered me in Euwan, yet I found myself agreeing with him more often than not. Eyan, and then Qisam, eavesdropped on our mobile lessons, and soon my entire escort began learning the unspoken language. I noticed that the random bouts of laughter increased as soldiers fingered jokes one to another. To my surprise, Lo let them laugh.

Closer to Shi'wanara, Lo rode ahead to scout for bandits, and I surprised myself by actually missing his company, not that I expected much more of it. Once Lo mastered my simple handtalk, I doubted he would care to speak to me again.

And he didn't, not even after our arrival in Shi'wanara. The city offered us a polite reception, much to my relief, though their reactions to me were more mixed. Fortunately, even the most suspicious of my guard had warmed to me after weeks of travel.

Many of them stayed up late with me that first night in Shi'wanara, though we sat around the fire of the inn where we were staying so the others could ward off my wintry aura.

"I heard," Qisam said in Hraric, his voice so low and accented I strained to understand him, "that in the Northlands, the earth waters itself every morning."

"How can the earth water itself?" asked Bakr, the youngest soldier in our group, three years my junior.

"I think he means *dew*," I said, using the Northlander word, which was easy to pronounce with the Zareedian accent. "Every morning its small droplets cling to the grass, only to vanish when the sun grows too strong."

Lo had not joined us for our fireside chat, but I spotted him at the far end of the room, handing coin to the innkeeper. He leaned against the wall with his arms folded against his chest, the firelight glinting off the gold rings and chains in his left ear. He would have looked a shadow if not for that jewelry. He was certainly as silent as one.

"I heard once," I said to Qisam, "that dew is fallen rain that yearns to return to heaven. Every night it struggles up from the earth that has claimed it, climbing the grass on its journey to the sky. But every day the sun, keeper of the heavens, forbids it from completing its journey and casts it back into the soil."

"A sad story," said Bakr.

I shook my head. "Were it not so, nothing would grow."

"And then we'd *all* go to the heavens!" Eyan shouted. I laughed with the others, though the thought of Death made me shiver. I had not seen Sadriel since catching a glimpse of him many days before, but I often felt as if I were being watched.

The night grew late, and the soldiers—my friends—retired to their beds, many of which were shared by two or three men. As my snow flurries swirled outside, I, too, took to my bed on the first floor of the inn. But the insomnia that often came with the cold dragged at me hard that night, and I soon returned to the hearth, this time alone. I stared into the depths of the flames and thought of my small campfires in the mountains. I did not miss my mountains—my safe haven—despite spending three long years there. Imad had saved me by bringing me back to the Southlands; he had reminded me what it was to be human.

I rolled up my mustard-colored sleeves, removed my gloves, and picked up one of the red coals and turned it over in my hands, careful not to let it crumble. Often, in my loneliness, I played with embers like these, imagining that I was not cursed but blessed—a woman who could touch fire and remain unscathed. I blew onto the coal softly, my cold breath dimming its red life.

"It does not hurt you?"

I nearly dropped the coal at the voice. Instead, I quickly tossed it into the fire and turned around, my braid falling off my shoulder. Lo stood behind me, still wearing his many layers of warmth, the indigo on the outside.

Instead of waiting for my reply, he said, "We move tomorrow. You need to sleep."

I turned and smiled at the flames. "I will in a moment, thank you."

"You cannot?"

I glanced back to him. He took a seat in one of the canvas chairs set around a sage-and-lavender-woven rug. Not wishing to burden him with my woes, I answered simply, "I am a little cold tonight."

"And the fire does not help."

He looked at my hands.

"When we were children," he said, watching the flames, "my mother would help warm us up by filling a goat bladder with hot water and pressing it to the backs of our necks. It always helped, even if it stunk."

I smiled. "I do not know what a goat bladder smells like."

"You do not want to."

"You have siblings?" I asked.

"I have nine, two in the past-lands."

"You are the eldest?"

"The youngest."

I considered him for a moment. "That surprises me."

He raised a black eyebrow.

"You seem like an older brother."

A smile threatened his lips. "Perhaps because Imad has given me the task of overseeing seventeen little boys."

I chuckled to myself, pulled down my sleeves, and replaced my gloves. "Are you from Mac'Hliah?"

"Djmal," he said. "It is closer to Kittat than anywhere we have been, in the canyons."

"Is it small?"

"Very."

"My town is small, too," I said. "There were three hundred people or so when I left."

His dark eyes shifted from the fire to me. He hesitated before speaking, but when he did it was without abashment.

"Tell me, if you will, why you are how you are. It is apparent you were not always Svara Idyah. Why has this winter come to follow you so intimately?"

I opened my mouth to speak, but only chilled air passed my lips. It would be a long time before I explained to someone Mordan's curse. Over the years I had realized I'd done many things to deserve his curse, whether or not he knew it.

After some thought, I answered, "Winter is the dearest friend to those who have chosen to be cold."

He narrowed his eyes, but I did not explain. Standing, I brushed off my skirt. Using my right hand, I signed, *Thank you for talking to me*, and excused myself to my quarters.

I do not know how late Lo stayed up, but I managed to get an hour of rest before Eyan banged against my door at dawn for our two-week return trip to Mac'Hliah.

I did not tell him how terrified I was of what would happen to me once we arrived.

CHAPTER 14

Lo did not slow the soldiers when we reached the city; they staggered to a halt on their own, awed at the sight before them. I peered over their tall shoulders to see it for myself, and a smile broke across my face.

Fresh water ran down the mountain slopes that cradled Mac'Hliah, and I dare say I saw a few struggling patches of green among the cliffs. Not enough time had passed for the water to bolster farming, but the market—the almost straight line of color that cut through the center of the city—seemed a little fuller, the people a little livelier.

Lo gave me an almost wry look before shouting to the men in Hraric and leading us down the sandy slopes into the capital, through the winding streets to that exquisite palace that shimmered against the breast of the mountains. Imad, dressed rather plainly for a prince in long *khalat* robes of teal and plum, welcomed us warmly on the steps of his home. He even embraced Lo, who stood a full head taller than

him, and bowed to me. He was a prince, so the gesture humbled me
and left me speechless.

"The pools have been refreshed, Smeesa," Imad exclaimed, gesturing to the mountains behind us. "The leopard pools have been dry so
long, but your snow has filled them, and will continue to fill them." He
clasped my gloved hands. "You must stay here; I beg you. Should you
wish to return to the Northlands, I will of course grant your wish, but I
beg you to stay. Even if the drought ends tomorrow, the water will make
Zareed prosper. Do you see?"

He released my hands and rubbed his own together, warming
them.

"But she cannot stay in the city," said an older man lingering behind
him, his head and face shaved clean like Eyan's. He was dressed more
richly than Imad, despite the heat. For a moment I supposed him to be
the king, but no one bowed, and Imad had described his father as being
very old. This man looked middle-aged at most.

Imad nodded, thumbing the hoop in his left ear. "I have considered
that. Smeesa, my adviser, Kechak."

The man nodded, as did I.

"Do not think me ungrateful," Kechak said in heavily accented
Northlander, "for your services here. But Mac'Hliah will not survive
under constant snowfall, and the cold will throw off the balance of the
land. Tar Tarra"—the term meant Mother Nature—"did not intend
for Zareed to be so temperate."

"Come inside, Smeesa," Imad said, gesturing with both hands.
"And we will all discuss it. Lo, please excuse your men—their journey
has been hard. A few days' paid rest will see them well."

Eyan yelped a solo cheer behind me.

I followed Imad and Kechak up to a wide room on the second floor,
where another adviser, Talim, sat waiting for us at a long table. I had
the impression that these men had been against Imad's mission to find

me. But if that had been the case, they regarded me much more warmly now that the land was thriving.

I, of course, agreed to stay in Zareed, for there was nothing in Iyoden I wanted to return to—nothing I *could* return to, save for the empty mountains, hunting dogs, and Sadriel's visits. After a meal and some discussion, Imad decided on some caves in the Ohpi, or "Finger," Mountains northeast of Mac'Hliah. They were far enough for my snowstorms not to affect the city but close enough that, should I be needed, I could be easily reached. That, and the mountains would continue to collect snow and provide runoff throughout the year. I was wary about my new home, but Imad gave me his word that it would be comfortable. I stayed in the palace for three more days while Imad's men made arrangements for me. During that time my storm refreshed the city's runoff but also drove families back into their mud-brick homes. I imagined many of them were happy to see me leave.

I did not see Imad the day of my move—Aamina told me he was working out border delegations in his father's stead with Paeil, a small coastal country to the west. Aamina, a woman in her late forties with hair dark as onyx and a mouth full of conversation, had been appointed as one of my suppliers, a servant of sorts who would bring food and other necessities to my new home. I felt awkward to accept such an arrangement—after all, I had learned to live on my own—but Imad had insisted on it. Before I left, Aamina introduced me to Rhono, a stout woman with a pursed mouth, and Havid, a tall, thin man with a long neck and short hair, both of whom would also assist me in my new residence. Neither seemed happy to meet me nor pleased with their new line of work. Rhono actually crossed herself and tapped her shoulders before I even left the room. I pretended not to notice, but anxiety pressed in on me from all sides until I was forced to breathe slowly through my mouth just to hold my calm. Aamina asked if I was all right, and I assured her that I was. I did not want her to worry, though I was relieved she would be the one to help me settle into my new home.

My belongings had already been loaded onto my choice camel, and when I left the palace with Aamina, I was surprised to find Lo securing my load—I had not expected him to be my escort. He had shaved and trimmed his hair, and donned a fresh uniform of indigo sewn with mail. A heavy, curved sword hung at his left hip.

"Do you have everything?" he asked in Northlander.

I glanced to Aamina, who didn't speak that tongue, and nodded. I had little to bring with me and could not bring myself to ask Imad for anything more.

The three of us walked down the steps of the palace, Lo guiding his camel and mine. My storm, which blew and twirled about us, had left the earth slick beneath the animals' feet. Aamina and I held on to the straps of my camel's saddle as we picked our way through the half-shoveled roads beneath the palace. The snow soaked my slippers, and I knew Aamina had to be freezing despite the extra layers she wore. I apologized to her, but she merely shook her head and reassured me that she was fine. Fortunately, after some walking, we outstripped the worst of the storm and the winds died down. The earth suddenly dried beneath our feet, and I imagined it felt much warmer to the others.

Lo halted the camels between a few low-roofed houses and had them both kneel down. He helped Aamina onto his own animal. As I approached my blanketed mount, however, I heard a noise that froze me in place.

Barking.

I whirled around, stumbling over my own feet, as two long-legged dogs came racing down the street, the wispy hair of their ears and tails blowing in their self-made wind. Three boys chased after them, waving sticks in the air.

I stopped breathing. My leg still bore the marks of the basset hound's bite from that long-ago day when the two hunters had come for me in the mountains. My mind screamed at me to run.

I cried, a mewing sound with no air, and stumbled backwards, tripping over the folded legs of my camel.

The dogs bolted for me. I flung both arms over my head and held an icy breath.

I heard the faint scraping of metal, and the dogs' gallop slowed. My heart racing, I glanced up and saw Lo standing over me, his thick, curved sword in his right hand. The tall dogs stopped and regarded him warily.

I shivered.

The three boys, none older than perhaps fourteen, caught up to the animals and snatched them by the thick woven collars around their necks. Their eyes bugged at the sight of Lo's sword.

He sheathed the toothed blade. "Keep your animals under control," he growled, "especially so close to the city limits. You disrespect these women who are in the service of your sheikh."

Trembling, I forced myself to my feet and gawked at Lo. The children's gazes moved between Lo and myself, and they gushed out an apology before darting back the way they had come, tugging their animals with them.

"I-I'm sorry," I said, covering my face and willing myself not to cry. "I'm sorry, I didn't mean to—"

"It's all right," Lo said, his tone softer than when he'd addressed the boys. "I would have gone around this area had I known dogs frighten you. There are a lot of them here."

I tried to swallow, to wet my frozen throat, but I couldn't. I only nodded, focusing my energy on keeping back my tears. Aamina watched me with an almost maternal concern, but she didn't speak.

"I do not think they would have hurt you," he offered.

"There were men in Iyoden who feared what I am," I said, my voice barely above a whisper as I scrambled onto my camel's saddle with little grace. "Men with dogs."

I left it at that, and Lo didn't ask me to explain, only nodded his understanding. He took his own seat behind Aamina and guided us out of the city, following the Finger Mountains north.

I recognized my cave before we reached it—its entrance stood high and narrow, much like the eye of a needle, and a wooden door had been fitted just inside of it. When we stopped and climbed off our camels, I hesitated to approach it, but Aamina led the way as Lo unpacked my belongings from the camel.

I had not known what to expect—after all, it was a cave—but the reality exceeded my wildest imaginings.

The room inside was about the size of my home in Euwan but narrower, stretching back about thirty paces. A bed with a thick mattress sat against the left wall, and a beautiful stone table was positioned against the right, complete with three chairs. Thick rugs hid the rocky floor, and long draperies masked most of the walls. They alternated red, cream, and white, some decorated with inky depictions of Mac'Hliah itself. A white drapery, ironically, depicted the profile of a dog. The cavern's ceiling did not quite meet itself, leaving a long crack overhead. It had been covered with what appeared to be a thick canvas, which let in the soft gray glow of storm-filtered sunlight.

"This . . . is amazing," I said as Aamina lit a tall glass lamp in the corner, illuminating a short red chair with high armrests and a plump-polished wooden cupboard. When I rushed over to look inside, I saw it held a variety of dishes and food. There were even animal skins filled with water, not that I needed it. My snow had always been enough for me. Closer to the door I noticed a small fireplace filled with coals, its chute drilled into the rock.

Lo opened the door, a load of blankets and clothing in one arm. I hurried to him and accepted the items myself, though he seemed hesitant to hand them over. His gold earrings glimmered in the lamplight.

He glanced around and smiled. "Our sheikh has outdone himself."

"It's beautiful," I agreed, turning in a full circle as I took in the effect once more. "I can't imagine what it must have cost . . ."

"Now, don't worry about that," chided Aamina. "I'll be back in three days; Rhono will come to you tomorrow, and Havid after that."

"Oh, I won't need—"

"They'll come all the same. Just in case."

I smiled. "Thank you. Really." I glanced to Lo, remembering his swift response with the dogs. Though I believed he was right and they had been no real threat to me, I appreciated how quick he had been to protect me. "Thank you."

He nodded. "I imagine Prince Imad will pay his respects shortly and see you settled in."

"I look forward to it."

Lo left to retrieve the rest of my things—my books from home and some medical supplies. Before he and Aamina left, he waved his hand at me, signing, *You will be safe here.*

I signed back, *Thank you*, but I didn't think he saw it.

CHAPTER 15

"You don't know what luxury is."

Sadriel startled me from my reading. Now that I was alone, he had wasted no time in coming to see me; the sun had not yet set behind my cavern.

He walked around the interior of the cave, studying the drapes. "You think this is *nice*? I suppose it's . . . quaint, in its own way."

"Imad put a lot of work into this for me."

Sadriel laughed. "Imad's *servants* put a lot of work into it, and they only did so to make a few coins." His amber eyes settled on me. "In my realm, your chamber pot would be made of rubies."

"Please don't say that."

"Why?" he asked, pacing the length of the room. "Because it insults your desert prince's interior decorating, or because it tempts you?"

I shut my book and glared at him. "Do you really think such a thing would tempt me? Where have you been the last three years, Sadriel?"

"Fine clothes will change a person," he said, rubbing his chin. "They might change you yet."

His words stuck in my ears. *But I have changed,* I thought. *Haven't I?*

I shook the thoughts from my head. "I am grateful for the clothes I've been given. They keep me from hurting anyone."

"But they do not warm you," he said. "I could take you somewhere where mortal concepts like warm and cold don't matter."

I picked up my book with gloved hands and squeezed it. "Please leave."

"You want to discard me for your new friends?" Sadriel laughed. "They're so unrefined."

"And the company of the dead would be preferable?"

He grinned.

I took a deep, cool breath. "Your tactics won't work on me, Sadriel. Why must you torture me so? Do I really still 'amuse' you after so long?"

"It would amuse me more if you danced. But I know others who are less prudish than you, Smitha. Until we meet again."

His chuckle echoed between the cavern walls as he faded away.

I tried to read my book again in my quiet cavern, but I could not focus. Imagining it to be weariness from travel, I turned down my lamplight—leaving it at a soft glow—and climbed beneath the covers of my lush bed. I did not need the blankets, but I relished the comfort of their weight. Shivering and aching, I fell asleep quickly.

I dreamed of Lo. When I awoke before dawn, I did not remember much of it, only that he and Ashlen had been in it, and we had been handtalking. Every time Lo said something, however, I couldn't read it.

I got a knock on the door while working a brush through my cold white hair. I hurried to it, eager for a visitor, and saw Rhono standing outside in the snow, her head scarf soaked. She carried a small tin bowl of soap, washcloths, and what looked like salt. Behind her I noticed a number of men out in my storm, digging long paths through the snow and shoveling the frozen clumps into stout leather bags, which they then piled into a large wagon. Snow harvesters, come for water. Or perhaps they had simply been sent to ensure the blizzard did not trap me inside this cave.

"Come in, come in," I urged Rhono. I stepped aside so she could enter. Her eyes marveled at the room for a moment before she stepped in out of the cold. I spied her camel not far off, its reins staked into the frosty ground.

"I'm sorry, I didn't think to light the fire. Actually, I'm not sure how, with coals . . ."

I knelt at my small fireplace and looked down at the coals, wondering if the rocks would just light if given a spark. I stood up to find my flint, but Rhono had already laid down her load and walked back into the snowfall, trekking toward her camel.

I watched her go. "Thank you!" I called. Without so much as turning, she mounted her camel smoothly and started back for the city at a trot.

After shutting the door, I took Rhono's gift and placed it with the tin tub I had found hanging on the wall in the very back of the cave. Afterward, I finished brushing my hair and ate some dates. With nothing else to do, I returned to my book of plays and started up where I had left off.

As Lo had predicted, Imad came that very afternoon. I could hear him talking before he even knocked. When I opened my door, Lo stood there with him—not surprising, as he was captain of the prince's guard. Both of them were dusted with snow. I hurried them inside.

"Smeesa, it's freezing in here!" Imad exclaimed, rubbing his hands together and looking over the walls. His words puffed in clouds of white. "But they did a decent job. Is it satisfactory?"

"Yes, yes, of course!" I said, tugging my gloves tighter over my hands. "And I'm sorry, I don't know how to light a fire with these kind of coals—"

Before I could even finish the sentence, Lo crouched at my fireplace and began rearranging the coals into a cone, not caring that they left black smudges on his riding gloves. He found a cask of oil that I had not seen and drizzled it in the coals' center, then struck a match to light it.

"Thank you," I said. He nodded.

"A little dark for my tastes," Imad said, examining the ceiling. "You're sure you like it? I can send more lamps."

"I love it. Really, truly. I could not have asked for better. Did your negotiations go well?"

Imad blinked for a moment. "Oh, with Paeil? Well enough; thank you for asking."

"You know Dideh Bab?"

Lo gestured to the open book of plays on my bed, its pages wrinkled, faded, and torn on the edges, the dye in its cloth cover patchy from having been left in the snow too many times.

"Dideh Bab?" I repeated.

He tilted his head. "These are his plays. *The Fool's Last Song.*"

I straightened at the title. He knew these? I'd always thought the book was some obscure volume collected by an eccentric merchant. To know someone else knew the stories that had kept me sane through my years of isolation kindled a strange sort of hope in me. "*The Basket Bearer* is my favorite," I said. "This is the book that helped me learn Hraric."

His stern, dark eyes considered me for a moment.

"If you need more books," Imad said, "I am happy to send them."

I perked further. "I-I would love that. This . . . I can't count how many times I've read this."

Imad laughed. "It shows!"

Lo smiled.

"Forgive me, but I must go," Imad said, running his fingers over one of his thin braids. "I will try to come again for longer, but—"

"You have responsibilities. I am grateful to you for making the trip so soon." Looking to Lo, I added, "Please see him to the palace safely."

"Of course."

It saddened me to see them go; I stood in my doorway and watched until the snowfall hid their retreating camels, not caring if snow dampened the rugs at my feet. I had no more visitors that day, and Havid's visit the next day was as quick as Rhono's had been, though he was gracious enough to leave me a package of flatbread. To my relief, Aamina came on the third day as promised and stayed several hours.

"And she, of course, will have nothing of it," she chattered as water boiled over my fireplace. She told me an animated story about a woman I did not know and would likely never meet. "She's smitten with that bricklayer, even if marrying him will mean living in a tent the rest of her life!" She clicked her tongue and brought the bubbling water over to the stone table. "You know how young girls are."

She seemed not to notice that I, too, was a young woman, having just turned twenty-one, but it did not surprise me that the dark circles around my eyes and white hair made me appear older to her. I thanked her for the water, dipped a rag into it, and began washing my hands.

"Goodness!" Aamina said, placing a hand on her heart. "Doesn't it burn you?"

I shook my head. "The hotter the better."

Aamina clicked her tongue again and started fussing with my bed linens, which did not need tidying. "You need to eat more. This food shouldn't be lasting so long."

"I will try."

"I'm going to need boots if this snow gets much deeper," she said, staring up at the canvas overhead. "I'm surprised that doesn't cave in."

I considered asking Aamina about Rhono's and Havid's apparent distaste for me but ultimately decided against it, not wanting to burden her with my problems. Instead I listened to her stories of how her husband had lost his little finger on his left hand and how the farmers were planting on the slopes again. Aamina enjoyed talking, and I enjoyed listening to her.

When she left, I brought my blankets over to the fire, undressed, and curled around the hearth, massaging my tense forearms and willing some small whisper of the heat to penetrate my muscles. The motion helped a little, but my teeth still chattered as they always did, and my frosty blood scraped its way through my veins.

"Perhaps I should announce myself, not that I mind the view."

I grabbed the corner of a blanket to cover myself before rolling over to glower at Sadriel, whose grin spanned more of his face than usual.

"Perhaps you should."

"Quite the company you're keeping," Death said, making himself comfortable in my red chair. "But they'll learn soon enough. Didn't I tell you about Marya?"

I waited.

"Marya from Kittat," he clarified. "A dyer, and a good one, with two little boys. I had to collect her a few days after your visit there. Pneumonia is a nasty thing, often brought on by the cold."

I sat up, the blanket sticking to me with frost. "Truth? You're telling me the truth?"

"Why would I lie to you, Smitha?"

It was strange to hear my name pronounced that way again. The way it was said back home. I turned from him, hugging the blanket to me.

"Two boys?" I asked. "Did . . . did the cold take any others?"

"Do you really want me to tell you?"

"Yes. Please."

He spoke of two newborns, a boy who had slid on the ice and cracked his head, and an elderly woman who'd died of fever. Each name ate at me, making me colder and colder until I lingered on the verge of numb. Tears came to my eyes and froze on my lashes. My very heart was sculpted in ice.

"I'm sorry," I whispered.

Sadriel stood. "No need to apologize to me," he said. He strolled over to my fire and crouched beside me. "These people," he continued, softer, "will turn their backs on you, eventually. I won't. You can't hurt anyone in my realm."

"Only watch as you do."

"What is life without Death?" he asked, tilting up the rim of his hat. "Will you punish me for doing that which I was created to do?"

I drew my knees up to my chest and shook my head, tears falling onto my cheeks, freezing to my chin.

"Come with me."

"I can still help them," I whispered, little more than a breath. "The drought—"

"The drought."

"I have a home here." I met his eyes. "I have friends."

He snorted. "For now, perhaps. But they can't change what you are any more than you can. They'll realize the consequences of your curse soon enough."

I squeezed my eyes shut and sobbed, the tears gluing my eyelids shut. By the time I had worked them off—losing a few eyelashes in the process—Sadriel had vanished.

I cried the rest of the night with my face pressed close to the fire. The coals sizzled faintly with each tear.

CHAPTER 16

I didn't sleep that night. I wished and prayed and begged for sleep, to blow myself out like a candle just for a little while, but sleep eluded me. Once I had cried myself dry, I tried to remind myself of all the people I had saved by curing the drought. I replayed Imad's praises over and over in my mind, but they did little to relieve my guilt.

At least I could hurt no one out here. The Finger Mountains were too steep for farming or habitation and too far from Mac'Hliah's community for any who lived there to fall prey to my storm. Here I could be sure my curse stayed only with me and did not touch anyone else.

The next morning I dressed in my fuchsia clothing and braided my hair over my shoulder. I admired the intricate plaits Aamina wore, but I doubted my fingers were deft enough to manage such a pattern. I left off my head scarf and waited for Rhono. The helpers Imad had appointed to me usually came mid- to late morning, but Rhono stayed away.

With little else to divert me, I decided to wash my laundry. I did not sweat, so the clothes only needed to be cleaned of stains. I soaked the hem of my mustard dress to get the snow-wetted dirt from it, handling it carefully with my gloves, then scrubbed it with my toothbrush. I didn't mind that it was my toothbrush—I had grown so accustomed to dirt in my years alone I honestly didn't think twice about it.

I left my clothes by the fire to dry and read through *The Basket Bearer* to cheer myself, for it was a pleasant tale with a happy ending. I reread *The Fool's Last Song* as well, a more complex story that held subtle commentary on the balance of justice and compassion, told from the point of view of an executioner on the verge of retirement. His last criminal to eliminate was the king's jester, who'd been thrown in prison for being too honest.

Fitting that this would be Lo's favorite.

A knock sounded at my door near sunset. After setting down my dinner, I hurried to the door, wondering why Rhono had come so close to dark.

When I opened the door, I was surprised to see Lo outside instead, warmly bundled with a mashadah wrapped around his head. Behind him a few snow harvesters with shovels cleared snow from the ground.

"Lo," I said, stepping aside. He had a heavy leather bag over his shoulder.

"I found this on your doorstep," he said, holding up a set of clothes, wet with snow. I recognized Kitora's handiwork.

"Thank you," I said, taking them from him. "Rhono must have left them outside." I must have been frightening to her, the poor woman. But she had come, and for that I was grateful.

I took the clothes—a lovely pale gray dress and salmon head scarf—to the fire to dry and took down my others, quickly tucking the undergarments out of sight. "It's late," I said, glancing at the cracks around the door. "Dark soon."

"Do you not stay up late?" Lo asked, removing his mashadah and coat. Instead of his usual indigo uniform, he wore a plain brown shirt with no markings, and loose *sirwal* slacks that cinched at the ankle.

I nodded, thinking of our exchange about goat bladders and curses in Shi'wanara. "But it isn't safe to travel in the dark, not through my storm."

"It doesn't concern me. I work long shifts; this was the best time for me to come. I can leave, if it bothers you."

"No!" I said, perhaps too animatedly. "No, it's fine. Please, sit."

He pulled out one of the chairs and sat, then reached into his heavy bag. I chose a spot on the bed across from him.

"Here," he said, handing me a thick hardbound book. I took it, surprised at its weight. "These are Dideh Bab's earlier works, before he was acclaimed."

My mouth formed an O as I ran my gloved fingers over the title, embossed into the front cover along with the outline of a bird. "Imad was willing to part with this?"

"It is my copy," he said, pulling a second book from his bag. Another hardcover, but covered in black cloth, with no title that I could see. "This is old Hraric," he explained, opening the front cover. On it had been written a sort of code in fine, slanted penmanship, scrawled with deep blue ink. "The Dideh Bab is . . . a thick read, but this will help you translate."

I accepted the book, smiling. "I . . . thank you. I'll take good care of them; I promise."

He glanced at the tattered volume at the end of my bed and smirked.

"Really," I insisted. "I . . . didn't have a safe place . . . for that one."

"Prince Imad will have to build you a shelf." He glanced around. "Though I'm not sure where you would put it. This room is more decoration than sense."

"It is, isn't it?" I laughed.

He smirked again, a sort of half smile that tugged on the left edge of his lips. Then he stood and shrugged on his coat.

"Thank you for coming," I said, though I was disappointed he was going so soon.

"I'm not leaving," he said, sitting back down. "It's cold in here."

"Oh. Oh!" I hurried to my fire and poured some extra oil on it. Removing my right glove, I rearranged the coals and tried to fan up a bright flame.

"I think it's warmer over here," I said, gesturing to the red chair.

Lo shook his head, his earrings glinting. "This is fine, thank you."

I paused, staring at him. He had never said that to me before— *thank you.*

He raised an eyebrow.

"Sorry. May I ask you an odd question?"

He waited.

"Prince Imad," I said. "If he is the prince, why doesn't he wear more earrings? They're a sign of wealth, correct? I've seen merchants with so many their ears touch their shoulders."

"It is because our sheikh is a good man," Lo said, his eyes following me as I retook my place on the bed. "He knows he has more wealth than any one man could ask, but he does not feel the need to exploit it."

"And yours?" I asked, counting the rings in his ear. Six of them, looped through with a gold chain.

He touched the rings with his fingertips. "The first three were given to me when I joined the king's guard," he said. "The others when I became captain of the prince's."

"The king, is he doing well?"

"As well as can be expected. His passing will not be long now."

I nodded, and a moment of silence fell between us.

"Why did you become a soldier?" I asked.

He leaned back in his chair and folded his arms. "Why did you become the Svara Idyah? You still haven't given me an answer."

The question caught me off guard. I shivered.

Lo let out a long breath. "About sixteen years ago, when I was thirteen, Undah-hi raiders attacked Zareed, Djmal and Kittat included. I did not think such a thing was right, so I signed up for the militia."

"Militia?" I asked, wide-eyed. "They take soldiers so young?"

His mouth formed a wry twist. "They did not know how young I was until I was old enough."

I nodded. "And . . . your siblings, who passed away. Was it from . . . ?"

"One, yes," he said. "The other from childbirth."

"I'm sorry."

"What of yours?" he asked, tapping his fingers against his arm. "Or is that a secret as well?"

"I have one sister, Marrine, who's younger than me. Almost sixteen now," I said, staring at the seams of my gloves, tracing each stitch with my thumb. "As far as I know, she is well." I hesitated. "She was sick, when I left. The cold . . . it—"

"It is all right," Lo interrupted, perhaps due to impatience, but I thought it for the quiver in my voice as I spoke of my sister, whom I had so often mistreated. "I did not come here to pry into the details of your life."

I glanced up at him.

"Numbers, with your handtalk," he said, unfolding his arms and going through digits zero through nine on his fingers. "What if they are unspecified quantities? What then?"

I smiled, relieved to change the subject. "Then you make your best guess and wiggle it," I said. I formed *nine* by touching my thumb and pinky together, and shook my hand back and forth. "There are a lot of men in the army," I said. I then flattened my hand, palm toward Lo, and curved my thumb inward, the sign for *zero*. "There are very few men in my bedroom."

Lo laughed, more heartily than I had ever heard him do so, and the rare, rich sound of it warmed me, in a manner of speaking. In truth, I licked my teeth to coax them to stop chattering.

"That is smart," he said. "You surprise me."

I mocked offense. "It surprises you that I am smart?"

He nodded. "For one so young."

"Unless years pass differently in Zareed, I am not," I protested. "I turned twenty-one not long ago."

"Hmm. Perhaps not so young, then. It is hard to tell with white women."

I gaped dramatically. "Aamina happens to think me an old woman, I'll have you know."

Lo stood. "Perhaps I ought to sign something with my left hand to show I am joking?" He wrapped his mashadah around his head. "Thank you, Smeesa, for enlightening me. I'm sure I will have more questions for you."

"And thank you for the books, very much. And for your company," I said, rising to my feet. "I appreciate it."

"Read 'Milkmaid' first," he said as he walked to the door. Snow flurries flew into the room when he opened it and stepped out. "You may find it amusing."

Despite last night's weariness drawing on me, I opened the larger of the two books Lo had given me and sifted through the pages until I found "Milkmaid"—a short story, not a play. It told of a spice merchant who traveled to the High-Top lands—I assumed he meant those farthest north—to sell his wares. I soon discovered the tale to be a comedy, for Dideh Bab wrote so openly of the strangeness of white folk—women especially—it was laughable. Some of the practices he described, like wearing rouge, were true. The rest, such as singing with the nose and drinking straight from a she-cow's teats, were entirely false.

I laughed through the story before carefully wrapping the book in a blanket and tucking it away. I turned off my light, and as my dying fire's rosy glow filled the cavern, I fell asleep and rested better than I had in weeks.

CHAPTER 17

Rhono and Havid soon got into the habit of dropping off their parcels, if they had any, at my front door, often early in the morning. Sometimes I heard them, and sometimes I did not, but I never opened the door when I suspected they were there. They hadn't asked to serve me, and I understood their fear. Had my life gone differently, I certainly would have feared the Svara Idyah, and I doubt I would have been so kind as to make the trip to her cave to deliver food, even if my sheikh had requested it of me.

But every third day Aamina came to see me, and she always stayed for several hours. She was not a superstitious woman, or perhaps she craved a listening ear. I did not mind in the slightest. Her chatter helped me to solidify my handle on Hraric, and she always explained more complex words and terms to me without malice, even though I often had to interrupt her babble for clarity.

Aamina brought me a small loom with which to occupy my time, since my fingers could not manage threading a needle, and every third day she fetched me new yarn and showed me tricks for creating different patterns and designs. I often undid my own weavings and started over, since I had the time to strive for perfection. My best pieces of work hung on the walls, and I soon began my own mosaic to cover the dog drapery near the head of my bed.

I had thought Lo's generous visit a special occasion, but he returned almost two weeks later on one of Havid's days. Night had already fallen over Mac'Hliah.

"It must be terribly boring, being the prince's guard," I commented as I let him into the cavern, "if you come all the way out here for recreation."

He smirked and set his mashadah by the fire to dry. "Most of my men are learning your handtalk; now the palace halls are eerily silent, even midday," he said, breath clouding in the air. "Have you read them?"

It took me a moment to realize he meant the books. "Oh, yes," I said, hurrying over to the fire to stoke it. I only built up the fire on Aamina's days, as it did not matter to me how chilly the cavern became. I spilled some oil on my glove, but fortunately pulled it back before it could catch on fire. I jogged to the other end of the room, removed my gloves, and grabbed a clean pair. Frost traced uneven lines over the fabric as I pulled them on. "I've read the plays twice, but I'm still working through the other. I'll admit, I didn't believe you when you called the language heavy."

Lo's eyes lingered on my gloves. I quickly brushed the frost away.

Clearing my throat, I unwrapped the two volumes from their blanket at the foot of my bed and opened the cloth-wrapped book of ancient Hraric. I had woven a thick bookmark for it, a simple striped pattern of black and sienna. I set the book carefully on the table and turned it toward Lo, who still lingered near the door. Worried my frost had frightened him, I said, "Would you mind . . . helping me? I marked a few places I couldn't understand."

Lo unbuttoned the top of his high-collared coat and joined me at the table and took a seat. He picked up my bookmark and, turning it over in his hands, said, "A new hobby of yours?"

"A *very* new one," I said, oddly embarrassed to see him handling such a mediocre show of my work. I reached for it, but he pulled it from my grasp, inspecting the woven yarn with his dark brown eyes—dark like wet mountain soil, though I noticed a lighter brown around his pupils, a color like the predawn desert, before the sun could turn it gold.

"You're making a blanket?" he asked.

"Blanket?"

He gestured with a tilt of his head to the unfinished drapery folded behind my bed. When had he noticed that?

"Oh." I pushed back my chair and collected the work in progress, unfurling it on my bed. "It's going to replace the dog drape. Aamina brings me the yarn."

"Why not ask Prince Imad for a new one?"

"Because," I said, refolding my amateur mosaic, "I like it when my hobbies have a purpose. And why bother Imad—*Prince* Imad—when I can take care of it myself?"

Lo set the bookmark on the table. "Show me where you struggle."

Smiling—I couldn't help it—I took a chair at the table and turned back to the first word that had given me trouble. I hadn't marked it, for I had spent so much time trying to decode each hiccup in my reading I could relocate them with little effort.

"Here," I said. "*Baadhi Suto.* 'Suto' is a chair, but . . ."

"It is a compound word," Lo explained, underlining the term with his fingertip, the nails cut short. "*Baadhi* is 'infant.' This is an old term for *basuto*, or 'rocking chair.'"

"Ah," I said, rereading the sentence. I turned a few more pages. "And this one?"

When Aamina arrived the next day, along with the newest party of snow harvesters, she brought with her a large basket filled with dried spices, rice, milk, and a small *kokud* chicken wrapped tightly in linen.

"I have decided," she said, winding her long braid back into a bun, "that you must learn to cook for yourself. I will teach you how to make the best curry in the Southlands."

I thanked her profusely. In all honesty, I knew how to cook only a few dishes, as I had taken very little interest in "slaving" over ovens and cook pots during my life in Euwan. I hesitated to participate, not wanting to botch Aamina's recipe, but after stretching a second pair of gloves over my fingers, I could slice meat and herbs with little damage. The recipe called for a number of bizarre-sounding vegetables, but due to the drought, those were in short supply. I hoped next year's harvest would prove more bountiful.

I still struggled with the spicy flavors Zareedians—Aamina especially—seemed to love. But beyond my occasional choking and running nose, the food tasted magnificent, and I couldn't help but think Marrine would love it.

Aamina left me enough supplies to make the dish on my own after she left, and I tried to the next day but to little avail. I burned the bottom of the pot—something horribly tricky to clean, when a decent scrub meant freezing the guck to the metal—and ice crystals swam through the finished product, but I ate it until my stomach ached. My meal seemed to solidify into one chunk of ice right at my center. For the first time since receiving my curse, I panicked over throwing up, worried that the bile would freeze in my throat and suffocate me. Fortunately, I kept it down, and Sadriel did not show up to tell me how close to his world I may have come.

After only a week, Lo visited once more, this time with the dawn. His pounding on the door woke me from a fitful sleep and lodged my heart right into the base of my skull, it frightened me so.

He looked tired, but smirked at me, the kind of look a man gets when he's up to no good. Whether in Iyoden, Zareed, or the world beyond, it was an expression common to all men.

He held several planks of a strange wood in his arms. He dropped them right there in the doorway, along with a small linen sack of nails, a handsaw, and an iron hammer.

"What on earth is this for?" I asked, panting. I still had not caught my breath from my frightful awakening.

"A bookshelf," he said. "Where you'll fit it is up to you."

I stared at him.

"You like your hobbies to have a purpose, hmm?" he asked, apparently thinking himself rather clever. "Build it, and I'll bring you more books."

I opened my mouth to say something but ended up just gaping as he turned from the cavern without another word, a gust of snowless wind tousling his black curls, unprotected without a mashadah. He rode swiftly back into the city. After all, the captain of the prince's guard had little time to spend on cursed white women.

I looked at the wooden pile before me and smiled. Though my father's trade was building wagons, I had never built a thing in my life. Still, I figured it would take a great deal of time, and time was something of which I had in abundance.

Shivering, I brought the supplies inside and tried to determine how I could piece them together. A bookshelf seemed simple enough, but I wanted to do it right, for I knew wood was a valuable commodity in Zareed, and I did not want to waste it.

When Aamina came again, I asked if she could bring me some writing utensils. In my wait for her return, I grew impatient and began nailing the shelves together on my own, which resulted in me splintering one of the boards.

Once I had a pencil and paper—the pencil hard to grip—I sketched out what I considered the best design for the shelf and went to work.

It was not easy.

My trembling hands and stiff fingers struggled with the tools. There was no one around to hold the boards for me while I nailed them together, so I ended up in many a strange position as I tried to work them out. I desperately wanted to finish the project before Lo's return, whenever that might be. I knew he would visit again, and I looked forward to it, though not entirely for the promise of reading material. Lo was a stern and quiet man, but I had already learned that he could say in a moment of silence what a normal man would take an hour to relate. None of my other friends among the guard had come to see me, though I could hardly blame them. I cherished Aamina's visits, but, deep down, I knew she came on Imad's orders. Lo came of his own volition, and that meant worlds to me.

Sadriel visited once while I was struggling with the bookshelf. Not to help, of course—he wouldn't lift a finger, not even when I entreated him with every kind and begging word I knew. He stretched out on my bed and watched me work, treating the cavern like a honeymooner's escape, making comments in whatever provocative manner he could contrive.

"It's crooked," he said. "If you really want a shelf, I'll give you one taller than the Itarian itself, and bring you the souls of your favorite authors."

"What is the Itarian?" I asked, wrenching a bent nail free of its wood.

"The largest tower in the world, across the seas in Gardinia. They're especially good at war there. Wouldn't you like to see it?"

I told him no, and he left.

Frowning at what must have seemed a foolish endeavor, Aamina, on her next visit, said, "Wouldn't it be easier with the gloves off?"

My first reaction was to shake my head. I had assumed the gloves were necessary to prevent the wood from freezing. But after thinking on it a moment, I wondered if Aamina was right. Did it really matter if frost laced my hammer or riddled my boards?

I slipped off the gloves, which improved my poor grip on the tools. I sawed the splintered board to make a small cubbyhole on top of my creation, which, in the end, stood three shelves high. I had nearly finished it when Lo returned, this time midday. Bright sun made the drifting snow flurries outside my door look like fairies behind him, twirling and glowing and gold.

He carried his side bag with him, laden with books. I wanted to grab each volume from his satchel and dance with them, but even the Svara Idyah could remember her manners.

"Impressive," he said, setting his mashadah by the dwindling fire. He poured some oil on the coals. "But will it hold?"

"It can hold me," I said, hammering a nail into the back of the cubbyhole.

He smiled and unloaded the books onto the table. He read the titles to me, each sounding like music—*The Word of Kings*, a philosopher's book and fairly recent; *River of Tears*, a short novel missing its back cover; and *Sun, Moon, Stars, Sand*, a book of—

Distracted, I let the last nail slip from my fragile grip as I hammered. Instead of pounding it into the wood, I smashed its point into and across my palm. I hissed and dropped the hammer, which hit the rug-strewn stone floor with a loud *thud*. Cold blood oozed from the gash and trickled down my wrist and the sides of my hand, congealing and then freezing to the skin. A drop stained the pale green rug underfoot.

Cradling my hand, I hurried to the half-filled pitcher of water and bowl on the table.

"What happened?" Lo asked, stepping toward me.

"I slipped, it's fine," I lied. It throbbed terribly, my coldness making the slash ache all the more. I reached for the pitcher.

"Let me see—"

He reached for my hand before I could stop him, before I could shout. His fingers grasped my wrist. Frost zigzagged over his hand in an instant. Wincing, he pulled his hand back as though struck by—what had Eyan called me?—a cobra.

I spilled the pitcher.

"I-I . . . I'm sorry," I choked out as Lo cradled his hand to his coat, rubbing warmth back into it. I repeated myself, quieter, and fumbled with the pitcher. I couldn't look at him. I couldn't bear to see that expression of hate and contempt I'd seen on so many faces play across Lo's familiar features. I averted my eyes from his injured hand and fled, not bothering to clean up the mess of blood and water.

I stumbled outside with the pitcher still clutched in my hand, biting my lower lip to force my emotions flat, but they swirled and looped inside of me until I barely knew up from down or east from west. My insides became stone. Kneeling, I bit the inside of my cheek as I scrubbed the cut with snow, shivering and shaking.

Careless, I thought to myself, wiping my eyes on my sleeve before tears could form. I clumped snow together and scoured frozen blood from the sides of my hand and wrist until the skin turned raw. I had gotten too comfortable here, too careless around people. I had thought I could no longer hurt anyone, tucked away in my cave. I had been so very wrong.

I took several deep breaths, trying to calm myself. I couldn't stay out there forever, just as Lo would not merely wait in the cave until I bridled my emotions. Clenching my injured left hand in a fist, I scooped snow with my pitcher and stepped inside, setting it by the fire to melt.

"I'm sorry," I murmured, again without looking at Lo. Instead, I stared into the coals, prodding them with my right hand to build a better flame.

"It is not your fault," Lo said from behind me, though I still didn't glance back to see him. "You warned me before, with the others. I was not thinking."

I forced more deep, chilly breaths into my lungs as I poured the melted water from the pitcher over my hand, keeping it over the flame so the liquid wouldn't freeze to my skin. I washed the new blood away, but it slowly bubbled up again.

Lo kneeled beside me, and I flinched away, not wanting to hurt him again.

He set bandages from my small store on the ground and retrieved his leather riding gloves from his coat pocket. After pulling them on—his hand didn't look damaged—he unrolled a length of bandage and held it taut, waiting for me. He said nothing.

Another deep breath, and I placed my hand on the middle of the bandage. He pressed gauze to my palm and carefully wrapped it, proficient even with the gloves. I imagined he'd had experience bandaging wounds, being a soldier. I wondered how many he had wrapped for others and how many for himself.

He smelled like sandalwood and cardamom.

I stifled a wince as he turned my hand over and tied a firm knot just below my knuckles.

"I'm sorry," I whispered.

"I chose today to come because it is especially hot in the city," he said, removing his gloves. "I appreciate the cold."

I laughed. It wasn't funny, not really, but I laughed anyway. It relieved some of the pressure in my chest.

Holding his gloves in his hands, he met my eyes. "How do you live, so cold?"

I rolled my lips together. Moved the pitcher from the fireplace before it got too hot. "One day at a time."

"You've grown accustomed to it?"

I shook my head, stray bits of hair falling from my braid. "In almost four years, I never have. I feel as cold now as the day winter fell upon me." Swallowing, I lifted up my bandaged hand. "Thank you."

"You're welcome." Then, moving his fingers, he signed, *I am not angry.*

Lo returned to the table—I noticed he had cleaned up my mess—and finished reading off the titles of the books he'd brought as though nothing had happened, then showed me the new signals his men had created over the past few weeks, including inappropriate ones I could not help but laugh at.

How wonderful it felt to have friends after so long. How much I wished I could see Ashlen again and embrace her, for I had not realized how good a friend she had been to me. Hers made one more debt on the list of those I could never repay.

Lo stayed for about an hour before placing my books on the shelf. It was no craftsman's piece. It stood plain, a little crooked, and scratched in the back from where I had missed my nail, but he smiled at it, and in that moment, I desperately wished I could touch him, this man who had ridden me down atop a horse of deepest ebony, who wore a helmet of ibex horns, and who spoke to me not as a person with an unfortunate curse but as a woman who loved literature and old tongues, who feared domesticated dogs and wove uneven rows of yarn and spilled pitchers of water over fine rugs. A man willing to forgo superstition to bring me a book, merely because he wanted to hear my thoughts on it.

I held my bandaged hand to my heart as he left.

CHAPTER 18

Nights later, I dreamed of dogs.

In my dream, I lived in my mountains again. The beasts were tracking me over muddy fields and rocky inclines, and I ran from them without looking back, my tattered dress blowing around me. I grabbed tree branches to pull myself up steep slopes, each touch sending frost skittering across the wood. The dogs howled in the distance.

I scrambled up a shelf, loose rocks cutting my hands and feet. A bank of snow suddenly appeared before me, slick and wet, and I tumbled into it. I didn't remember falling, only pushing myself back up and running across endless blankets of snow, desperately looking for a tree with branches low enough to climb.

When I finally turned to look, two bassets and a saluki sight hound—the tall dog portrayed on my drapery—were chasing me, teeth bared. A tree root snagged my foot, and I tumbled to the earth. I willed myself to rise, but the cold had frozen me in place.

I saw footprints in the snow and followed them with my eyes. Suddenly Lo was there, standing between me and the dogs. He drew his sword, and the dogs stopped, eyeing him and then me, as if trying to decide if I were worth the fight.

The dogs vanished. Turning to me, Lo offered his hand, but when I clasped it, his entire body turned to ice—

I gasped and sat up in my bed, my cavern illuminated only by a dying fire and the softest glow of my oil lamp. My shoulders and thighs ached with a strange tautness, as though someone had taken a wrench to me and tightened my muscles until they could stretch no more. My skin tingled with the cold and my toes burned with it, as though I had stubbed each one before crawling into bed. Teeth chattering, I rubbed icy fingers into my icy shoulders and spied two shining amber eyes near the table.

Flinging back my blankets, I hurried to my lamp and cranked it to full light.

"Such an animated sleeper," Sadriel said, though his voice was mirthless, his smile nowhere to be seen. "I thought it was the forest that made it so, but even here, in your new 'home,' you fret more than a babe in the night."

Trembling, I grabbed my pitcher and set it by the coals to melt the water inside. "How long have you been here?"

"Does it matter?" he asked, running his fingers along the chain of his ruby amulet. "You were much more receptive to me before you came to this wasteland. Don't tell me it doesn't still hurt, Smitha. I see the curse inside you; I know how it devours you. How much more pain will you bear before you give in? Is it so much better to waste away in this realm than to be my companion?"

I peered at the door, the faint glows of early dawn. I busied myself with the fire, coaxing it to life.

Within moments, he appeared to my left. He seized my injured hand and pulled it back from the hearth, squeezing it until I grit my teeth against the pain. He glowered at me, a dark and twisted expression only Death could wear. "Doesn't it *hurt* you, Smitha? Stop playing games with me! I know mortals, and I know you. Will you wait until it crushes you? Come with me."

I stared into the embers. "I thought you could wait more than a few years for men to fall to you," I whispered.

They were the wrong words. What Sadriel did next, I had not seen coming.

He hit me.

I fell backwards, banging my head on the end of the red chair. The room swirled. My cheek stung; my blood pulsed through the bone. I touched it and stared at where Sadriel had been, now just empty space. No one had ever struck me before. Not my father, not my teachers. Not even Mordan.

Sitting upright, I spied Death's boots on my other side, near my bed. "You are a senseless woman," he growled.

Standing, I pulled my hand from my cheek and said, "Get out."

He laughed.

I pointed to the door, though he hardly needed to use it. "Get out!" I shouted, my voice echoing between walls. "What do you *want* with me, Sadriel? Amusement? Sex? Not love, never love. You are Death; you don't have a heart! But I do!" I pounded my uninjured fist into my chest, tears welling in the corners of my eyes. "It's cold and cursed, but I still have a heart! How many times must I say it before you hear me? I. Will. *Never*. Go. With. You!"

It happened so quickly. One moment I was screaming at him and the next my back crashed against the cavern wall beside my bookshelf. Sadriel's pale hand wrapped around my throat, just as Mordan's had that day in the willow-wacks. Books tumbled to the floor at my feet.

The brim of his hat brushed my forehead.

The front door burst open, snapping its lock.

"Smeesa?"

Sadriel vanished.

I stood there, back against the wall, my chest heaving with every quickened breath. Blue dawn light flooded the cavern, along with icy winds and light flurries of snow.

I touched my neck. Heavy gooseflesh covered my skin.

The sound of footsteps drew my attention back to the present. Lo hurried to me, his eyes searching every shadow in the cavern.

I swallowed and blurted out the first coherent thought that came to mind. "What are you doing here?"

I asked in Northlander, and he replied the same, though not to answer my question. "I heard shouting. Who was here?"

His hand clutched the hilt of a dagger still sheathed on his belt, a knife long enough to pass clean through a man. He passed me and examined every cranny and corner where a person could possibly hide. The cavern had only one entrance, so his confusion was palpable when he found nothing. My mind scrambled to recall what language I had used with Sadriel. Angrean or Northlander? What had Lo heard, and what had he understood?

"Who?" he asked, brows knitted tightly together.

I swallowed ice down my throat and shook my head. "No one." A deep breath. "No one."

He glanced at me, his eyes falling to my cheek. "No one did that?" he asked almost darkly, gesturing with his chin.

"I tripped over the carpet and fell," I said. "Onto the red chair."

"Smeesa—"

"Please, don't . . ." I started, trying to regain my wits, pulling my hair forward to mask any marks that might appear on my neck. "I can't explain. Please, it's fine. I'm fine."

I wanted to run to him, to cry, to thank him and God in heaven that he had come when he did, for the thought of what Sadriel might have done scared—no, *terrified*—me. I had known Sadriel for years, but there was no understanding him. He was an ever-changing being, unpredictable. I had always been wary of him, but I hadn't feared him since our first meeting. I couldn't bear to think of him, not then. Oh, what a beautiful sight Lo was to me at that moment.

He stared at me, suspicion dripping from him. I started to repeat myself, but he shook his head and returned to the door. I thought he would leave, but he only shut it and fiddled with the lock until he had it working again. He did not apologize—not for breaking the lock, the dent in the door's wood, or for barging in at the earliest hours of morning. He merely walked to the table and pulled a bag off his belt. Though it resembled a coin pouch, the sound it made when it hit the stone tabletop was more like the rattling of dried beans.

The tension in the air made it hard to breathe.

"What is that?" I asked, trying as hard as I could to relax, to sound casual.

Lo's eyes surveyed the room once more before he said, "Coffee. It is meant to be brewed hot—perhaps it will be more comfortable to drink."

How I wanted to cry.

"Thank you," I whispered.

He nodded to me—mashadah still wrapped around his head—and headed for the door.

"Wait!" I called, sure I flushed somewhere beneath the layers of cold that embraced me.

He paused.

"Could you . . . stay, for a while?" I asked, embarrassment dripping down my spine like ice water. My heart still pounded from my encounter with Sadriel, and I didn't want to be left alone, so soon. "A-Aamina will be here, today, but . . . I know you're busy . . . and thank you, for the coffee—"

"Who was here?" he asked.

Words jumbled in my throat. "You wouldn't . . . believe me, if I told you."

"Try."

But I just shook my head and looked at the floor.

I felt the intensity of his gaze on me, then heard him sigh, a long escape of breath. When I finally glanced up to look at him, he seemed to be deep in thought. He rubbed his chin—he had begun growing in his half beard again, I noticed. I shivered.

He walked toward me until we stood no more than a pace apart. "You are sure you're all right?" he asked, stooping to see my face better. He focused on my bruise.

I nodded.

"I can stay until Aamina comes," he said, stepping past me to pick up the fallen books.

I winced, thinking of my promise to care for them. "I'm sorry, I can—"

"Do you want to heat water? For the coffee?"

I remembered the pitcher left in the fire and hurried over to it. Its base had begun to scorch black, and the handle sizzled under my cold touch. I set it down on the table and retrieved a clean pair of gloves.

As I pulled them on, Lo untied the small bag and said, in Hraric, "Tell me about your home in Iyoden."

"Euwan?" I glanced at him. His countenance seemed darker than usual—worry, perhaps, or distrust. But I felt so glad to have someone with me—*him* with me—that I didn't care if he glared swords at me.

"Well," I said, pouring water, my trembling now nearly invisible, "It's small, with a lot of spaces between houses, not like here. And the homes are larger, made of wood. There are a lot of trees weaving through it. A mercantile, a school, a turnery where my father worked, crafting wagon wheels and some personal commissions."

I thought of Mordan and stopped pouring.

"Your home?"

I sat down, facing him. Cleared my throat. "A single-story home with three bedrooms, much larger than the ones here. Near a lake—Heaven's

Tear Lake. There were a lot of mosquitoes in the summer: small flies that leave itchy bumps on your skin when they bite you. We had a small kitchen with a wood-burning stove, a big living room, and a barn . . ."

When Aamina came midmorning, she nearly startled herself to death at the sight of Lo. Lo had relaxed, somewhat, though he remained watchful and spoke little, leaving me to do most of the talking. He excused himself before Aamina could even sit down, bidding me a quick good-bye with handtalk. And though I was grateful Aamina was there to keep me company, I found myself wishing he had stayed, even in his silence. The cavern seemed . . . empty . . . without him.

I half expected Aamina to begin lecturing me on propriety the way my mother would have, but she merely launched into a monologue about how her youngest child was faring in school. I wondered at that. Then again, why would anyone worry about the wiles of a woman who could kill a man just by holding his hand?

Thinking of the Northlander hunter, I remained quiet for the rest of Aamina's stay.

In the following days, I found myself looking forward to Lo's next visit—planning passages to discuss with him, stories to share. I even tucked the remaining coffee beans into the cubby of my bookshelf, hoping to share them with him again. Any time I heard, or thought I heard, footsteps outside my door, I ran to it with a girlish excitement fit for any winter solstice, but it was never him. I'd always find Rhono or Havid quickly retreating to their camels, or a new set of snow harvesters loading up their wagons.

But the days between Lo's visits rolled by empty, one week, then two, then three. I began to fret that I had somehow offended him, or lost his trust by withholding information on Sadriel, whom I also had not seen, thankfully. As yet more time passed, the fear that Sadriel might have something to do with Lo's absence started to eat into me.

I asked Aamina about it on one of her early winter visits, winter being no different than summer in Zareed, other than the nights growing longer. And my winter, of course, never gave way to any other season.

"He is captain of the guard, so he is very busy," Aamina explained to me as she helped me pin my new mosaic drape over the one of the sight hound. With its simple yet vibrant squares, it resembled a quilt, and I was proud to have finished what I considered a grand piece of art. "And the dissenters are marching again, which always increases the guard."

"Dissenters?"

"Grouches who want a king from the old line. They think our sheikh's declining health is a good excuse to shuffle things around."

I thought of Eyan's words during our trip to Kittat, of the men riding out to scout the mountains, and felt cold metal pierce my lungs.

She stepped off her chair and looked at the new drape. "Very well done. I'll bring you extra yarn next time I come."

I hopped down, my head scarf falling to my shoulders. "Why extra?"

"My sister is pregnant as a melon—didn't I tell you?"

She had, several times.

"She's ripe as one, too, due to give birth any day now, and I need to be at her side when she does."

"That's wonderful news."

Aamina nodded. "It's a boy; I can feel it in my hips. Aunt's intuition. I will be away until they're on their feet, but Rhono and Havid will take care of you until I return, and oh, will I have stories when I come back! That farmer's daughter eyes my sister's husband like he's a fresh-plucked chicken, so this new child will rile her well."

Aamina chuckled, and I smiled, though the thought of not seeing her for so long tasted bitter.

Keeping true to her word, Aamina brought me a surplus of yarn in saffron, violet, and jade on her next visit, along with extra paper and extra rice. Three days later, no one came to my door—not Aamina, and not Lo.

My cavern became frightfully silent, save for the blowing—sometimes howling—winds outside. When my storm grew fitful, I spied neither Havid nor Rhono. When it calmed, I tried to invite both of them inside, desperate for company, but both refused without word. After that, Havid stopped coming altogether. I turned to my weaving for comfort and diversion and completed a simple, square-patterned tapestry the size of my bed, then unpicked all of it and started again. Sadriel did not reappear, not that I could see, but twice I had dreams in which I felt his eyes on me. When I woke, I could not tell if the sensations had been real or imagined. It made me tremble, and not from the cold.

I wove a tapestry of birds flying over the Finger Mountains, then unraveled the bottom half to include my cave and snow clouds. It was a picture I took pride in, and I eagerly wanted to show it to Aamina or Lo, but still they did not come.

The empty days drew by. One week, two weeks, three. I had spent years with no company other than Sadriel's, but for some reason this loneliness stung harder and faster than all that time in the mountains. Perhaps because I had finally been accepted, curse and all—I had actually *made* friends and *enjoyed* company, and to lose all that now created a contrast for which I was not prepared. But I knew Aamina would return soon enough, and I kept the coffee beans in my cubby for Lo, as if doing so might summon him.

I struggled to keep myself busy. I wove bookmarks until I ran out of yarn. I tried once more to talk to Rhono, but I terrified her to the point that I worried she would stop coming entirely as Havid had done, and then I would be without food, for I could not walk into Mac'Hliah. I did not want to risk it, and I did not want Imad angry with me. The thought of the dogs alone was enough to keep me in my quarters.

I began to wait for the snow harvesters to arrive, for surely one of them would be willing to talk with me. I did not know their schedule, if they even had one, but I listened for their camels and wagons, and stepped outside my door countless times to search for them on the horizon. They did come, but by the time I realized it and rushed outside, they had already retreated. I ran after them and called, but the angry winds of winter carried my voice back to the mountains, and I lost my chance.

More days passed, and I spent them alone. I could feel darkness begin to brew in the recesses of my mind, the same darkness that had nearly driven me to accept Sadriel's offer, and it terrified me. Though my fingers had little deftness to them, I began to write in my shaky and unruly penmanship, as small as I could manage the letters. I wrote to my father, my mother, and my sister, then transcribed the letters into Hraric, which read even worse than my Northlander. I even wrote a letter to Mordan telling him that he had made me, deep down, a better person. I truly believed it, and I clung to those words every time my hands cramped with the chill, or a shudder drew my pen down and ruined my script, or my pen became so cold the ink refused to flow.

When I ran out of paper, I began to read. I read *The Fool's Last Song* so many times I memorized it, and I even took the liberty of acting it out on my own, playing each part myself, as I had loved to do back in Euwan, for I had craved the attention of others. I acted it out in Hraric and in Northlander, but between the bits of dialogue I always heard the silence of my cavern and the whistling of the never-ending storm outside.

When I could not bear the stillness of my cave a moment longer, I went outside and began sculpting snow as I had often done in the mountains, this time making depictions of hens and scorpions and spiders and ibexes. I gazed out at the distant city of Mac'Hliah and watched the sun's shadows slowly trace their way across the mud-brick buildings, longing to be there with my friends. It was Rhono's day to bring me supplies, and when she saw me standing outside the cave, she pulled her camel short and dropped my parcel of food right there in the snow. I called out to her, begging her to stay, but she only tapped her shoulder with her free hand and sped away. From there on out, she no longer left her parcels on my doorstep but on the edge of the snow.

Large parcels, so she would not have to come as often. I did not bother to collect them. Part of me feared moving my storm, but in honesty, I lacked the motivation to eat much, so I did not need the things she brought me.

I read and reread Lo's books and forced myself to push them away when I cried, for I had promised to take care of them, and I could not tolerate a single tear marring their pages. My darkness taunted me, creeping into my thoughts during my few hours of sleep. My cavern, so beautifully decorated, became a cage. I let my fire die. When my lamp dimmed, I did not fetch Rhono's supplies to get more oil.

Though I urged myself—shouted at myself—to be happy and to be content, for Aamina would soon return, and perhaps Lo would, too, if only for his books, I shriveled inside my shell of ice and skin. I was so grateful for all Imad and Lo and the others had given me, but my cold heart splintered more with each passing day, until I could feel its shattered pieces rattling down my rib cage and settling somewhere in the hungry pit of my stomach.

Late one night, fear and seclusion feeding my insomnia, I realized I was not stationary. I was not made of stone. Seven weeks alone in my cavern had left me wearier than I can describe, and I needed to escape, if only for a while. I needed to use my legs, to discover something new. I realize now, looking back on it, that I must not have been of sound mind, for I barely drank and had stopped eating with the last of my rations gone and the rest a mile away.

I left in the dim light of predawn, my storm especially violent and blowing heavy snows in all directions, nearly concealing my mountain in purest white. I wore my gray dress and my patterned head scarf and gloves, and I walked away from Mac'Hliah, away from anyone I could hurt.

I walked, and the snow and wind calmed. I walked until I found sand under my feet instead of snow. I thought of climbing the mountains to see what lay on the other side, but their slopes proved too steep.

I had to wait for a pass, for surely someone had built a pass somewhere in this range.

I walked and walked and walked, until the sand turned gold around me and not so much as a gust from my storm tousled my hair. I stayed close to the mountains at first, but the rocks tore at my slippers, so I moved away, into the open plains of sand. I walked until plains became hills. I passed a few twisted plants, none higher than my knee. The air tasted strange here, thicker in my throat. Perhaps from the heat—heat I could not feel. How I yearned to feel it. At that moment, I could not remember what warmth felt like.

On I walked, folding my arms against the cold, breathing through a dry, parched throat. I felt light-headed, but I continued onward, needing to get away. Needing . . . something.

Sometime in the day—I cannot remember when—my foot slipped off the ridge of a hill of golden sand, and I tumbled down, down, down the ripples of gold, landing in a void of black.

CHAPTER 19

I couldn't breathe.

I woke up choking, coughing as water ran over my mouth, freezing in uneven streams down my cheek and neck. I felt so cold, a sculpture of snow, but with the weight of a boulder crushing me. Darkness. Gray. Darkness. My head pounded rhythmically, as if someone were pounding nails into my temples.

I heard shouting in the distance, then again right over me.

My eyes fluttered open. Storm clouds, orange light. Snow and sand. A blur of brown and black over me that looked remarkably like Lo. I heard his voice, but I didn't understand his words.

Darkness threatened to descend again, but I fought through it and forced my eyes open. Where was I? A chill stiffened my back, and I coughed, droplets of ice hitting my tongue.

I heard Lo's voice again, shouting to someone I couldn't see. He disappeared for a moment, and then indigo cloth draped over me, covering my eyes. He pushed it behind my head. The snow and sand fell away from me, and I floated, cradled in someone's arms. I bobbed and swayed in a sea of black, swallowed by the intoxicating scents of cardamom and sandalwood.

⟫⟩———⟨⟨

Again I woke up coughing.

Strength outside my own helped me sit up, and I choked and rasped through a cold and raw throat, as though I had swallowed briars. My head spun.

"She's awake?" A female voice.

"Here, it's hot." Another.

Trying to swallow, I glanced up and saw two women I did not recognize: one in her midthirties with a heavy braid over her shoulder and a white head scarf, the other much older, with deep wrinkles and more gray hairs than black. I stared at them for a long moment, picking at my memories. Where was I?

My cavern, my bed, though the fire near the door burned brightly now, as did the oil lamp. What time was it?

I tried to ask my visitors what had happened, but my words were too hoarse.

The older woman held a tin cup in a towel, steam rising from its lip. She handed it to someone beside me—the one who had helped me sit up.

Lo.

I gaped, but he pressed the hot cup into my hands. It smelled like flowers—rose water—and still bubbled. They had boiled it for me.

"Drink," he said.

I lifted the cup to my lips and drank quickly, the liquid filling my mouth and running down my throat. The last swallow went down the wrong pipe, and I coughed again, covering my mouth with a gloved hand.

"Slowly!" Lo said, exasperated. He handed the cup back to the woman. I cleared my throat enough to manage an "I'm sorry."

"You should be," he snapped. "You have proved yourself a fool, Smeesa."

Those words stung me more than they should have. I glanced at him, at his hard eyes, his mouth set in a firm line.

Then I remembered. The desert, my fall. Lo. Lo had saved me.

Oh, how wildly I would have blushed if the curse had not hidden it.

The younger of the two women asked, "Can you eat?"

I nodded, and she handed me a steaming bowl of some sort of bland mush, but I hardly complained. Despite her warning to eat slowly, I shoveled the goop into my mouth as quickly as I could, partially due to hunger, partially because I did not want the food to freeze. Lo stood from his chair and ran a hand through his hair before pacing to the back of the cavern. The older woman set a mug of hot coffee in his place.

The last few bites of the meal froze to the bottom of the bowl, but I scraped them off with my spoon and crunched the almost milky ice between my teeth before reaching for the coffee. It was a different blend than what Lo had given me—spicier and less sweet. I coughed a little as I swallowed it, liquid, and then slush. My stomach turned into a rock inside me, and I winced at the nausea.

"Thank you," I said.

"You should not eat so quickly," scolded the older woman.

"There was no food in the cavern," Lo murmured, low and quiet. "I found your supplies nearly a mile away."

Biting my lip, I glanced over at him. His bronze arms were folded against his chest, and he glowered at me with a face that could curdle fresh milk.

The younger of the two women said, "Perhaps now is not the time—"

"You are excused," Lo quipped, not taking his stony glare off me. I shrank under his scrutiny and wished I could disappear into the mattress.

The two women frowned, but they gathered their things and stepped outside into the calm falling snow. Judging from the light, it looked to be midday.

"Why were your supplies so far out?"

I looked away, not wanting to answer.

Lo slammed his fist on the table, making me jump. "*Why* were your supplies so far out?"

"Rhono left them there, but it's not her fault," I said, twisting the index finger of my left glove. "I scared her."

Lo snorted. "And Havid? Aamina?"

"Aamina's sister just had a baby." I hoped everything had gone all right with the birth. What if it hadn't? What if that was why Aamina had not been back to see me? A new sickness bloomed in my gut at the thought.

"Havid?"

"I don't know."

Lo released a long breath that ended in something like a growl. "Why didn't you pick up the supplies? Half the food was spoiled! How long did you leave it sitting there?"

I didn't answer.

"*Khuso*, Smeesa!" he swore, pacing to the front of the cavern. He pushed both hands into his hair, ready to rip it out. "Why did you leave the cavern? Alha knows how far out you were before I noticed the clouds were gone!"

I shivered and glanced up to the canvas roof, heavy with snow. That was how he had found me—the clouds. Of course.

"The desert would claim you as quickly as it does anyone else," he almost shouted, pointing a finger at me. "Do you think you're immortal?"

"No," I whispered. "I'm sorry. I'm so sorry for the trouble."

"For the trouble," he repeated, scoffing. He took a deep breath and asked again, "Why did you leave?"

I stared at the bedcovers.

He stalked closer to me. "Why did you leave?"

"I just . . ." I started, forcing down a sudden lump in my throat. "I needed to stretch my legs."

"Stretch your legs for *thirteen miles*?"

I shook my head and rested it in my hands. "I needed . . . to get out. To do something."

"You couldn't weave? You couldn't read?"

"How many times can a person read the same books?" I asked. Tears threatened my eyes, and I blinked them back. "I've read the Dideh Bab volume thirty-six times, alone! I ran out of yarn, out of paper. I just . . ."

I turned away from him and tried to swallow the stinging lump in my throat, willing myself not to cry. I clenched my jaw to keep my teeth still.

"Smeesa—"

"I've been alone," I said, trying not to let the words choke, "for so long. What you . . . Imad, and Aamina . . . have done for me has meant . . . so much." I swallowed, but the lump still refused to budge. I waited a moment, urging it down. Whispering, I said, "I don't want to be alone anymore."

Lo stood near the foot of my bed, staring at something I could not see, his lips pursed.

"I'm sorry," I managed. I wiped my eyes with the back of my glove. It was dirty from my trek and my fall.

After a long silence, Lo said, "No, I am sorry, for not coming."

"You have no obligation to me. And the prince—"

"Prince Imad has more guards than spiders have eggs," Lo said. There was something else he was not telling me, though—I could see it in the way his eyes shifted away from me, in the tenseness of his broad shoulders. He seemed to be deep in thought, and I did not interrupt, content to sit in silent companionship with him. Content to have someone here with me.

After several minutes he pulled up a chair and sat, leveling his face with mine. "I will see you taken care of, Smeesa. Zareed needs you."

I nodded, truly feeling the fool. Had I forgotten all the people my snowfall had helped, even saved? Would I really forget the thousands for fear of hurting the few? Had I really been willing to throw away everything I'd achieved in this land because I could not wait just a little longer for companionship?

The guilt of the situation struck me like a blizzard's gale, and cold tears wet my eyes once more. How could I have been so *selfish* . . . and after everything I had thought I'd learned.

"You are right," Lo said, the anger gone from his voice. "I have no obligation to you. But I come because I enjoy your company." He touched my swathed shoulder, and a chill colder than ice rushed into my collar and down my arm, raising gooseflesh on gooseflesh. My slow heart quickened, and I desperately hoped he did not notice.

"I will come again," he said, pulling back his hand. It had been such a fleeting touch, and through layers of fabric, yet he still needed to rub his fingers together to warm them. "Our sheikh is no doubt worried about you, so I must return to the city. And you must rest."

I did not think all the gold and fine things in the world could have coaxed me to sleep at that moment, but I nodded anyway.

Lo paused halfway to the door and looked over his shoulder. "I will see if I can't help you 'stretch your legs.' Prince Imad speaks of you often, and he will listen to any pleas made on your behalf."

"Thank you."

The smallest smile touched his lips, and he left, closing the door quietly behind him.

I touched my shoulder, still feeling his fingertips there, but it was the look in his eyes that had left me in a stupor. When was the last time someone had looked at me like that, with genuine concern? Years. It had been *years*. And his eyes . . . They were so much different than Sadriel's.

The thought of Death made me stiffen, and I half expected him to appear from the carpets. He had not spoken with me since our . . . argument . . . but I did not think him gone for a moment. I wondered if Death could take the life of someone free from age or sickness, if he could force them into the underworld, or if such a thing broke the laws by which he operated.

Regardless, I would not let him take me, for my life belonged to me, and I would only put it on the line one more time, and then of my own will and choice.

CHAPTER 20

To my surprise, the next morning Qisam and Eyan arrived at my door, wearing their full soldier's gear, including a leopard helmet on Qisam and the scorpion helmet for Eyan. I invited them inside, but they declined.

"Got it backwards," Eyan said with a grin. "We're here to take you to the city."

I stared at him, thinking for a moment I must have misheard his Hraric.

Qisam pulled a tightly rolled scroll from his belt and read it, perhaps double-checking his instructions. "Prince Imad has granted you access to his city, though your stays must be brief."

"You know," Eyan added, "so you don't freeze our crops or children."

"And we're here to escort you for your first visit. Captain said you didn't like dogs." Qisam shoved the scroll back into his belt.

My astonishment hindered my words. "Lo?" Had Lo spoken to Imad on my behalf? I felt both embarrassed and rejuvenated, a strange combination of emotions that left me light-headed.

Eyan said, "We can come back, if—"

"No, now, I'd like to go now!" I exclaimed, clasping my hands together. I half stumbled into my cavern, tripping over the upturned corner of a rug. I snagged my mustard-colored head scarf, draped it over my hair the way Aamina wore hers, and hurried out the door.

"Feels like I'm taking my daughter to the storm festival!" Eyan exclaimed with a laugh. He brushed snow off his shoulders. "We'll take you through the market if you'd like."

Qisam handed me a small money pouch filled with gold coins. I tried to hand it back, but he refused to take it.

"Our sheikh says it is your share for the water, from the snow catchers' harvest," the young soldier explained. "Do with it what you will."

"I . . . thank you," I said, tucking the pouch into my bodice. I didn't know how to count Zareedian coin then, but I got the impression that the amount was more than generous.

Qisam and Eyan had brought a third, blanket-laden camel with them, and I recognized her as the beast I had ridden in from the Unclaimed Lands and through Kittat, Ir, and Shi'wanara. I decided then that the animal deserved a name for its loyalty, so I called it Leikah, the Hraric word for *faithful*. Eyan joked that I should have instead named it Leipo, which meant *unfortunate*.

My mile-wide storm cloud followed us back into Mac'Hliah snowless, perhaps just as eager as I was to see the winding roads, clustered homes, and real, living people. My insides twisted as we neared the city, making me almost sick with anxiety. Not for the fear of dogs, but for the regard of the people—what they might think of me and what accidents might befall them because of my presence. But my trip into the city would be short. With any luck, not a single crystal would fall from my pale clouds.

The people of Mac'Hliah watched our approach from a distance. As before, I saw some of them cross their chests and tap their shoulders. Others regarded me with curious or unreadable expressions. I held the greatest unspoken gratitude for those few who simply glanced my way for a moment before continuing with their own work, for I did not want to be a spectacle. More than anything, I wanted to be normal. Almost a year had passed since I first came to Zareed, and I wanted to feel some semblance of belonging here.

I asked Eyan if we could dismount, for I desired the exercise and did not want to ride so high above the others. Perhaps, though it was wishful thinking given the cloud that followed me everywhere, it would allow me to blend in. He helped coax Leikah down and took her reins, then fell in step behind me. Qisam walked ahead of us, scanning the streets with disinterest. I suppose even a city as grand as Mac'Hliah would seem commonplace to someone who had lived in Zareed all his life.

But it was not to me.

I marveled at the people who filled the streets, though they gave me and my companions a wide berth. Men carried yokes laden with clay water jugs. Women balanced baskets atop their heads with one hand. Children played with tops and buttons on strings and small clay flutes in the shapes of animals. They all talked freely among themselves, the chatter filling the air and tumbling over itself, like the city was breathing. Scents of cinnamon and curry flooded my nose as we passed a few round tents, one of which had a small cook fire outside its door with the leg of a goat roasting over it.

I heard the whispers, of course. Hands shielded mouths as we walked past. I assured myself that the prattle did not concern me—or if it did, it didn't matter—and did my best to smile at those we passed, which seemed to unnerve quite a few.

We came to the market. Comparing it to the market I had seen last spring was like comparing a snake to a snakeskin. So many people filled the street we could barely pass in most places, even *with* the wide berth. I pulled up my gloves and wrapped the ends of my head scarf around my neck to ensure I covered all my skin, save for my face. I did not want to accidentally bump into someone and hurt them, though in the jubilance of the market, I almost forgot about the cold.

Swaths of green, scarlet, maroon, white, gold . . . every possible color of fabric draped merchant shops and a few stationary wagons. The barrels of dates, nuts, and spices were still not full, but they were considerably fuller, and the prices were lower than what I remembered. The boldest of sellers even called out to me, Qisam, and Eyan, trying to sell wares of dishes, beads, even daggers and leatherworks. I began to feel I should buy something, for I wanted to be part of the city, not just a bystander, but there were so many people bartering and dealing, and so many items on display, I hardly knew what.

Halfway through the market I spied a coffee seller. Thinking of Lo, I chose a paler bean on Qisam's recommendation, enough for four cups. Perhaps, if I put on an extra pair of gloves, I could successfully brew the drink without freezing it the next time Lo came by.

A man in a mashadah tapped his shoulders at me as we turned the corner, and I waved at him, which made his hands move all the faster. I couldn't help but laugh. Who would have thought a simple girl from Euwan could drive such fear into a grown man, and a Zareedian at that?

Qisam, in front of me, suddenly veered to the far right side of the street. I was about to ask why when I saw a cluster of guards up ahead, surrounding the bright tangerine tent of what appeared to be a silk merchant. A few civilians hovered close by, standing on their toes for a better look. I heard the word *sheikh* as we passed, and when I peered between the armored guards—a few of whom I recognized—I saw Imad comparing belts at a table.

One of the guards nodded to me—his name was Vi, if I remembered right. I wanted to talk to Imad, if only to say thank you, but my friends appeared to be leading me in the opposite direction, which I took to mean that it was not the right time to bother the prince. I did, however, spot Lo just before we turned the corner. He wore his ibex helmet, which must have been very hot in the direct sun, and his indigo uniform. It looked darker than usual—unfaded. A new shirt, perhaps. A heavy sword hung at his left hip and a dagger at his right. He stood beside the merchant who spoke to Imad, his back pressed against the merchant's large, three-wheeled wagon. Despite the overcast sky, I did not think he had seen me, but before I stepped out of view, his dark eyes glanced up the street.

I signed *Thank you*, and then, *I named my camel Leikah.* I did not have a sign for *faithful*, so I spelled the word out.

Lo laughed, startling the merchant beside him.

We turned the corner and lost sight of the prince and his entourage, but how my cold, slow-beating heart fluttered at the distant sound of Lo's laugh. I felt I had swallowed a bird—a very lively one. A strange feeling, reminiscent of ones I had experienced before, yet . . . unique. And undeniable, despite how I might have tried to mask or discredit it.

I knew then that Lo's kindness was more than just kindness to me. His laughter made me laugh, his thoughts made me think, and his silence made me listen to each intake of his breath. It seemed absurd, as I mounted Leikah and started back for my cave in the Finger Mountains, that I had once been so fearful of him. He was beautiful.

And no matter how I tried to reason my way out of it, I was falling for him.

CHAPTER 21

Humming a child's song my mother had often sung while doing housework, I mixed rice and water in a pan and set it on a small metal rack over my fire, a little away from the flame so I would not burn the bottom, as I was prone to do. Rice was an easy food for me to eat if I cooked it myself—so long as I continued to add water, I could scoop it out of the hot pan and swallow it before it froze in my mouth, and it required little chewing. True, my last bites were often little more than mush, but with a little pepper it tasted more or less like breakfast porridge.

I ate at the fire until my stomach stretched to its limit, then fetched water to wash the pan. The hotter the pan, the easier I could clean it before my wash water froze. But as soon as I stood, I saw Sadriel on my bed, propped up against my pillows—the book of ancient Hraric Lo had given me clutched in his long, unadorned fingers.

The cold rooted me to the floor.

He turned the page. Without looking up, he said, "That Southlander of yours is rather interesting."

So long since our last encounter—I had dared to think he'd left for good. Touching my once-bruised cheek, I glanced over my shoulder to the door. If I ran, would he follow me? Yet how could I hope to best Sadriel if I lost the courage to face him alone?

Straightening my stiff shoulders, I met his gaze.

Death set the book down and regarded me from beneath the rim of his hat. "Come closer, Smitha. Surely you're not afraid of me."

I removed my head scarf, hoping he attributed the shaking of my hands to my usual bitter chill.

"You've been gone a long while," I said. "Was it because you thought I feared you?"

He laughed. "I wanted you to see what it meant to be truly alone, love. Not pleasant, is it?"

I frowned and busied myself turning up the flame in the oil lamp. "I'm only human."

"No need to remind me."

I watched him, his first words itching at me. Fortunately, he explained without my asking.

"Twice he's kept you from me." Sadriel flashed and reappeared standing, taller even than Lo. "I really thought I had you, in the desert. But then, your death would just make you like all the other lost souls in my realm. You wouldn't be the same, then."

"What did you intend, the last time?" I asked, touching my cheek where he had struck me. "Does Death have the power to take me against my will?"

He smiled. "As far as I'm concerned, Smitha, you've got one boot in the grave. No ordinary mortal could survive in your state."

"Is that why you still come to me, Sadriel?" I asked, watching the flickering flames of the lamp for a moment. "Because I'm live bait? Or because you can't entertain yourself with a true corpse?"

His smile shrunk but did not disappear. In three strides he closed the gap between us and touched my face with his fingers—fingers that felt as cold to me as anything else, and perhaps they were. I bit my tongue to keep myself from flinching. I would not fear Death, and I would not allow him to wield any power over me.

"I've told you, haven't I?" he said, studying me. He wore a peculiar expression. He looked almost . . . lonely. "Yet in recent months I've often wondered the same thing. What *were* the words of that young man's curse, hmm? Do remind me."

I had not forgotten them, even now. Mordan's spell had etched itself in my memory.

"I don't remember the spell itself," I said quietly, pulling away from his touch. "It was in a language I didn't recognize." I shivered, thinking of the rest. "'I curse you . . . to be as cold as your heart.'"

Sadriel smirked at that.

"'May winter follow you wherever you go,'" I recited, and my eyes widened. I stared hard at Sadriel and finished, "and with the cold, death.'"

His amber gaze glimmered with amusement.

"But mortal curses don't affect you," I said, stepping back. "You said so yourself."

"Correct you are, love," he said. "But it's interesting to think about, hmm? Perhaps that was a hint to breaking it."

"If it takes death to break my curse . . ."

He touched my chin, tilted my head to the side, and released me. "Something to ponder on."

He turned around and walked toward the back of the cave, stretching out his arms. "I am bored. Perhaps if you cannot entertain me, I'll find someone else to catch my interest."

I stalked after him, my skirt flapping around my ankles. "Sadriel—"

"Who shall I go visit in the city?" he continued, glancing back at me.

"They can't even see you!"

"Oh, but I can make them."

I gaped and pressed a hand to my frozen chest. "Don't you dare, Sadriel!"

He began to fade.

"Sadriel!"

I rushed for him, but he vanished before I could grab him, and my violet fingernails clawed only air.

"Sadriel!" I shouted, spinning around. Surely he didn't have the power to take a healthy soul for no other reason than to taunt me . . . but who was I to question the strength of Death?

I snatched my head scarf from beside the hearth and ran out into the desert, my feet skidding along fresh snow made golden by the distant evening sun. I did not see Sadriel outside. Then again, he had a quicker method of travel than I did.

Running across the snow as fast as my cold-cramped legs would carry me, I wrapped the head scarf around my head and neck, constantly searching for the flourish of a black cape or the gleam of his ruby necklace. I called out his name once more, hoping he was merely toying with me, but he did not reappear. He had never been the sort of man to come when called.

Snow thinned beneath my feet and made way for sand as I broke through the perimeter of my winter. The cloud floated above me as always, tethered to me by unseen threads. My heart thudded in my chest, pumping icy blood to icy muscles. I ran, desperately searching. Why had he drawn me to the city? Had he been bluffing? Was it too late to stop him if not?

To my surprise, I reached Mac'Hliah without stopping for a rest, though my lungs burned with each frosty breath and needles filled my legs. It was twilight, and there were few people on the streets.

A man hammering a small nail into a shoe glanced up at me through thinning black hair as I struggled for breath. I brushed sand from my dress and swallowed. My legs ached, but I hurried at a quick walk, searching up and down lanes and between homes. I heard a dog bark not far off and quickly changed direction, hugging myself against the chill.

I dared not call Death's name, but as I weaved between homes and tents I began to feel sure Sadriel had only meant to rile me—or at least I prayed he only meant to rile me. If he truly wanted to hurt someone, I had little hope of stopping him. I would not have put it past him to frame me for such a thing, either.

I stepped aside to let a short man with a handcart pass me, his eyes wide with earnest wonder. Kneading a tight muscle in my shoulder, I allowed myself a moment to catch my breath and calm myself. Surely I would return to the cavern to find Sadriel laughing at me.

I turned around and navigated my way back through the northmost homes of Mac'Hliah, not entirely sure which route I had taken into the city, but I could see the white-crusted peak of my mountain, so I had no fear of getting lost. Yet as I made my way through narrow alleys and winding streets, I knew I tread new ground, for I saw people I would have remembered my first time through, even in my panic.

An old man, too old for me to name his age, sat huddled against some sort of shop with dark windows, his stringy beard long gone gray, a dirty mashadah draped over his head and shoulders. Filth lined his wrinkles, and he reached for me with a wrist so thin a wintry gust from my storm could have broken it. Not far from him, on the other side of the road, huddled another man, slightly younger but in no better condition.

Beggars. My heart grew heavy at the sight of them. During my few trips into the city, I had always taken the main roads either to the market or to the palace and always with others to distract me. I had never stepped foot on this edge of town. How many more homeless wandered the streets without help or home? Did Imad know about them?

I reached into my dress for my coin pouch and pulled it free, working open the cord-closed mouth. The first man looked at me hopefully, but when I poured out half the coins into his hand, his eyes turned round and awed. It was as if he had never seen so much money in his life. Perhaps he hadn't. I had unknowingly given him enough to buy a camel. He seemed unfazed by the cold emanating from my gloved hand. I smiled at him, feeling the weariness of my long walk drain away.

The rest I handed to the second man, who mumbled something incoherent and bowed to me. I shook my head and said, "*Jya*," meaning *no*, for I made no sacrifice; I had everything I needed, and the coins I'd been given were excessive. I glanced over my shoulder before continuing on my way.

I had almost reached the city's edge when I saw one last beggar, a woman who looked to be in her forties, with a mashadah of her own wrapped about her head, and a tattered shirt and skirt covering skin riddled with stretch marks. She was washing what looked like a long sock in a shallow puddle in the street. Where the water had come from, I wasn't sure. My guess was that it must be from one of the camel troughs around the corner.

She glanced to me, unperturbed by my appearance, and continued kneading and folding the sock in the muddy water.

I had no coin to give her, and I dared not ask the others to spare some of what I had given them, but I could not walk by and do nothing. My cold heart wrenched itself, sending shivers down my back and arms.

I searched myself for something to give her—even my head scarf would be an improvement over what she wore. But as I reached for it, I touched my braid and had a thought. An uneasy thought, for I had always been fond of my hair, and despite its grandmotherly color, I considered it to be one of the last vestiges of beauty I had left.

I stepped forward and in Hraric said, "May I talk to you? I won't hurt you."

She glimpsed me for only a moment and nodded her head, tirelessly working on that sock that would never get clean.

"I come from Iyoden, in the north," I explained slowly. "In Iyoden, girls sometimes sell their hair for money. Do they do that here?"

She paused in her washing; I noticed her cracked knuckles. With a frown she pulled up the edge of her mashadah, revealing a scalp almost void of hair, save for a few scraggly pieces. I could only imagine such a thing coming from either abuse or illness, but I did not inquire.

I pulled my own braid over my shoulder and rubbed it between my fingers. I took a deep breath and said, "Could you use this?"

Now she looked at me with the sort of stare to which I had grown accustomed.

"It won't hurt you, and you can dye it," I said. "Could you sell this?"

She hesitated for a long moment, glancing between my face and my braid. She finally nodded slowly, unsure.

"Do you have a knife?"

Hesitant to take her eyes off me, the woman reached behind her and pulled out a small paring knife, the dull blade barely two inches long and rusted at that, the sort of knife used in a kitchen for things like potatoes and radishes. I took it from her. Though she flinched at my cold aura, she did not move away from me.

I grabbed my hair at the nape of my neck and set the knife against the top of the braid. I admit I hesitated for a moment, but I knew the hair would grow back. Besides, I really had no need for it. I carefully sawed through it with the dull blade until the last strand came free— about three feet of hair. To my own shock, when I held it out to her, it was not white as an old woman's, but a soft blond, the color my hair had been when I was seventeen. I marveled at it for a moment. Severed from me, the locks no longer held the curse.

"Gold," she murmured, for blond hair was nowhere to be seen in the Southlands.

I smiled and handed her the braid, which she took with delicate fingers. "Sell it for as high as you can," I insisted.

She nodded and quickly scrubbed her eyes with the back of her hands.

I smiled, feeling light within, and for a fleeting moment I did not feel cold. Standing, I handed her my head scarf as well. I didn't need that, either; I hardly had trouble keeping off the sun.

I walked back to the caverns without a real path to follow, but I felt so glad inside, sweeter than a hundred honey taffies. Almost enough to forget the soreness in my joints, my bones of ice. The cheer morphed into a strange sort of fullness as I continued on my way, so much so that I almost wanted to thank Sadriel the next time I saw him.

The trek to the cave, much of which was uphill, would have made a normal woman sweaty and sunburnt, but I was just breathless, and my thinning slippers and the hem of my dress were dirty. I hated to do it, but I would have to ask for new shoes the next time I saw Aamina. Preferably sturdier ones.

As I neared the mountains, I spied someone leaning against the lip of the cavern by my door, feeding his camel from a wide canvas sack. I could not help but smile when I recognized Lo, still dressed in his indigo uniform, but free of his helmet and mashadah. When he saw me, my short, uneven hair tousled by the wind, he made no gesture other than raising one eyebrow.

"What is this?" he asked, fastening the feeding bag to his camel's saddle.

I touched the frayed ends and shrugged, pausing a moment to catch my breath. "It's a long walk back here; I didn't want to carry the extra weight."

He smirked. "I would not say it is becoming, but it suits you. But why have you gone to the city again, and without a ride or escort?"

"I . . ." I couldn't think of an excuse. Scarlet sunlight far to the west cast a red glow over Lo, making his uniform look violet and his earrings orange. "Do you want to come inside? Do you have long?"

He narrowed his eyes but followed me inside and waited silently as I built up the fire.

"I bought some coffee today. I . . . Qisam thought you might like this kind," I said, going to the small table where my purchase sat. I could smell its richness before I even reached the bag. "If you'd like, I—"

"Misa," he said, dropping the *s* from my name, "why did you go into the city?"

I glanced at him, subconsciously working the muscles of my frozen hands. "Is that not all right? I was only there for a few minutes. And thank you, for speaking to Imad. It means—"

"Only a few minutes. I know; I saw the cloud. Why?"

I didn't answer. I used to be such a good liar. Where had those skills gone?

I fumbled an answer. "I was worried. About Aamina."

He frowned. "If that's true, then tell me where Aamina lives."

I hesitated too long.

He stepped toward me. Perhaps it was a trick of the firelight, but he seemed very, very tall. "Who was in here, that day I heard you shouting?"

I glanced down at the carpets, then forced myself to meet his eyes. "That was two months ago, Lo."

He stared at me so intensely I thought I could feel a hole drilling right into my forehead.

He dropped his hands to his hips. "If you do not trust me—"

"No," I interrupted. "No, I . . . trust you." My pulse throbbed from breast to chin. Could he hear it?

"You said I would not believe you if you told me," he said, pulling out a chair and sitting in it. "I am listening."

I bit my lower lip and shivered, chills running laps between my toes and ears. I ran through every possible excuse, anything I could think of that might convince him to drop the topic, perhaps even play the "trust" tactic myself. My heart feared what Sadriel might do if I were to tell anyone about his visits. There was the chance he wouldn't care. But there was the possibility he would be angry with me, and the last time he had gotten angry . . .

Yet something inside me rioted from the idea of lying to Lo. I *did* trust him. Truly, I did.

So I told him about Sadriel. I told him everything.

The words flew from my mouth and crashed into the cavern around me. I told him about Mordan and my harsh rejection of him. I told him about the curse, Euwan, Bennion Hutches, and the first time I had seen Death. I told him how I left home and my conversations with Sadriel. I described him in such detail that, even with the skewed stare Lo gave me, I knew he had to believe me.

Once I started, I could not stop. I told Lo about the dogs and the hunters from the coast, even about that weak, awful moment when I almost gave in to Sadriel, and once more I was grateful my frigid skin forbade me from flushing.

I told him about the mountains and the villages and crossing the northern border, and how terrified I was when he and Imad and the others chased me down . . . and how very afraid I was that they were more hunters come to kill me. I told him why I had been shouting that day he broke the lock on my door, why I had the bruise, and why I had feared telling him the truth. Why I still feared telling it to him. And I told him Sadriel's threat about hurting someone within Mac'Hliah.

"And I realized I had no sway over him, so I came back," I said, filling a cup with trembling hands and wetting my throat until the water froze.

Rather than respond right away, Lo stared past the cavern walls, taking his time to think, as he always did. I rolled my lips together, massaged my hands, and offered him water—a gesture that went unnoticed. His silence went on for so long that I went to my bookshelf and selected my book of Hraric plays to keep me occupied. My hands shook as I turned the pages but not from the cold. I read three of them before he finally spoke.

"Aluhra."

I lifted my eyes.

"That is his name . . . in Hraric," he explained slowly, dark gaze shifting to me. "Aluhra."

I closed the book in my lap. "You believe me?"

"Should I not?"

I shook my head and blinked quickly to chase away tears. "Thank you. I haven't told anyone. I don't know . . . what he'll do if he finds out. With any luck, he won't."

Clasping his hands, Lo leaned forward in his chair. "Will he come tonight?"

Again I shook my head. "I don't know. I can't depend on anything with him."

Shivering, I took a deep breath, trying to calm my nerves. Without thinking of it, I touched my cheek where Death had struck me, but Lo noticed.

"You are afraid." It wasn't a question.

I didn't want to be, but I nodded. "But he won't come, not now. He stays away from the living. The uncursed living."

Lo considered this for a moment before standing and rolling his neck, the bones popping several times. "How much oil do you have left for the fire?"

I watched him. "Enough for a few days. Why?"

"Do you want me to stay?"

Blood rushed to my cheeks even without the heat.

He motioned to the front of the cave with a jerk of his head. "Over there," he clarified. "If you are afraid, I will stay."

My heart threatened to break my ribs. "But won't Imad—"

"Even my sheikh cannot keep me every hour. There are men to fill in for me. Misa, do you want me to stay?"

I nodded.

He moved to the north wall, ready to pull down a drapery, but I scurried to my feet and pulled the blankets from my bed. "Use these," I said, holding them up. "They make no difference to me."

"For my camel?"

"I don't mind."

Lo accepted them, then studied the one I had woven of the Finger Mountains, my storm, and the birds. "Your talent is growing."

I smiled.

He stepped outside, brought his camel into the lip of the cave, and covered it, then set the last blanket beside the fire, rolling it at one end to form a pillow. When he had finished, he glanced at me as though we hadn't just had a conversation about Death and him staying the night and asked, "What coffee?"

Smiling, I tossed him the bag and set the pitcher by the fire to warm.

CHAPTER 22

I did not sleep well that night. It was in part due to the cold, in part my determination not to let my teeth chatter in the silence between wintry gusts that swooped over the cavern, and in part because I was very aware of Lo's presence on my floor. He lay far from my reach, and I could not see him unless I sat up, but my thoughts ran rampant, and I could not—or, perhaps, did not want to—rein them in.

I do not think he slept well, either. The moment I dimmed the lamp he went into guard mode—utterly silent, his body tense and ready to spring at any moment, much like a panther. His eyes had a way of seeing everything at once, while never looking at anything directly, and I knew even the faintest shiver would not escape his watch. I listened to his breathing as I massaged the cramps in my calves and sides. It did not sound like the breathing of a sleeping man. I felt guilty for stealing away his sleep. But I hadn't felt so safe since before I left Euwan, when I had a sturdy home to sleep in and a strong-armed father just down the hall.

Sadriel did not come.

Not long before dawn I selected *River of Tears* from my bookshelf and began reading through it—it was a short novel about an old man who loses everything in a fire and, using the roof of his ruined house as a boat, travels upstream until he can find a new home. What he finds is an ancient burial ground, where he lies down and dies among the bodies of his unknown ancestors. It was my least favorite of my books and the least read among my small collection. I preferred happy endings, though I appreciated that the story was rich with symbolism.

At the first pink light of dawn Lo rose wordlessly from his bed and took his time folding his blanket and stacking it at the foot of the bed. I set down my book and poured oil on the coals to light the fire. I found myself constantly tucking strands of hair behind my ears—I had cut it too short to tie.

"Are you cold?" I asked.

"I am fine."

"Do you want some coffee?"

I stood up and grabbed the pitcher before he could answer, then slipped outside to gather fresh snow. It fell in wide, soft flakes, silent and beautiful, catching the colors of the sunrise. I watched it for a moment before heading back into the cavern, shutting the door quickly behind me.

Lo was sitting on the edge of my bed, turning over *River of Tears* in his hands, running a calloused finger down its broken spine. He regarded me with a faint grin, and I smiled back at him. I set the tarnished pitcher on the coals to warm.

"You never told me what you thought of this one."

I took my patterned head scarf—I had given away the mustard one—wrapped it around my forehead, and knotted it at the nape of my neck to hold back my hair. "It's well written and thoughtful, but it's a sad story with a sad ending." A tale of a man truly alone.

"Hmm." He turned the book over. "I always read it when I became too aware of myself. When I 'could not see the big picture,' as you might say in the Northlands. I find it . . . realistic."

"Realism is what philosophy is for," I said, wetting a rag to wipe out the previous night's cups. The water froze on the fingers of my gloves. Lo put down the book and took the rag from me, cleaning the cups himself. "Fiction is for dreamers."

He smirked. "Is it?"

I turned up the flame in the oil lamp. "Why else would one read unbelievable stories but in hopes of believing? I always saw novels as an outlet for which the mind can escape this world, not be tethered to it."

"I think I know an author you may like, in that case," Lo said, placing the cups on either end of the table. "I will have to bring you his works."

He looked at me with those rich, dark eyes. I forced myself to look away, if only to hide a girlish grin.

To my surprise and great joy, Aamina arrived later that morning, her arms wrapped around a basket nearly too large for her to carry. Lo took it from her, and her eyes popped at the sight of him, then goggled at me in astonishment. Thankfully, she said nothing while he was present.

"I was so worried," I said as Aamina stepped in from the snow, her shoulders and head scarf nearly soaked. "Your sister, is she well?"

"Yes, yes, she's healthy as a wild pig. But child, that babe wanted to come into this world feetfirst, and you must know what a poor idea that is, and bad luck at that. Oh goodness, if that midwife had arrived ten heartbeats later—"

Lo gathered his things as Aamina prattled, silently excusing himself. However, as Aamina began unloading yarn and foodstuffs from her basket, Lo leaned down to me, his fingers brushing my scarf, and whispered, "You do not have a cold heart, Misa."

My pulse quickened at the feel of his breath on my skin, and his words stopped my heart completely.

He left without a second glance back, disappearing into the drifting snow.

Aamina continued her story behind me, but I admit I did not hear it. My body had fixed itself to the ground, as though the cavern floor had risen and solidified about my ankles. I stood there, barely breathing, staring at the door. Staring at the place Lo had been just moments before.

"You do not have a cold heart."

My lips quivered, and tears blurred my vision. I pressed one palm to my lips and the other over my heart, shivering and aching and feeling . . . light. A sort of airy relief I can't describe passed through me at those words, words I hadn't realized I needed to hear. Words that answered the question buried in the deepest part of me—the one I had never thought to ask.

And Lo . . . oh, Lo. How had he known the one simple phrase that could relieve such weight from my shoulders?

Aamina gasped. "Goodness, your hair! What have you done?"

I swallowed hard and blinked back my tears before turning around. Clearing my throat, I touched the short, uneven locks.

Aamina's eyes bugged. "What is wrong? Are you ill?" Her brows skewed and nearly crossed each other. "Did that man do something?"

I shook my head, wiping away half-frozen tears. "No . . . no, Aamina. I'm just glad you're back."

She rolled her eyes, but her face lifted into a smug smile. "I told you I would be. I sent a letter with Rhono—didn't you get it? Anyway, you're skinnier than I remember, and I have a treat for you. Ever heard of chocolate? It comes from a funny sort of tree that grows in the Hurot

Isles, and you wouldn't think much of it on its own, but get your hands on some honey and it will do *wonders* for the soul."

Using her sewing scissors, Aamina very carefully fixed my hair while wearing a pair of my gloves, evening it out so it looked acceptable, even cropped as it was. She talked a great deal about her sister and her new nephew, and I was glad to hear they were in good health, though try as I might, half my mind lingered in Mac'Hliah, a bird perched on Lo's shoulder, unable to fly away.

CHAPTER 23

The next time Aamina came she brought me leather shoes with hardy soles and long stockings, as well as a new mauve dress with especially baggy sleeves and a white head scarf trimmed with olive. She was insistent that I try out my new shoes, so we used my newfound mobility to journey into Mac'Hliah together for the afternoon, she on her camel and me walking alongside. The idea of me riding on the back of the saddle didn't bother Aamina, but I did not want to risk harming her, and her camel looked at me with the sort of knowing eye that affirmed my decision to walk. Walking or riding, I was elated to leave the cavern.

When we reached Mac'Hliah, we walked through the vibrant market, which brimmed with a surprising number of soldiers. Aamina chatted about anything and everything, from how to select the best melons to the strange shapes of moles on her husband's body. She often spoke of her husband, who worked as a trader between countries in the Southlands and was often away. Aamina painted a laughable picture of a short, stout, dark-skinned man with half a head of hair, but I could tell from her small smiles that she cared for him deeply. I hoped I could meet him someday.

Aamina had a strange way of shopping. She stopped at nearly every booth to gander at its wares, often prodding produce or examining strings of beads against her wrist, completely ignoring the merchants' sales pitches. She fondled this and sniffed at that but rarely pulled a coin from her purse. I wondered if she was picky or just curious. I stayed close to her, constantly aware of my surroundings, stepping this way or that to avoid brushing shoulders or startling a camel. I tried my best to smile when others stared, to laugh at the few who still crossed their chests and tapped their shoulders at the sight of me, and to nod to those who greeted me. I recognized a few of the soldiers from my spring trek to Zareed's largest cities and waved. A few signed to me in handtalk, simple things like *Hello* or *Nice to have some shade.*

Nearly an hour into our jaunt in the city Aamina took great interest in a shop that sold clay pottery. Not wanting to hold still, and seeing the shopkeeper's wariness over my presence, I excused myself to await Aamina outside. As I paced the store's perimeter, I noticed a group of women across the street and down a ways, eyeing me and whispering. I paid them little mind at first, but their eyes followed my every move. While I could not hear them from such a distance, particularly over the noise of bartering and gossip, I saw them constantly shake their heads and gesture with their hands, always in my direction.

I was about to fetch Aamina when she stepped out of the shop of her own volition, a chilly breeze from my storm nearly tossing back her head scarf. She carried in her hands two bowls carefully wrapped in linen and began explaining her bargain to me when one of the women who'd been watching me, apparently startled to see us leaving, cut off a man pulling a handcart to cross the road and hurried after us. I paused and waited for her. It must have unnerved her, for she hesitated before approaching me. The other women gawked from their cluster.

"Svara Idyah," she said, her voice quivering, "forgive my interruption"—she nodded to Aamina—"but I have a son sick at home with fever, and when I saw the clouds . . ."

She stared at me for a moment before dropping her eyes. "His body is so hot; I thought perhaps you could cool him. Anything will help."

Astonished, I glanced back to the woman's friends, who quickly separated and went their separate ways. Had this been their discussion? I had assumed they were eager to see the back of me.

Aamina shook her head. "Terrible news—how old is he?"

"Seven," the woman answered, eyeing me.

"I am no doctor," I said, "but I will try my best to help."

The woman seemed both terrified and relieved. She wet her lips and said, "This way," and wove back through the market, leading us around tents and down a dirt road that meandered through the homes on Mac'Hliah's north side, closer to the mountains than the rest of the city. She said nothing as she led us, only wrung her hands together and occasionally glanced over her shoulder at me. I noticed bags under her eyes. There must have been a great deal of worry hiding beneath her skin.

She stopped at a single-level brick house and led us through a door made of hanging cloth. A few pieces of wicker furniture lined the walls of the front room, and an elaborate but faded oval rug lay over the center of the floor, a few dishes scattered atop it. The woman led us into a second, smaller room filled with narrow beds. A young boy lay on one in the corner, his black hair matted to his forehead with sweat. His eyes did not open when we entered the room, and his stomach heaved with each breath. A young woman—I can only assume his sister—knelt beside him, wiping his face with a wet rag. My presence obviously rattled her, but she did not move from her brother's side.

The woman—her name was Boani—quickly crossed the room and knelt at her son's side, pressing her palm first to his cheek, then to his neck.

I swallowed. This reminded me too much of Bennion Hutches.

Boani waved to me. "See? His head is too hot. Come, feel."

"I cannot," I said at the same time Aamina spurted, "No!"

Boani and her daughter gazed at me with wild eyes.

In careful Hraric, I explained that my direct touch would do more harm than good. I noticed a dented pail half-filled with water at the bedside.

"Do you have a sack?" I asked.

Boani nodded and hurried out of the room, careful not to brush me as she went.

I neared the bed, Aamina behind me. The daughter shivered.

"I'm sorry," I said. "How long has he been sick?"

She held up two fingers. Two days.

"It looks different."

I whirled around at the voice, causing Aamina to start, seeking that honey-slick voice that spoke the dead tongue of Angrean. Death stood in the corner of the room, his arms folded over his chest, his back leaning against the wall.

"Smeesa?" Aamina asked, studying my face. I remembered that she and the others could not see the man in the corner.

Boani returned with a burlap bag that smelled something like chicory, and I forced my attention off Sadriel. I took the bag and placed its base in the pail, twisting it until most of the water was inside its netting.

"I do not want it to snow on Mac'Hliah," I explained as I pulled off my gloves and tucked them into the broad sleeves of my dress. "But I will do what I can to help you cool him. Has he seen a doctor?"

Boani stared at the pail and nodded.

I knelt and clasped the metal bucket between my hands. Frost etched up its sides, and for a quarter second condensation formed along the rim of the pail, but within moments the water inside it froze, clinging to the burlap.

Death appeared beside me, blocking my view of Aamina. "It's different. What did you do?"

"Now is not the time to talk about my hair," I snapped quietly in Angrean, though not low enough to avoid being heard. Boani eyed me strangely, likely suspecting some form of witchcraft. "Why are you—"

The truth came to me in a sudden rush of understanding, and I ripped my hands away from the bucket and glared at Sadriel. He wasn't here for me. He was here for the boy.

"You cannot take him," I hissed.

From behind Sadriel, Aamina whispered, "What are you saying?"

"Just talking myself through what I'm doing," I answered in Hraric. "Boani, take this."

Boani hurried over to me and grasped the top of the sack while I held the pail, and she lifted the solid block of ice after a few tugs.

"Not your hair," Sadriel said, oblivious to the mortals around him. "Your curse. It looks . . . different."

I stiffened and glanced at him, then forced my eyes away. I did not want the others to think me insane.

To Boani, I said, "Do you have more water? For more ice?"

The word for *ice* was the same in Hraric and Northlander, though I pronounced it with the Zareedian accent. She nodded and nearly tripped over herself in her haste to rush out of the room.

"Are you all right?" Aamina asked, rubbing her chin.

I nodded and murmured in Angrean, "What do you mean, it's different?"

Sadriel only shook his head and shrugged. "I can't explain it in a way you would understand."

My teeth chattered, and I clenched them tight. Different or no, I felt as cold as the day Mordan had cursed me. Cold as the water of Heaven's Tear Lake, when the ice broke beneath my feet when I was ten years old. Cold as the deepest layers of snow on the highest peaks. Cold as my heart.

"You do not have a cold heart, Misa."

I shivered. "You cannot have him."

Without intending to, I had spoken in Northlander. Boani's daughter narrowed her eyes and repeated in a thick accent, "Have him?"

Giving her my attention, I said, "Get some clean cloth to wrap that ice in; it will hurt him if you put it directly on his skin. I will make more for a cold-water bath to help lower his temperature." At least, that's what my mother had done for us when our fevers ran too high.

Winter wind swept through the windows, and Aamina hugged herself in a futile attempt to get warm. I needed to leave, soon. I nodded to the young girl and left the bedroom with the pail to search for Boani. She had already returned to the main room with a jug of water.

"Do you have a hammer?" I asked.

She nodded.

Kneeling, I poured the water into the pail and froze it. "Use the hammer to break off pieces. If you have a cellar, or even a deep hole, the ice will keep for longer there. I need to leave before snow starts to fall on the city. Can I do anything else?"

Boani shook her head, and I saw tears in her eyes, which instantly made me regret the need to make haste. "No, thank you," she said, bowing slightly at the waist. "This has helped so much."

I smiled and pulled on my gloves. "I will check back and pray for him. Call the doctor again—it cannot hurt."

Boani smiled and picked up the pail of ice before hurrying into the bedroom. I spied after her, but I did not see Sadriel, which relieved me in more ways than one.

I thanked Aamina for her time with me and told her I would return to the cavern on my own. She insisted on escorting me, but I stood my ground and she was cold, so my argument won out. I arranged my head scarf so it would keep the short strands off my face, then hurried outside and back the way we had come. A few tiny crystals of snow already danced on chilled winds. The streets were largely clear, and I imagined many had returned to their homes to wait out the storm. I walked briskly, encouraging the patch of white sky to follow me. Any stragglers in the street stepped aside for me; it was not hard to recognize the Svara Idyah and her cloud.

Thankfully, I saw no dogs, and therefore took a main road around the marketplace and northward, toward the edge of the city. I had only just passed the last of the stores when a familiar voice called out my name.

"Smeesa!"

Despite my hurry, I stopped and looked back at a band of guards moving toward me. I noticed Eyan first, but he had not been the one to speak my name.

Imad waved at me from the center of the group. He was dressed in simple clothes, and his hair was longer than the last time I'd seen him, though he still wore the two narrow braids over each ear. His pale eyes were a startling contrast to those around him.

I spied Lo behind him, taller than the entire guard save for one of the men. He smiled at me, and my heart sped.

I bowed as Imad neared. "Forgive me, I've been in the city too long. I was just returning home."

"I had hoped to find you before you left," Imad said with a wide smile, speaking Northlander. "I saw the cloud. How have you been? I have not been to see you as promised, and I apologize."

"No, it's fine!" I said, putting up my gloved hands. "You have done so much for me; I could not ask more. I am very comfortable."

Imad nodded and walked beside me, his guard fanning out around us. I stole a glance at Lo. Our eyes met for the briefest moment.

"My second cook has created the most remarkable dessert, thanks to you," Imad said, clasping his hands behind his back. "He uses your snow and salt to harden sweet cream. Do you have anything like that in the Northlands?"

I grinned. "Not that I know of. It sounds . . . interesting."

Imad made a grand gesture toward the sky. "You will have to make it snow hard so we can have more ice. I want to serve it at my birthday dinner, which I insist you attend. I will have Havid deliver an official invitation, of course."

"Aamina may be better . . . Birthday? When is it?"

"Next week, but the celebration will be in two," he answered. He clapped his hands together. "It will be spectacular. The doctors say even Father will be able to attend, so you will finally get to meet him. He is impressed with you."

I bowed my head. "Thank you, but helping Zareed requires no effort on my part. If it will cause no harm, I would love to attend your dinner." Eating in front of so many would prove a challenge, but I could have an early dinner in my cave and come just to watch. How exciting it would be to attend a prince's party! I could not believe such blessings existed for me. And though I seldom spoke to him, I still cherished Imad's friendship.

Imad slowed. "I best get back, but I'm glad I found you. Lo, would you send an escort with Smeesa?"

"I will take her myself, my sheikh," Lo said with a short bow.

Imad nodded and clapped his hands once more. "Then I will see you in two weeks, Smeesa." He shivered, then laughed. "I will have to remember to bring a coat the next time I hunt you down."

I smiled as Imad and his guard took the next fork in the road to make their way back to the palace. For an outing such as this, many nobles would probably have ridden on a litter or in a carriage, but as Lo had said, the prince was a humble man. A man to be admired.

Lo moved beside me, a hand resting on the large sword at his hip. "Has *he* returned?"

I shook my head, knowing he referred to Sadriel. "Not to the cavern. I saw him not an hour ago, in the home of a woman named Boani. Her son is sick with fever, and I fear he came for him." My step slowed, and I peered up to him. "Lo, can I ask you a great favor?"

"Of course."

"She lives on the northwest side of the city, by the mountains. Aamina knows where. If the opportunity arises, would you visit her? See if she needs anything—a doctor, medicine, food? See if her son is recovering, or . . ."

"I will," he said, adjusting his uniform closer to his skin, attempting to ward off the cold without being obvious about it.

"Thank you."

We crossed an intersection, and two soldiers nodded to Lo from their station on the corner. Once they were out of earshot, I asked, "There are more guards in the city than usual. Why?"

"Dissenters." He frowned. "They've been . . . louder . . . than usual. Prince Imad is the great grandson of the man who overtook the throne through war. That generation has passed, but there are still those who support the old regime, who want it restored."

"But Imad is a good ruler."

Lo nodded. "Do not ask me to explain it, because it is as senseless as snow in the summer." He chuckled a little.

"But they wouldn't hurt him, would they?"

The mirth faded. Taking a deep breath, Lo said, "There has already been one attempt on Imad's life, though the assassin never got close enough to draw his dagger. We caught him in the receiving room of the palace."

I gasped and pressed a hand to my lips. "When? Was anyone hurt?"

Pressing a hand to my back, Lo guided me around a short wagon parked in the street, then returned the hand to his sword hilt. I shivered at that brief moment of contact. Rolling my lips together, I busied my hands with the ends of my head scarf.

"No one," he said as we reached the last homes of the city. "Do not worry yourself; Imad is well protected."

"But are you?"

His dark eyes met mine for a moment. A smile tugged at one corner of his mouth. "I will be fine."

We walked in silence for a while—not an uncomfortable silence, just a thoughtful one. We passed two more soldiers, both of whom nodded at Lo, before leaving the perimeter of the city and starting the trek to my cavern. I found myself wishing we would never reach my little home in the Finger Mountains.

Home. My home. When did I start thinking of it that way?

My cavern came into view, and I could not help but share my thoughts. "When I first agreed to come to Zareed, I was scared," I said, ignoring a chill that bit hard at my arms. "We have stories back home of Southlander mercenaries, though I always enjoyed the honey taffies they sold."

Lo smiled.

"But the strange thing is, despite living in Iyoden all my life, when I think of home, I think of Mac'Hliah. I love the land, the culture, the language, the people."

"Most Northlanders do not."

"I don't know how to describe it, but Zareed is beautiful. When I'm here . . . I can almost feel the sun on my face."

He paused not ten paces from my cavern door and studied me, a light winter breeze tousling the ringlets of his black hair. Several seconds passed before he chuckled, as though hearing a joke carried on the wind.

"You are peculiar," he said. "But I hope you will feel the sun again, Misa. If I could have Garen's wish, I would ask for that."

My stomach fluttered. "Garen's wish?"

He nodded. "I will bring that book for you the next time I come. It is more suited for children, but perhaps you will enjoy it."

"I would like that."

"And I will find this Boani," he said.

"Thank you."

He smiled at me, nodded once more, and left for the city. Though I stepped into the darkness of the cave, I left the door open a crack and watched him walk away until he vanished entirely from sight.

CHAPTER 24

Time rarely passed swiftly for me, but the days leading up to Imad's royal celebration flew by. In Zareed, the monarch's birthday was somewhat like a winter solstice back home, where everyone participated, decorated, and gave gifts, only I was one lucky enough to experience the celebration firsthand.

In preparation for the event, Kitora herself braved the storm to come to my cavern to deliver a dress—a beautiful high-waisted, aquamarine gown that fell to my toes, made of the softest cotton I had ever touched. Kitora had layered a sheer, pale green fabric over it, and the same fabric also formed drooping sleeves and a shawl sewn in at the shoulders. Thick gold thread lined the collar, cuffs, and skirt, and gold appliqués fanned over my ribs like butterfly wings, centered around a large amethyst just under my breasts. I had never seen a dress so intricate and lovely.

I told Kitora I could not accept such a dress, but she insisted, saying that even the Svara Idyah had to look respectable at the sheikh's banquet. She made me feel so guilty for trying to reject the dress that I agreed to try it on for her so she could make any necessary adjustments. I warned her about my skin, but fortunately the dress covered most of it, though I knew the sheer material over my arms and shoulders would provide little protection for those brushing past me.

Kitora fussed over my hair, which she said looked like an ibis's nest, and returned the next day with a scarf to hide it. She had originally wanted me to wear hair ornaments, but I refused to wear a wig, so this was our compromise. I thanked her until she snapped at me to keep quiet.

Lo also came to see me before the celebration, once the day after I saw Imad in the city, and again a week later to bring me another book in ancient Hraric, though not the one that referenced "Garen's wish." On that first visit, he came bearing wonderful news: Boani's son's fever had broken, and the boy was recovering nicely. I did not know if Sadriel had played any part in deciding the child's fate, for I did not see him before Imad's celebration. Because he stayed away, I did not have the opportunity to ask him.

A troop of four guards, Qisam and Eyan among them, came to my cavern in the early afternoon the day of the celebration, their camels' saddles and tails decorated in braided wool. They wore bright bronze armor and swords with gem-studded hilts in honor of the occasion. The armor was obviously not meant for protection, being too thin, but I imagined it shined brilliantly when not in the shadow of my storm.

I dressed quickly, hoping the stiffening fabric around my body did not look too obvious. Kitora had made such a beautiful dress; I hated not being able to do it justice. I put on my gray gloves and tied back my hair in the scarf before mounting Leikah, who wore a red and black wreath around her long neck and bells on the back of her saddle.

"You look ripe as a sheila's daughter," Eyan said with a laugh as we started for the city.

"What does that mean?" I asked, but Eyan only laughed more, and colorless blood rose to my cheeks. Did I look foolish? But Kitora had made this dress for me, so I would wear it and be proud, regardless of what anyone else thought. I asked him to ride closer so I could check my head scarf in his armor, which made Qisam snicker. Truly, though, I rode into the city between four men made of mirrors.

Oh, how lively the city was! Unlit lanterns stretched between buildings and windows like clothes on a line, each with a different ink painting—tigers and mountains and spiders, even snowflakes. Women wore elaborate dresses with silver hairpieces that chimed when they turned their heads, or hats nearly an arm-span tall. A few wore gowns similar to mine, with the hems tied up nearly to their waists to keep them from dragging in the dirt. Men and women alike wore long jeweled earrings and carved stone necklaces, beads in braids and beards, and kohl to outline their eyes. Many women wore bright red lip stain, emphasizing their already full lips. People sang in houses and on corners, and even danced right in the middle of the road until harried travelers or camels forced them out of the way.

For once, the markets did not bustle with merchants and customers. Nearly every shop was closed, save for a few manned by especially determined salesmen bartering off last-minute jewelry or makeup, gold-tinted chains, and wide embroidered belts. The smell of yogurt and meat drew my eyes to a street vendor who had several feet of sausage roasting over a small fire. He cut pieces off the end, then skewered them on sticks and handed them out to passersby.

So much jubilation surrounded us that few people noticed me, even when my storm blocked out their sun or a cool breeze brushed through mashadah. It felt wrong to bring in my storm when so many were enjoying themselves in the warm streets. I decided then to leave the banquet early, if only to keep my storm from snowing too much on this blessed day. At least those who did not live close to the palace would not bear the brunt of my chill. Perhaps, if the day had been hot, they would even enjoy it . . . or so I hoped.

A stage had been erected near the palace, and women dressed in sheer veils and broad pants lined with bells were performing a complicated dance, holding glimmering batons in either hand. A crowd had gathered around them, and the spectators clapped their hands to the beat of music that sang from two hammered dulcimers and a goatskin drum. I laughed at the sight of them. How marvelous it all was! Nothing in Euwan compared to the grandeur of Imad's Nameday Festival. Nothing.

I was not the only guest to arrive at the palace with an escort, nor was I the first. Four men carrying a litter draped in magenta lace approached the front of the well-guarded palace well before me. A beautiful young woman in heavily beaded silks emerged from the curtains, her ribbon-braided hair hanging to her ankles. A small caravan came after her, though the wagons were too tall for me to see their guests. Eyan led us behind a cluster of camels ridden by men in bright yellows and whites, each with an ornamental sword at his side. Unlike Lo's, their swords were narrow and slender, with brass handles that looked like frozen fire.

I searched the indigo-clad guards who were helping guests at the front of the palace, but did not see Lo among them.

Eyan waved off a few soldiers and guided Leikah down himself, even offering me an armored elbow. I smiled at him but dismounted on my own.

"There's a show going on while the guests arrive," Eyan said. "My niece is playing the *arghul*. She's excited to see the Svara Idyah in person. I told her you weren't that great."

"So kind," I chuckled, clasping my gloved hands beside me and following him through the entrance. Qisam stayed behind. I tried not to marvel at the palace, for I still found its beauty enchanting. Many of the guests took notice of me—if not by sight, then by the chill—but fortunately none were blatant enough to make the signal for warding off demons in my line of sight. They either did not wish to offend me or did not wish to offend Imad, who had invited me. A few donned violet coats, all of the same make. Perhaps Imad had passed them out earlier. I stayed close to Eyan and adjusted my stride to ensure I gave everyone else plenty of space.

I could hear the music as we trailed our way up the broad, winding stairs—engrossing melodies with dozens of harmonies and heavy, methodic percussion. It was the sort of music that could coax life into even a slow-beating heart like mine, the kind you could taste just by breathing. But the minute I entered the throne room, I forgot how to breathe altogether.

How beautiful it was.

Flowers clustered in tall, hip-height urns in the room's corners and on the windowsills, and sheer fabric not unlike the material of my dress hung in loose, bobbing drapes from the ceiling in carmine and beige. Tables so narrow people could only be seated on one side of them wove around the perimeter of the room, leaving the center of the floor and the throne exposed. Several musicians sat in the open space, and Eyan pointed out the young woman in brown who was playing a flute with two chutes. She could be no older than fourteen, but the way her fingers moved across the instrument's round holes dizzied me. Such talent for one so young. For anyone!

To my surprise, several braziers also lined the room, though only a few had been lit, wafting off scents of cinnamon and mint. Considering that Zareed was always hot, even in the middle of the night, I could only assume these had been arranged in anticipation of my arrival. Imad had proven himself, once again, a thoughtful man.

I scanned the room for Lo but did not see him anywhere, nor did I see Imad or anyone who looked like his father. Several faces turned my way, and hushed whispers harmonized with the music.

Eyan gestured to the right corner of the room. "If you want—"

"Could I sit somewhere more distant from the others?" I asked. "Maybe outside?"

"Outside you'll get snowed on," Eyan said with a snort. Still, he motioned for me to follow him to the balcony, where a heavy canvas had been erected to keep *off* the snow. It relieved me to see that the tall doors were also edged with thick drapes to dampen the wind, ensuring I could enjoy the festival without ruining it for anyone else. Imad had truly thought of everything. I'd have kissed him for it had the curse allowed it.

The balcony was lined with smaller round tables, many of them unoccupied. I took a seat at a table at the far end of the balcony, with my back to the draperies. I could still see the musicians through the glassless windows ahead of me, and since I was sitting so close to the mountain, I hoped more of the city would be outside the range of my snowstorm. I had chosen the perfect seat, where I could watch everything and everyone without being much of a bother or a spectacle.

"Would you like me to stay?" Eyan asked, peering up the balcony.

"Thank you, but please go enjoy the party. I'm very content."

He smiled. "My 'enjoying' is standing guard at the top of the stairs, but enjoy it I will."

He bowed flamboyantly—which made two women several tables away laugh—and headed back into the throne room, walking like a man who had ridden a camel for too long.

I watched other guests filter into the throne room until they filled all the tables, though many of the tables on the balcony remained empty. Dancers similar to the ones I had seen outside joined the musicians, and they skipped in a small circle before the throne where Imad had taken a seat, waving their arms in synchronous patterns. I could not see their feet.

The chill spread around me, and a handful of guests moved inside where it was warmer. Before long, a few servants came out to the balcony to light braziers while others began to pass out small plates of yellow rice topped with a green vegetable I did not recognize. I thanked the one who served me, and when I knew no one was watching me, I dared to take a bite. It tasted strange and delicious, salty. The rice turned hard in my mouth as I chewed, but I swallowed without problem.

"How is it?"

I nearly dropped the spoon at the sound of Lo's voice. Wiping my mouth to make sure I had not missed anything, I stood. "I was wondering where . . . Lo, you look so . . ." What word to say?

His facial hair was coming in again around his mouth and chin, but he had shaved his cheeks clean. Rather than his usual indigo uniform, he wore an umber shirt that wrapped around his torso and was tied with a coral sash, white vine-like embroidery running down his collar, which opened to expose part of his chest. Dark, rust-colored slacks bagged around his thighs and cropped close to his calves.

He looked so . . . handsome.

"Different," I finished, unsure of the word.

But he didn't answer right away. He studied me, and my cheeks burned cold. I had nearly forgotten the gorgeous dress Kitora had sewn for me, like something a storybook princess would wear. A head scarf that exposed my neck, sheer fabric over my shoulders, and a high waistline that emphasized my bust.

His eyes flickered back to mine almost too quickly. Thank Mordan I couldn't blush, for so much blood rushed to my head I thought I would faint.

He cleared his throat and said, "Your food?"

I smiled and moved to tuck away a strand of hair that wasn't there. "It's delicious. Are you going to eat?"

"I will," he answered, shifting the drapery behind me to peek outside. Soft snow flurries fell from the clouds above.

"No guard duty tonight?"

He shook his head and smiled. "Imad insisted I attend the celebration as a guest."

Twisting, he patted the hilt of a gold knife sticking out from his waistband, resting against the small of his back.

I chuckled. "He is in good hands."

"Can I get you anything, Misa?" he asked, eyes on mine. "You can come inside—we have braziers for a reason."

I wanted to reach out to him, touch his hand, but I kept my own hands firmly clasped in front of me. "I'm fine," I said, assuring him with a smile. "I can see and hear everything, and I don't think the guests want to wear heavy coats."

He smiled, faintly. "If you do—"

"I'll ask one of the servants," I said. Laughing, I added, "Go enjoy your night off, Lo! Before your food gets cold."

He nodded and graced me with one last smile before heading back inside. I tried to watch him through the windows, but he sat just out of view.

Hands trembling, I managed three more bites of rice before it grew too cold, and I didn't touch the wine in front of me. Not only did I want to avoid it freezing to my lips, but the thought of staining Kitora's dress made me nearly ill. When a servant came to claim my plate, I told him I was fine for the night, but he still brought me roasted chicken with rosemary, which smelled intoxicating. I managed a few small bites. God bless the men and women who had divined such an amazing dish. I hated to waste it, but curse aside, my stomach had tied itself into knots, and I doubted I could have eaten much more anyway.

The guests began clapping, and I leaned back in my chair enough to see Imad addressing them. For once he wore the garb of a prince—gold robes and a thin crown, though his earrings remained unchanged. I could not catch everything he said, but excitement flavored his tone, and he even glanced out the window near the end of his speech to wave at me.

When he sat down again, out of sight, I caught a glimpse of Lo and leaned forward a little to get a better look at him. He was sitting beside one of the most beautiful women I had ever seen—my age or perhaps a little younger, with skin smooth as a babe's and a long braid of hair the color of rich coffee. She wore red with bright orange appliqués, a sheer orange head scarf pinned above either ear, and several beaded necklaces of varying lengths. She had large eyes and a small nose. Perfect, red-stained lips. Petite. She looked like a painting.

A plate of yellow rice sat half-eaten on the table before her. She hadn't been served the chicken yet, so perhaps she had arrived late.

I paused, watching her. Who was she, and why was she beside Lo? They seemed . . . familiar with each other.

I couldn't ignore the pulling in my gut, like half of me was sinking.

Lo spoke with her and the older woman beside her, who was also still picking at the first course. Judging by their facial features, I assumed she was the younger woman's mother, but neither of them resembled Lo. So they were not family. At least, not immediate.

My eyes returned to the young woman. She had to be the most beautiful person I had ever seen.

I touched my own face, envisioning its pallor in my mind, the darkness around my eyes and the whiteness of my hair, cut short at an odd angle—the exact opposite of what was considered pretty for Zareedian women.

Just then, the young woman at Lo's side glanced up and spied me through the window. I snapped back to my upright position, and, fortunately, a new round of dancers filled the floor, drawing the audience's attention there.

I rubbed my chest, frowning at the uneasy feeling that lingered there, beneath the ever-present cold.

To my surprise, as evening settled over Mac'Hliah, the young woman who had been with Lo came out to the balcony. Seeing me, she smiled and quickened her step until she stood at the other end of the table. She bowed.

Her beauty was even more astonishing close up.

"You are the Svara Idyah, Smeesa?" she asked.

I nodded and tugged on the edge of my head scarf.

"May I sit with you?"

Stunned, I nodded again.

She pulled out a chair—her fingers smooth and slender—and sat. She had hazel eyes fringed with dark lashes.

"My name is Faida," she said, "from Djmal, near Kittat, where you visited."

"Djmal," I repeated, and cleared my dry throat. "That's where Lo—the captain of the guard—is from." Family, then? I prayed she was one of Lo's many siblings, or perhaps a cousin. Could the older woman be his aunt?

She lit up. "Yes! Yes, you know it!"

I nodded and fought the urge to chew on my lip.

"I wanted to thank you," she said. I saw gooseflesh spread across her neck from my chill, but she didn't flinch away. "For coming last spring and bringing us water. My father is a merchant, and my brothers are farmers. It has helped us such a great deal. Our lands are green again because of you." She bowed her head once more. "I would have brought a gift had I known you'd be here. Please accept my utmost gratitude in its stead."

I couldn't believe her words. Only Imad had ever thanked me in such a manner. "I . . . I didn't . . ." Swallowing, I settled on, "You're welcome."

She smiled at me. "I am glad to have met you, Smeesa. Lo has spoken well of you. Please do not hesitate to return to our lands. You are a blessing to Zareed."

Stuttering, I thanked her again for her kind words, and she retreated back to the throne room, bowing in my direction once more before leaving the balcony.

I shivered and rubbed my arms to smooth the icy pinpricks on my skin. Had Lo been telling these women about *me*? Had Faida asked? I could not feel warm, but Faida's words had softened me. The thought that I'd helped people, made an actual difference in their lives, soothed me as any warm drink should. I felt a heaviness leave my shoulders—it had settled so gradually that I hadn't noticed its weight.

A bitter wind pressed against the draperies and crept onto the balcony. Sticking my tongue between my teeth so they wouldn't chatter, I stood from my chair and walked past the line of braziers to the throne room, slipping past the dancers relatively unnoticed. I hoped moving around would calm the hovering winter, and perhaps I would not need to leave so early. I also wanted to see Lo one more time, if possible.

I saw Eyan on the stairs and waved, then took the steps down to the main room, where a few guests stood clustered in conversation. I caught sight of Aamina out of the corner of my eye, carrying an empty pitcher toward what I assumed were the kitchens. Quickening my pace, I called out to her.

"Smeesa!" she exclaimed, eyeing me from head to toe. "What a beautiful dress! How my daughter would be jealous of such a thing!"

"Thank you. Kitora made it, but if it fits your daughter, it's hers. I will have no need of it past tonight."

She gasped dramatically. "No, it is yours!"

"Then I will slip it into your bag on your next visit," I said, laughing. "You look lovely," I added, and she did, draped in dark pinks with small beads wound through her braid.

"I look old," she joked. "Are you leaving?"

"Walking, for now. This is all so wonderful, but the snow . . ."

Aamina nodded. "A little too chilly in the kitchens for me. But you must stay for dessert. We are having snow cream."

I grinned and massaged a cold knot in my shoulder. "Aamina, I met a woman from Djmal upstairs. Lo's village—"

"Faida?"

"Yes," I said, relieved that she knew of whom I spoke. "She was very kind to me . . . I was wondering if you knew anything about her."

But deep down, I knew I didn't ask because she had been kind to me. A tendril of fear had begun to worm itself around my diaphragm, and I sought the assurance that would squelch it.

"She is the most beautiful child I have ever seen," Aamina said with a nod. "Lo is lucky to have her, though I don't know why they've waited so long."

Her words made my heart tremor. "What do you mean?"

Another servant passed, and Aamina waved with her free hand. "She is the captain's betrothed."

My bones splintered within me, and I pressed a hand to the wall to hold myself steady. The worm grew into a snake. Breathless, I asked, "They're . . . engaged?"

"It is different in the Northlands, isn't it?" Aamina asked, waving to someone behind me. "Yes, yes, from a very young age. It's customary for marriages to be arranged between the young. Her family is well off, and he is highly esteemed. A good match."

How much effort it took to keep my face expressionless as her words passed over me, colder than winter's heart.

"I think she leaves in the morning," Aamina said.

I nodded numbly. "Th-Thank you," I managed, though it was little louder than a whisper. Forcing a smile, I said, "I need to take a walk before it gets too cold."

Aamina nodded and hurried down the hall to refill her pitcher.

I took a few steps before pressing a hunched shoulder against the wall, the banquet's music fading from my ears. My heart beat slow and cold, and my body shivered uncontrollably.

Betrothed.

What had I expected? That my life in Zareed would go on unchanged? That Lo would continue to discuss books with me into his old age? That he could ever love me, a woman whom he could never touch? I was a child cursed for her cold heart, a woman who flirted with death at every turn. Lo was captain of the prince's guard. And Faida . . . Faida was beautiful and kind and selfless. Everything I was not.

A good match, Aamina had said, and they were. Faida and Lo. My name hadn't made the list.

I took several deep breaths and forced my clenched hands to relax, but I could not reason myself from my stupor. The mind and heart are two separate entities, and one cannot control the other—Dideh Bab had said so much in *The Fool's Last Song*. I took in a shuddering breath and pushed myself off the wall. I couldn't stay for the rest of the celebration, not now. I could barely stand.

Dazed, I started for the palace doors, but before I reached them I heard someone call out my name.

Turning, I saw Faida on the stairs, her skirts dancing about her small feet as she hurried toward me. I saw her and admired her and hated her. She stopped a pace short and took a second to catch her breath.

"Are you leaving already?" she asked, her red lips smiling. "I went to find you again to introduce you to my mother—surely you will stay a little longer?"

I stared at her for a moment, wishing I could *be* her, just for this night, warm and beautiful, with Lo at my right arm.

The sincerity of her smile shamed me.

Yet I managed to return it. Clasping my gloved hands together, I bowed to her and said, "Thank you for your kindness to me; it has lifted my spirits." *Don't cry.* I couldn't cry now.

I met her eyes. "I wish you the most happiness in your upcoming marriage."

That surprised her, but she smiled warmly. "Thank you."

After bowing once more, I stepped through the doors and out into my storm, not bothering to find Leikah. The sun had begun its western descent, casting gold and red shadows over the lively city. A guard called out to me, but I did not slow. I was content to make the trip home on my own two legs. I passed dancers and painters and clouds of delicious scents from food vendors. Staring at the ground, ignoring any who took notice of me, I changed direction only once when I heard the bark of a dog. My feet kicked up snow, and then sand, my cloud slowly tracing my path northward.

And despite the way my heart ached so terribly I could barely move one foot in front of the other, despite the overwhelming sadness that made me cry before I could reach the city's border, I truly meant every word I had said to Faida. I barely knew her, yet I wanted her to be happy. No, not her. I wished that for Lo. I wished him every grace life could offer, and I would do anything to give it to him.

Oh, how I loved him.

CHAPTER 25

After four years, I finally grasped the entirety of Mordan's curse.

The curse's physical effects were obvious, of course. Every day, hour, and second of my life would be spent encased in an unbearable chill that no human—no living thing—should be able to endure. The kind of cold that freezes to the bones, to the spirit itself. The cold that stills the heart and crystallizes the blood. The kind of cold that even fire fears, that can turn a woman to glass.

But only now did I understand the implications. Just as I had broken Mordan's heart, so would my heart be broken, for I could not so much as touch a man without hurting him. No matter where I went or who I met, conversation would be the uttermost limit of intimacy I could hope to achieve with another human being, and only then if they were willing to brave the eternal cold of my presence.

In a way I was glad it had taken me so long to internalize the cost of the curse, for if I had understood the deeper implications of the curse from the beginning, I might never have survived my first year. If my inner darkness hadn't consumed me, Death would have.

Lying on my bed in the sanctuary of my cavern, the fire burning and the lamp turned low, I did not face my darkness, for truly I had banished it from me, and even with a broken heart, my will was forever strong enough to keep it at bay. At first I felt angry with the bid fate had made for me, angry at the injustice of it all. Then shame swept over me for thinking such selfish thoughts. Finally came clarity, and with clarity came a sorrow that spun itself like wool around me. I knew I could not have Lo—I could *never* have Lo—and any thought or action to the contrary would only bring him and Faida pain. Who was I to jeopardize their happiness? I forced myself to relinquish him, prying free one finger at a time, until a cold, dead ache rested solidly in my core. The kind of ache that only time can heal.

I wept over my fire throughout the night to keep the tears from clinging to my eyelashes and cheeks; then I carefully folded Kitora's beautiful dress and placed it with my others, at the bottom of the drawer. All my tears spent, I curled up, shivering, on my bed, too blank-minded to read, alone with only my thoughts and the new heaviness that had pressed into my body.

Oh, how often I had played the part of the fool, but I learned from it every time. This new pain would ultimately help me grow stronger; I knew that. But it ached so terribly, and I felt so very, very cold.

In the morning I ate a breakfast of dates and flatbread and selected some yarn to weave on my small loom, for I had not yet received a larger one. But my hands shook terribly, and I could not bring myself to focus on the task, so I lay down. If I could not sleep, at least I could rest, though the winter chill pulled and wrenched the muscles in my body, my legs especially. The walk from the palace had been a long one.

I don't know when I started humming, but I did, working through the tunes I'd heard at the Nameday Festival as I ran my gloved fingers over the patterns in my blanket, the one that depicted my storm cloud and a flock of birds over the Finger Mountains. I hummed one song after another, improvising the parts I had forgotten. I sensed Sadriel when he appeared at the far end of my cave, but I did not look up. I only hummed and traced the lines of my blanket, one by one.

"You *are* intriguing, love," he said, taking a seat in one of the chairs, studying me.

I traced a black bird and smiled, though I'm not sure it showed on my lips. "Thank you."

"Was that a compliment?"

"No," I said, a little hoarse. "Thank you for sparing the boy in the village."

Sadriel frowned. Crossing one leg over the other, he said, "Mercy is not in my domain, Smitha. A man either dies or he does not. My only role is as the gatekeeper."

"I thought so," I said, running my fingers over another bird's wings. "When I chased you into the city, that's what I thought."

He laughed. "You chased me? I should have stayed around for long enough to see that."

We were silent for a moment, but then Sadriel leaned forward, narrowing his shining, amber eyes at me. "It looks different, Smitha. What happened to you?"

"A very sad thing," I said, stilling my hand. "But it will pass."

Yet at the moment I struggled to believe my own words. Unshed tears lingered behind my eyes, but I was too tired to keep crying. Still, no distraction could dull the hurt in my chest that throbbed in tune with my heart. Only time could heal me. Only time.

I loved him.

I sat up, pulled my loose head scarf from my hair, and set it on my pillow, then tugged my right hand free of its long glove. I inspected the pale skin and violet nail beds, the veins that looked too blue and too dark. I stood, stepped toward Sadriel, and took his hand in mine, squeezing it. I relished his touch for a long moment before letting go and returning to my glove, working the cold-stiffened fabric back over my skin.

Sadriel watched me with a knotted brow. As I lay down, he asked, "What was that about?"

I traced the white, woven lines of my storm with my index finger. "I just wanted to remember what it felt like to touch someone," I said. A shiver coursed through my body, up my back and into my shoulders. "For a moment, I was scared I had forgotten. Thank you."

He frowned, and after a minute, shook his head. "You will not come with me?"

"No, Sadriel."

And he vanished.

That evening, or perhaps late afternoon, Lo came.

I recognized his knock—firm, quick, and loud—but he had to knock twice before I found the courage to answer the door.

"I wasn't expecting you," I said, drawing on all my years acting out plays for friends and family, all my years of lying to fake a smile. I had been a good actress then, and judging by the levelness of my voice, I had not entirely lost the talent.

"I had my shift covered," he said. "May I come in?"

"Of course."

He walked in. I closed the door and poured oil on the fire.

"That isn't necessary," he said.

"I don't mind."

The coals glowed orange with the heat. I took my time with the fire, and Lo remained silent. Finally I stood and brushed off my skirt. "What is that?" I said, gesturing to his hand.

He lifted the book as though he had forgotten he carried it. "*Garen's Wish*," he answered, setting it on the table.

Again I smiled. "I had begun to think you had forgotten—"

"I did not know Faida was coming to the palace," he interrupted, addressing the wall. "Imad extended the invitation without informing me."

Why was he telling me this? Did it matter how Faida had made her way to the festival? I swallowed and poured as much effort as possible into controlling my response. "Faida? I met her, but you have nothing to explain to me."

His dark eyes fell on me. "Misa—"

"She spoke to me, at the banquet," I said, moving to the bed and folding the blanket, if only to keep my focus on something besides him. "She wasn't scared, not even hesitant. She came right up to me and talked with me as if I were a normal person. She even thanked me for bringing water to her village! I can't imagine a better woman for you, Lo. I wish you had told me about her." I blinked rapidly, forbidding fresh tears. Clearing my throat, I asked, "Have you set a date?"

My voice quivered at that last word. I cleared my throat and tried to play it off as a shiver.

He snatched the blanket from my hands and dropped it onto the floor. He looked at me as though he had struck me and regretted it. "It is custom, in Zareed, for children to be sworn to one another."

"I know your customs," I lied, picking up the blanket. Keeping my eyes on the design. I took a deep breath to steady myself. "I've lived here for a year already."

He ran a hand through his hair. "So you have."

"How is Imad?" I asked. He looked at me, his eyes hard. When he didn't answer, I added, "Are the dissenters still a problem? Nothing happened at the banquet, did it?"

"I did not come here to talk about the banquet."

I refolded the blanket. "It was just a question."

Silence.

"Did you want your books back?" I asked, stepping past him to the bookshelf. "I've had them for so long . . ."

He seized my arm and stopped me, but the cold forced him to release me just as quickly. That alone almost broke me, but I would not cry in front of him. I pursed my lips and swallowed. Lo didn't know—*couldn't* know—how I felt about him. He had no obligation to me, and a wonderful woman in his future. He had such a future. I could never give him what Faida could.

"Misa," he said, his voice accenting my nickname so beautifully, "I want to talk about Faida."

"Is she ill?" I asked, feigning alarm. At least I hoped it sounded like alarm. "Are her brothers' crops drying?"

"No—"

"Then you have nothing to explain to me, Lo," I said, almost pleading. I trembled. But I only had to stay strong a little longer. "Thank you for the book," I continued. "I'll read it and let you know what I think, but I understand if you can't visit as often. You're captain of the guard, and well past marrying age, if I may say so."

He looked at me. I couldn't describe it beyond that. It was an unreadable gaze.

I just want you to be happy. Couldn't he see that?

Silence lingered between us for several minutes. I could feel myself crumbling, and it was all I could do to pick up the pieces before they hit the floor.

"Then I will go," he said finally. He crossed the room in long strides. Opened the door to torrents of wind.

I found my voice.

"Lo."

He paused.

"That was why I didn't see you, those two months," I said, fingering the cubby of my bookshelf. "Because of Faida."

His eyes met mine—the last time I would see them for a while. "She was part of it," he answered, and closed the door behind him.

I managed to hold myself together for a moment longer—long enough for him to mount his camel and start back for the city—before I collapsed onto the floor and cried, droplets of ice rolling over Imad's rugs.

When Aamina came the next day, she told me Lo had left Mac'Hliah for Djmal, where Faida awaited him.

CHAPTER 26

I turned to the last page of *Garen's Wish*, its string-bound papers crinkled and yellow. It was an old book, well worn, its bindings not the original. A book read multiple times, pages torn in a few places, likely by an eager child's hands. Perhaps it had belonged to Lo's mother and she had read it countless nights to him and his siblings.

The story was about a boy who had everything—a big house, clothes in every color, enough food to last a lifetime, toys, family, everything—but he wasn't happy, and he didn't know why. To cheer him up, his mother bought him a wooden doll that separated in the middle to reveal a smaller doll, which separated to reveal a smaller and a smaller. When Garen opened the last doll, a genie appeared before him and offered him one wish. But Garen didn't use the wish right away. He wanted to know the "wish of his heart": the one thing that would make him happy. However, because his heart could not speak, Garen could not hear what it wanted.

After days of tribulation, he went to the genie and asked to know the wish of his heart. This was a risk, for if the one thing Garen needed to be happy was unattainable by ordinary means, he would never have it, for he would have already used his one wish. Still, it was a risk he was willing to take.

The genie obliged, and Garen learned the wish of his heart: to be unburdened. Garen thought hard on this, and in the end, he gave away all his clothes, fine food, and toys until he was very poor, but because of the joy his generosity brought the community, he made lifetime friends and found happiness.

I stared at the last page, to a passage highlighted with smeared charcoal. *For happiness has wings, and when burdened by the things a man should want, Garen could not reach it.*

It was the only marked passage in the book, and I wondered who had underlined it and how long ago. I thought perhaps Lo had drawn attention to those words before giving the book to me. Maybe they had been his favorite as a child. Maybe he had intended it as a message for me. A week had passed since Aamina had brought the news of his departure for Djmal. I wondered if he had married Faida, or if he were still preparing for the ceremony. I was glad for him, truly. Happiness had wings; I could only hope to be the wind that helped him fly.

Rhono left a package at my door that included a letter from Imad himself, sealed with blue wax and stamped with the image of a spider. He had the best handwriting I had ever seen, each letter perfectly tilted and shaped. The hand of a king, asking me if I would once more rendezvous at the palace to make the journey to Kittat, Ir, and Shi'wanara and bring them water for the spring crops. My first impulse was to say yes, for I would do anything for Imad, but I admit my second thought was for that conversation I'd had with Sadriel—for those whom my cold had hurt, killed.

Pinching the letter in my hands, I took a deep breath and nodded to myself. I would go. Further precautions could be made this time, and the water helped so many. Surely Imad knew of the dangers that lurked with my curse, but it was his duty to protect his country as a whole. I could not let Zareed wither in a drought for fear of harming a few. Perhaps this time, all would be well.

In honesty, I was eager for the trip. I needed something to occupy my time, and I needed space from Mac'Hliah and its memories. This time, the trek would not be led by Lo. Zareedian weddings involved a great deal of pomp and circumstance, or so Aamina had told me, and it was likely I would not see Lo for a month or more. If nothing else, the journey would give me more time to heal.

A few days later Eyan and Qisam braved my storm to retrieve me. After wrapping my things in my woven blanket, I mounted Leikah and rode into the city.

I had not been in Mac'Hliah since the Nameday Festival. The lanterns had been stripped from the eaves of the buildings, and the civilians donned their normal garb, which still looked brighter and grander than most holiday wear in Euwan. Very few people crossed themselves as I rode by this time. Most continued on their way without taking particular notice of the clouds or the cold, and a few even cheered or clapped at the sight of me. One bearded man called out, "Praise the gods, it is damned hot out here!"

I laughed, but not as boldly as Eyan did. He slapped his thigh as though that were the funniest thing he had ever heard.

"You are coming again, aren't you?" I asked as we weaved through the market, Qisam riding just ahead of us to part the crowds.

"I'm in charge," Eyan said with a wide, toothy grin. "I think we'll head south first, to Shi'wanara. Get the grumpy ones out of the way and finish with the pleasant. Then the ride back to the capital won't be so long."

"Genius," I said.

"I'm still trying to figure out what to do wrong," he added, scratching at stubble along his jaw. "I'd hate to break a camel's leg or get a soldier lost, so I'll need to get creative."

I eyed him and shivered. "Wrong?"

"I'm worried I'll be promoted. I spend enough time at work as it is!"

Shaking my head, I chuckled at him, glad for his good humor. I still nursed a sore hollowness within me, but at least Eyan would help me take my mind off it.

"Perhaps you should get food poisoning in Ir," I offered.

Eyan snapped his fingers. "And have Qisam lead the party home! Then he'll get promoted and I can stay comfortable. There's Northlander smarts, right there."

We wove through the streets, the palace looming larger as we neared it. I led Leikah on my own, having grown accustomed to the reins and her movements. I patted her neck with a gloved hand as we passed a group of children playing marbles, and Leikah shook her head and glared back at me with an almost indignant expression. Perhaps she could feel the cold through glove and fur. Or perhaps "faithful" did not equal "friendly."

I thought about the first time I rode Leikah in the Unclaimed Lands, when Lo had pulled down her muzzle and restrained her so I could board. His eyes had been hard, but the gesture had been thoughtful and kind. If only I had known then.

I trembled with cold, wincing as the sensation spiraled through my chest and stomach.

I didn't dismount immediately when we reached the palace. From atop Leikah's back I had a wonderful view of the sandy carvings that covered the palace's facade—spirals and roses, faces of kings past, great lizards with wings. It seemed impossible one man could have created each and every engraving, but the style persisted as far as I could see. How long must it have taken to create such a masterpiece? If my hands could remain still long enough to hold a chisel, I would have loved to learn to carve stone—my snow sculptures were so fragile, not that they could compare to the majesty of these carvings. I guided Leikah down and slid off her back. Perhaps Aamina could find a history on it for me. Perhaps I would dare to enter a library myself when we returned from our journey.

Several guards in indigo filtered in and out of the palace, loading packs onto their camels while stable hands held feed bags and filled troughs with warm water. I recognized a few of the guards from my last trip and nodded to them as they passed.

"Smeesa!"

I turned as Imad approached, garbed in a maroon robe and white slacks that looked almost Iyodian.

I bowed. "It is good to see you again."

He waved his hands at me. "Don't do that. Haven't I told you before not to do that?" He bowed to me and smiled. "My greatest appreciation to you for agreeing to do this a second time, Smeesa. I have high hopes that next year the natural rain might favor us. But you must stay even then, if only for the sweet cream!"

I laughed. "I would like to stay indefinitely, if the people do not mind."

Imad clapped his hands. "Perfect! Another celebration is in order. We will dine with my father when you return, yes? But now I must speak to Eyan. If you'll excuse me?"

I nodded, and he walked to the head of the line, where Eyan was tightening the straps of his camel's saddle. He straightened immediately in Imad's presence and saluted. Imad shook his head and said something, and Eyan's laughter echoed off the surrounding mountains.

I smiled and turned back to Leikah, and barely managed to restrain my shriek at the sight of Sadriel standing not an arm's width away from me.

Glancing around to ensure no one could hear me, I hissed, "What are you doing here?"

He tilted his head and stared at me as though my question were obvious. And it was. Sadriel went where death called, which meant death lingered nearby.

I shivered and stepped back, frantically searching the area around me, my eyes darting from soldier to soldier. All lively, healthy. I turned back to Sadriel and asked, "What, what is it?"

Sadriel lifted one long finger and pointed. Not at a soldier, but at a tall domed building behind me, lined with beige columns and topped with a green-rusted copper spire. A government building. But beside that spire I saw movement. Squinting, I spied a man dressed in white to blend in with the snow cloud above us. He wore a white hat to hide his hair and a white veil to conceal his face.

And in his hands he held a brown bow, arrow nocked and string pulled back to his ear.

Lo's words resonated in my memory. *"There has already been one attempt on Imad's life . . ."*

It all ran through my mind so fast my vision blurred. Imad. The extra guards. The dissenters. The assassin.

And no one else saw him.

I spun on my leather-soled shoes, the city blurring around me. My body moved too slowly. I forced my cold muscles into action, pushing myself harder than I ever had before. Running. Running. Screaming.

"Imad!" I rushed toward him. *"Ki Pah'al e Vrara!"* *Get out of the way!*

He looked up, confused. Eyan, confused. The stable hands, alarmed.

But I ran for him until we collided, and as we fell lightning exploded through my back, piercing me deeper and deeper, ripping through skin and muscle and bone.

We hit the stone ground, me on top of him, the air expelling from my lungs. Red leaked into my vision. I tried to reclaim my air, but the hurt dug, seared, and burned down to the core of my being. My head floated.

Imad's face muddled in my vision, swirling and darkening.

Sticky, *hot* blood gushed down my back, and I was gone.

CHAPTER 27

My body felt very heavy when I opened my eyes, as though I had been asleep a long time. I lay on a large, soft bed with mustard-colored drapes hanging from its frame, mauve blankets piled atop me. A wooden chest sat at the foot of the bed, and beside me rested a small, round table littered with glasses, bottles, bowls, and bandages. I had the distinct feeling I had been here before, though it took a moment for my sluggish mind to register it.

The palace. The room where I had spent my first night in Mac'Hliah.

My mouth tasted strange. I turned my head, my neck stiff, and tried to sit up. A dull pain thudded in my back. I reached behind me and touched the layers of bandages wrapped around my ribs. I realized I was naked.

And I was warm.

I gasped and pulled my hand away, staring at its peachy flesh and pale nail beds, the faint pink scar running across my palm. No hard veins beneath the flesh. No shivering. No cold. No sign of frost.

Ignoring the pain in my back, I sat upright and touched my face. *Warm.* My neck, *warm.* My chest and stomach were hot from the blankets, the skin soft. Strands of blond hair swept into my eyes.

I shrieked, and I cried, warm tears filling my eyes and falling down my face, running smoothly along my cheeks without freezing. I threw back my covers and looked over my hips and legs, warm and healthy and smooth. I pressed a hand to my mouth and laughed and sobbed, warm tears gushing from my eyes and falling in wet droplets onto my breasts and covers.

The door opened. I pulled up the covers, but it was only Aamina, gasping and rushing into the room.

"Lay down, child!" she hissed, pushing my bare shoulders back to the mattress. It was the first time in years another human had touched me without so much as a wince. "You'll pull a stitch!"

I threw my arms around her and laughed into her neck. How wonderful she felt! How warm, how soft! "I'm warm, Aamina!" I shouted. "It's gone, look at me!" That spot in my back protested with dull pain as I sat up and leaned against her. "Look at me!"

Instead of scolding me, she smiled. "I forgot that you didn't know. You look as fresh as a Northlander should look. How do you feel?"

"Amazing!" I shouted, touching my cheeks, my arms, my hair, which seemed a little longer than I remembered it being. "Amazing . . ."

I stiffened as more memories flooded me. "Imad? Imad, is he . . . ?"

"Imad is fine, thanks to you," she said, eyes wrinkling with her grin. "But that was three weeks ago, Smeesa. We've kept you asleep to help you heal."

I tried to process her words. That explained the strange taste in my mouth. What herbs had they given me?

But I didn't care. I. Felt. So. *Warm.* Like the very sun radiated inside me, its rays spreading from crown to toes.

I hugged Aamina again, and she pushed me back onto my pillows.

"I'm glad you're so well," she said, suddenly maternal, "but they had to cut pieces of you out and sew pieces of you up, so you have to be careful until you're fully healed, hear me?"

I nodded and laughed, eager as a child on winter solstice. Warm. So warm!

"I'll get you something proper to wear. Stay put." She shook her index finger at me and stepped into the hall, shutting the door silently behind her.

Despite her warnings, I sat up again, shaking my head in wonderment. I touched my feet, the cracks in my heels already mending. I wiggled my toes and giggled like a little girl. I touched my bandages, carefully prodding that sore spot to the left of my spine. It ached like a deep bruise.

"I don't understand," I murmured, pulling locks of my hair in front of my face. There was not a white strand among them. How had my curse broken? How could I have woken up my old self? Why had I been freed?

"It looked different," a faint voice crooned.

Tugging up my blankets, I searched the room but found it empty. "Sadriel?" I whispered.

"Your curse," he said, somewhere to my right. "I told you it was different."

I scanned the room, the carpet and the ceiling. Still there was no sign of him. "Where are you?"

"Always amusing," he chirped. "You of all people should know mortals can't see me."

My lips parted. Mortal. Normal. I really had broken the curse.

I swallowed, though my throat was dry. "How was it different?"

"Cursed to be as cold as your heart," Sadriel said, his voice moving toward the end of the bed. "It seems the warmth of the truly selfless broke it." He sighed. "Yet another one lost."

I shook my head. "But I'm not . . . The things I've done—"

"Your hair," he said, closer. Right beside me. A cool finger brushed the side of my head. "That's when I noticed it. Giving up beauty, I suppose. And that savage soldier of yours. You let him go rather easily, hmm?"

Lo. The thought of him made my heart wring. "Love," I whispered. Giving up love. Had I done that? What had Aamina said? Three weeks? He must be married by now. A new pain ached beneath my bandages, growing until it pressed against my ribs. Had he yet returned to Mac'Hliah?

"And the prince," Sadriel said. "I had come for him, not for you. I almost had you in my realm once again, Smitha."

I reached my hand out, but it met only open air. "Thank you," I said, blinking away tears. "Thank you, for warning me. Thank you, with all my heart."

He scoffed. "I did nothing of the sort."

I smiled.

I heard a rustling of fabric, perhaps a flourishing of a cape, or an exaggerated tipping of a wide-brimmed hat.

"We would have been grand, you and I," he said, voice fainter. "Till we meet again."

I waited for a last quip, a last promise, but only silence settled over the room, impenetrable.

I wiped my eyes with the back of my hand. "Thank you, Sadriel."

The door opened, and Aamina hurried in with a soft brown dress and pale rose head scarf. And sandals. Sandals! No gloves, no socks. I almost burst into tears again at the sight of them.

She began laying out the clothes on the bed. Leaning forward, I grabbed her wrist—her skin was so *warm*—and said, "Aamina, can I ask you a favor?"

She eyed me suspiciously but nodded.

My cheeks hurt, I smiled so hard. "Could I . . . have a bath? A warm bath?"

She snorted, nodded. "I'll draw one up for you."

Four years. It had been four years since I had last enjoyed a real bath.

I slipped into the copper tub until the hot water—almost too hot—flooded up to my chin, and my knees poked out from the surface.

"Careful now," Aamina warned me, rolling up my dirty bandages. "You'll pull a stitch!"

I reached back and touched the wound, a curved line under my left shoulder blade, rough with stitches and a few lingering scabs. It throbbed at first as I curled up in the bathtub, but the hot water soothed it. It soothed all of me.

Steam rose up from the water's surface. I sighed. "Aamina, you are a stunning woman."

"Ha!" she laughed. "That's what my husband says when he's done something wrong." She tossed me a bar of sandalwood-scented soap. I held it in my hands, and my chest constricted. It smelled like Lo.

"Wash up, scream if you break anything," Aamina said. She stepped out of the bathroom, leaving the door cracked open.

I rested the base of my head against the rim of the tub, soaking in the heat, watching my skin redden with it. It all seemed so unreal, yet even in my dreams I couldn't fathom something as simple as a hot bath. I soaked for a long time, until the water cooled, before running the soap over my wrinkled toes, legs, torso, and gingerly over my back, relishing its scent. I smiled, and then a thought occurred to me. The soap slipped from my hands.

My family. I could see my family now.

I could return to Euwan.

I stared into the water, gaping and smiling. Father. Mother. Marrine. I had feared I would never see them again, never hear their voices or taste my mother's home cooking. And Ashlen!

I thought of Imad and the tour, but it couldn't happen, not anymore. The storm no longer followed me. But the Finger Mountains still held an abundance of water, and Imad had said next year should bring rain. Surely Zareed would thrive without me.

The thought of leaving the place that had saved me, the place I had called home for so long, spurred a cold pain at my center. But Euwan didn't have to be forever. I could come back. I could feel the desert sun on my face day after day after day.

I jumped up from the tub, sloshing water over the floor, and grabbed my towel. I wrapped it around my body and rushed into the bedroom, dripping water. Aamina was changing the sheets and shouted something at me, but I didn't hear what she said. I rushed to the window and threw the panes open.

Sunlight poured over me, golden and blinding and warm, as if God's own breath washed over me.

"Have you lost your mind?" Aamina asked, hurrying to my side and feeling my forehead for a fever.

I shook my head, new tears trailing down my cheeks. The sun.

Your wish came true, Lo, I thought, a single tear cascading down my cheek. *I can feel the sun.*

"Of course you should go home!" Imad exclaimed, grabbing both of my hands in his. The action jarred the healing wound on my back, but my smile hid the wince. He had a firm, warm grip free of calluses and lotion-smooth. "Smeesa, you've given us enough water to last through this drought and more besides. I will see you have everything you need, including an escort. There are bandits ready and willing to prey on pretty Northlander girls!"

I laughed and squeezed his hands. Warm. "It means more than you can know. But I don't want to bother anyone—"

"I insist you bother all of us." Imad laughed and released my hands. "I think Kitora can design some decent Northlander clothes, but you may need to direct her."

"Oh, no! These are enough!"

He waved his hand like he was swatting a fly. "It is a long journey, and I know how Northlanders are." He winked. "You can take your camel and retrieve a horse at the way station for the rest of the journey. You are good friends with Eyan, yes? He knows the way, and now that he won't be manning the tour, he can escort you. With a few others, of course."

I nodded, my cheeks sore from grinning. It seemed Eyan wouldn't get the promotion he feared after all.

"But take your time, Smeesa," he said, touching my arm. "It would devastate me if anything happened to you—I owe you my life. I want you fully healed before you make the trek there. And back. You *must* come back."

I smiled. "And I owe you mine," I said. I didn't reply to his request to return . . . I didn't know if I could, yet. Touching my face, I reassured myself that I hadn't reverted back to my cursed self in the last twenty-four hours.

"You will dine with my father and me tonight, won't you?" Imad asked, stepping aside to let Aamina fold my clothes. I would have stopped her and done it myself had Imad not demanded my attention.

"Yes," I said, overeager. My first meal after waking had been the best one of my life. I had almost forgotten how to eat like a normal person. And I had never realized how *spicy* Zareedian curry really was! My tongue burned just at the thought of it.

Imad clapped his hands. "Excellent. Until tonight, then."

"Imad?"

He paused at the door.

"Lo hasn't returned yet, has he?"

"Not yet, but soon. I'm sure you'll see him before you leave. Have you met Faida?"

A twinge. "Yes. She was very kind to me at your banquet."

He smiled and stepped out of the room. The two guards who had followed him into the room trailed behind.

I *did* want to see Lo again, if only to say good-bye. Regardless of where either of us went in life, I considered him my dearest friend, the man who didn't fear my curse and who brought me books to ease endless hours of free time. I still labored to fit the pieces of my heart back together, but I knew that, if I saw him again, I would not have to feign a smile.

I turned to Aamina, who had finished putting away my laundry. "How much longer will it take before I'm healed enough for travel?" I asked.

She thought for a moment. "A week, perhaps. The doctor can let us know for sure."

"A week. That's enough time for me to make a wedding gift, isn't it?" A pang. "And something for my sister and my parents. You'll help me, won't you, Aamina? Oh! And I can see your nephew now!"

Aamina laughed. "Yes, you can! He's such a fussy little babe, but he has his father's face, so no one can stay mad at him for long. I worry I'll be the only one with the heart to discipline him when he gets older, and he'll run rampant through the city, stealing things and making the poor girls swoon. But how do beads sound? I bet you can hold a needle now. I'll show you. Women love necklaces, even Northlander ones, so I hear. But is a necklace a proper wedding gift? Perhaps we should get you that big loom and work on a baby blanket! That's as appropriate a wedding gift as any. The wee ones tend to come along awful quickly with the way Zareedian blood flows. Ha!"

I laughed with her, though the thought of Lo and Faida's children pulled at those delicate pieces in my chest. How beautiful he would be, especially if he had his father's eyes. Surely it would be a boy. For some reason, I pictured Lo first with a son, then a daughter.

Taking a deep breath, I agreed to rest while Aamina gathered yarn and beads for the gifts. She stayed with me the entire day, helping me plan the necklaces and the pattern of the blanket until a servant summoned me for my dinner with Imad. We ate with his father, who looked tired but well. He spoke in the cleanest Northlander I had heard since coming to Zareed, and he told me of a time he had gotten lost in the mountains of Iyoden as a boy. What a blessing it was to dine with a king and a prince—my dear friend—without worrying about causing them discomfort.

That night the doctor affirmed that my wound would take another week for it to heal enough for travel, and though I wanted to skip and play and dance in the sunlight, I focused on resting and eating well to build up my strength. Every day Aamina joined me in one of the palace's sitting rooms to work on the gifts I was preparing. The fifth day after I awoke, I went to her sister's small home and met Shukri, who was indeed the handsomest babe I had ever seen, and the sister a bigger gossip than Aamina herself!

Day six, I began packing my things and working with Kitora on a pattern for a Northlander dress, which she claimed would be much easier than her usual designs.

Day eight, I would leave Mac'Hliah.

On day seven, Lo returned to the palace.

CHAPTER 28

I heard his voice in the dining hall on my way to my bedroom for my last fitting with Kitora. My heart thrummed so quickly my head swirled, and I had to pause for a moment to regain my bearings. I had come to believe that I would not see him before I left for Euwan. Aamina had already agreed to deliver the baby blanket to him on my behalf.

My chest seemed to stretch downward like pulled taffy at the thought.

For a moment I held my breath, debating. Would it be better not to see him, to focus on the new opportunities before me, rather than on the one I had lost? I left tomorrow . . . Surely I could avoid him and Faida until then.

But my body already inched toward the dining hall. Lo's voice draped over me like a warm blanket. He was talking to Imad. I peeked inside, but while I could see Imad, a drapery hid Lo from my view.

"—in the caverns. They're empty."

"That's because she's here, Lo, and leaving tomorrow."

I pressed my palm to my drumming heart. They were talking about me.

"For Kittat?"

Imad laughed. "For Euwan!"

"What?"

"You haven't heard? The captain of my own guard hasn't heard so much as a rumor about the man who nearly killed me?"

Lo's feet shifted forward, and his reply came out gruff. "Of course I heard; I rushed back to Mac'Hliah for that very reason. Imad, you are leading me in circles! What transpired while I was away?"

"A failed one, and the perpetrator was shot down before he could escape the city, thanks to Smeesa. Didn't you notice the clear sky, Lo? Her curse has been lifted."

Lo didn't say anything. The room became silent, save for the sound of my own pulse in my ears.

I stepped inside and peered past the drapery, the sight of Lo making me blush—how strange it felt to actually blush again! I touched my cheeks to cool them. My pulse thrummed in the deep scar the arrow had left behind. He had trimmed his hair but still wore the short half beard. He didn't wear his uniform, but commoner's clothes in beige and tan. His gaze was fixed on Imad, his dark brows skewed. He did not see me.

I cleared my throat, and both men turned.

"I heard you were back, Lo," I said, so nervous my voice trembled.

He stared at me as though looking at a stranger before his eyes went wide, but he maintained the rest of his composure.

Imad laughed. "I haven't seen a face like that for weeks." Clapping me on the shoulder, he said, "You've missed a lot, Lo. Seems as soon as you leave, the excitement arrives."

I offered him a faint smile, but he only stared at me. I noticed a gold bracelet around his left wrist. One of Dideh Bab's plays talked about a man who gave a woman a bracelet during a marriage ceremony. Was this the same?

The despair resurfaced in my chest, as fresh as it had been the day I met Faida. I swallowed hard as a lump formed in my throat. If only those three weeks of sleep had counted as time to heal this! His eyes on me . . . I felt like a frostbitten dagger was being plunged into my heart, twisting with my every breath. I thought I would be able to see him again, without it hurting . . .

How wrong I had been.

I cleared my throat again. "You look well. I hope you met no troubles on your trip."

Perhaps noticing the discomfort that hung thick as a storm cloud, Imad began discussing the guard with Lo—something about their rounds and the newly hired men in training. Taking advantage of the opening, I excused myself and escaped into the hallway, brushing past a servant carrying an empty tray. I made it around the corner before a tear escaped me, but I brushed it away before it could so much as graze my nose. Taking a deep breath and clenching my jaw, I straightened my back and walked tall, blinking rapidly to dry my eyes.

Lo was happy. He had no bags under his eyes, no scruff, no stains on his clothes. Nothing to indicate stress. And despite my tears, I was relieved to see him looking so well and healthy. I wondered if Faida had come to the palace with him, and if she would move here for the sake of Lo's work, or if they would find a house within the city.

I paused outside my bedroom door and glanced over my shoulder. No one had followed me. I took a moment to master myself—taking deep breaths, smiling, rolling my shoulders—before stepping inside.

"You're late," Kitora said, snipping a thread from the hem of my dress. It was another with a high waist, and was pale blue, with sleeves that cuffed with pearl buttons at the wrists. Lace adorned the high collar and the hem, which fell midcalf. It looked like something my mother would have made.

"Oh, Kitora," I said, touching the finespun wool. "It's wonderful."

⁂

That night I treated myself to another bath to relax and prepare myself for the next day's journey. Come morning, I would be leaving for the Unclaimed Lands with three soldiers, including Eyan. My things were already packed in saddlebags arranged at the foot of my bed. After drying my short hair on a towel, I slipped into the simple nightdress Aamina had given me: plain off-white cotton with loose sleeves meant to keep off the heat, for I could finally feel the hot, dry climate of Zareed. Outside, in the afternoon, it was almost blistering. Despite that, I loved the heat. I even loved sweating, for I had not been able to sweat for so long.

I ran a comb through my hair and pulled aside the curtain over my window, revealing a city half-asleep, with a few sparkling lights from houses brightening the mountains. My last night in Mac'Hliah. But I planned to return. Aamina had offered me a room in her home, and perhaps I could bring my family along, show them where I had been for the past year. I think Marrine would like it once she adjusted to the culture. And Ashlen, if she were not married and tending to children of her own. Ashlen with children . . . How strange that would be. Then again, Marrine could very well be married, too. A lot could happen in four years.

I knit my fingers together and pressed them to my mouth. In a matter of weeks I would see them all again. See Euwan again. See the Hutcheses . . . Such a debt I owed them. I would understand if my presence pained them, and I would not stay in Euwan long if I caused any grief. I did have a home and many new opportunities in Zareed. What would it be like to live in this city?

These thoughts had wound their way around my consciousness, capturing all my attention, so when a knock sounded on my door, I jumped.

"Come—" I began, then stopped. I *knew* that knock.

The door opened and Lo appeared in the doorway, still wearing his commoner's clothes.

"—in," I whispered.

He smiled at me and shut the door behind him. "I did not recognize you earlier. I did not think . . . such a thing was possible."

I softened and returned his smile. "Neither did I. Had I known, I would have shot myself a long time ago."

He chuckled. "I heard about that. I'm glad you are all right."

"I was unconscious for most of it," I admitted, though the moment the arrow pierced my skin lived fresh in my memory. A red-hot pain like that was hard to forget. "They drugged me with Oki-leaf."

His lips twisted. "I cannot think of a worse thing to put into a person's mouth."

I laughed. "So you've tried it?"

"Once, when I was in the militia," he said, lingering by the door. "I don't know if it was the taste or an allergy, but . . . I did not react well to it."

"Were you hurt?"

"Not badly." He touched his side. "Knife wound, but not deep."

"Scar?"

He nodded.

I reached back and touched my own puckered scar. The stitches had been removed the night before. "We have something in common, then."

Lo smirked. "I would hope you do not have so many."

I pulled away from the window, letting the curtain fall back in place. I searched for somewhere to look besides at *him*, something to focus on that would keep tremors from my hands and those sharp twinges from my chest. I moved to my trunk, tucked my skirt under my legs, and sat. I focused on the folds in my skirt. "How is Faida?"

I asked. If I did return to Zareed, I would have to learn to love her as much as I loved him. I wouldn't be able to bear it otherwise. "Did she return with you to the city, or will you live in Djmal?"

He shook his head. "She is not here."

"When will she arrive?"

"She will not."

I tilted my head. "Are you here to retrieve your things, then? Surely you're not retiring as captain of the guard! Imad would be—"

"I am not married, Misa."

My next words caught in my throat, stuck into the flesh like cattle wire. Had I heard him correctly? My pulse beat in my ears.

Lo stepped away from the door and paced over to the adjoining bathroom, his calloused hands clasped behind his back. "I went back to Djmal to break off the engagement—a very dishonorable thing, for us. That is why it took so long for me to return. I had a lot of arguing to do and promises to make to smooth things over between my family and Faida's. I am not sure I'll be welcomed back any time soon. My mother is especially upset with me."

I listened, my mind blank, staring so hard at my skirt it should have ignited. I shook my head as he talked, and long after he finished, unable to digest the news.

"But . . . why?" I croaked.

"Because it would not be fair to Faida," he murmured, "to trap her in a marriage when I have such feelings for another. It would not be fair to either of us."

I couldn't breathe.

"I love you, Misa."

"No!" I shouted, jumping to my feet, finally looking at him. Tears rimmed my eyes. "You couldn't have known . . . You didn't know I had broken the curse!"

"I did not," he said, strangely calm. "But that changes nothing."

"But it makes no sense!" I cried. "I thought you were happy. I wanted you to be happy! Faida . . . How could anyone not love Faida? And me, a cursed woman who couldn't even touch you!"

He smirked—*smirked*!

I shook my head. "The bracelet. What about . . . ?" I pointed to his wrist.

He lifted the hand with the gold band. "It only means that I have been spoken for." He smiled. "Did you read the book? The passage I underlined?"

I gaped at him, wild-eyed. *For happiness has wings, and when burdened by the things a man should want, Garen could not reach it.*

I took in a shaky breath. "M-Me?" He had meant me? But how could a cursed woman be the one with wings?

"I did not mean to upset you," he said, stepping toward me. "You have no obligation to me, Misa. If you do not feel—"

"H-How I feel," I stuttered, sobs choking my voice. "If only you knew how I feel about you."

He smiled. How beautiful his smile was.

I could not stop the tears. "It's not fair, you coming to me now," I whispered, my back hitting the wall. I had not realized I had been moving away from him. "I gave you up. I broke the curse because I gave you up!"

That froze him in his steps.

Another sob shook me, and I wiped my eyes on the sleeve of my gown, for all the good it did me. "It was everything. I had to be selfless. I didn't know—I had to give it all up. My hair . . . my life . . . *you*. It was the only way to warm a cold heart."

"You do not have a cold heart, Misa."

"But I did!" I cried. "I did, and I-I don't know . . . I don't know . . ."

He looked at me with glossy, forlorn eyes, his shoulders slumping. "You don't know if accepting me will bring the curse back."

I pressed my lips together in a futile effort to keep from crying and nodded.

I couldn't bear the agony on his face. I slid down the wall to the floor and covered my face with my hands, tears pouring over my fingers. My face grew hot and swollen, and my breaths came in short chokes, but I could not stop.

Then he knelt in front of me, gently pulling my hand away from my face.

Liquid thunder raced from each of his fingertips through my skin, boiling my blood and turning my pounding heart inside out. My breath caught in my throat. My tears stopped. The lightest touch . . . but it engulfed me.

Hesitant, I closed my trembling fingers around his. How did I think I knew what warmth truly felt like before this moment?

"Misa," he whispered.

"I love you," I said, those three words bringing tears anew.

His lips pulled into a sad smile, and he touched my cheek, wiping away a tear with his thumb. His skin burned against mine. How dearly I wanted to lunge into his arms, to cry into his neck, to kiss his full lips and forget I had ever existed before that moment.

But I had been cold for *so long.*

"The last thing I want is to hurt you," he said, lowering his head so he could look directly into my eyes. "Take whatever time you need to consider; I don't need an answer now. Whatever you decide, I will be content. Nothing you can say will change my heart."

I lifted my hand to touch his, but fear urged me to drop it. "Tomorrow—"

"They will wait for you, if you wish it."

I swallowed, my throat sore and tight. "I'm sorry," I whispered.

But he shook his head. "You have nothing to apologize for. Please, for once, consider yourself before me or anyone else." He pulled his hand away, and I grew cold without it—a different kind of cold than what had plagued me for four years. A hollow, winding cold. "Take your time. I will be waiting."

He stood and moved for the door. I reached for him but not before he had vanished from my sight, the door closing between us. A door only I could open. I stared at it a long time, empty and lost, tears running steady rivers down my cheeks.

My crying and the sludge of emotions fatigued me greatly, but I did not sleep that night. I felt a heavy scale hanging from either arm. I only needed to lean one way or another, but which way was right?

I questioned if my conversation with Lo had actually happened, or if I were in some cruel torrent of a dream. Loved me. He loved me. The most remarkable, kind, generous, and beautiful man I had ever known *loved me*. I could not have mistranslated his words, for he had spoken them in Northlander.

Yet the shadow of the curse haunted me, and even with my windows open and the night's warm breeze filtering into the room, it only took closing my eyes to feel my blood turn to ice, to feel the unyielding sting of winter on my skin, to see the gloom of that perpetual storm over my head. I feared that, should my curse return, I would never be rid of it again. I would never feel the sun on my face or the warmth of a bed. I would never enjoy a meal or a bath. I would never see my family or Euwan. And I would never savor the touch of Lo's hand on my cheek, for he would be unable to touch me without a shield.

But the love I held for him defied everything I knew. I had fancied men before, but never had I experienced a sentiment like this, a passion that could rip me in two if I breathed too quickly.

I stood and paced the room by starlight, the thick fibers of the carpeting brushing my feet, nearly healed of their cold-caused cracks. Healed. I hugged myself, warm arms against a warm chest with a lively, if vexed, heart. Could I risk losing that now that I was whole?

Yet Lo had shamed himself and broken a centuries-long tradition for the sake of being with a woman whom he believed had no chance of being normal again. But no matter how strong his feelings for me, no man could be happy with a woman followed by frost, who could not be intimate with him or bear him children, who could not so much as sit down for tea without summoning the sharp winds and frigid snows of a deep-winter tempest.

I considered my curse and recited Mordan's wording of it over and over again to a dark room lit by a single candle, but I found nothing within it to help me. When a curse broke, was it gone? Or could the breaking be undone, just as the curse had been undone? Did a curse last forever, lingering in remission like a lifelong disease, or could it be cured for good? Did my curse have a treatment, or an antidote?

I dressed and left my room with the first light of dawn, the sun still well hidden behind Zareed's sandy hills and jagged mountains. I passed several guards on duty, none of which were Lo. Fortunately the guards did not ask me to explain myself—I had proven my loyalty to Imad—and let me outside without question.

A cooler breeze caressed my face as I descended the steps into a dim and empty city. I adjusted my head scarf. I had no specific destination in mind; I merely walked east, keeping the jagged mountains behind the palace close to my right as my guide.

My thoughts ran rampant. I had already given up Lo once. I should be content with that and return to my home. But hadn't I already given up that, too? My home, my family, my life before Mordan? My winter had given water to Zareed. What if Imad had miscalculated, and the drought lasted through next year, and the next, and the next?

I looked out over the brick homes and canvas tents of the city, large and small, lit by a growing, rosy light. If my curse returned, I could continue to help Zareed and its people. They would never go hungry or thirsty again. Lo, Imad, Aamina, Eyan . . . all of them. I could care for them until death claimed me.

My steps slowed. The pain and the cold would be with me forever, and with them, Sadriel. I owed Sadriel a great debt, in the end, but could I knowingly invite Death back into my life, and into Lo's? Could I balance those two men, one who could kill me and one whom I could kill? I thought of the hunter from the mountains and grimaced.

Pausing in my walk, I found myself near a natural alcove in the rocks, a camel stable not far to my left. One of the great animals regarded me briefly. No fear in its eyes. I peered toward the eastern horizon, red and pink and gold. The sunrises here were so beautiful. So full of color. As I watched, the first sliver of sunlight slipped over the horizon, washing away shadows and fighting back the deep blue of night. It touched me, and I closed my eyes, savoring its warmth. The sun on my face. That had been Lo's wish for me.

I returned to the palace as the city awakened, my body weary and begging me for rest. After slipping through the entrance, I started up the grand stairs to the second floor just as the new shift of guards came to replace the ones at the door. I turned back and spied Lo among them. My stomach fluttered. He looked tired, older. He must not have slept, either.

He glanced my way, unsurprised to see me. Our eyes met, and in his I saw a strange depth, as though I stared into a black and stormy sea. Pressing my lips together, I turned away and hurried up the stairs, a hard lump rising in my throat.

When Aamina came to my chambers, I told her I was ill, and I surely looked it. She brought me water and broth and left me to sleep, which I did—in and out, hardly able to tell dream from reality. Waking or sleeping, I thought of Lo. And Mordan, Sadriel, my parents, my sister, Ashlen, and Euwan. I thought of Imad and Zareed, and the weights on my arms continued to tug me back and forth, cracking the foundation that held me.

Hours passed this way. Aamina brought me more food, but I had little appetite and could barely stomach a mouthful. I closed my eyes and saw Lo crouching before me, felt his fingers on my jaw. I traced the touch. I saw him at the front doors of the palace, meeting my gaze with such . . . pain. How I loved him. How it hurt.

After some time I stood at my window, looking out onto Mac'Hliah, which glowed with the late afternoon. I opened the window and reached out my hand as far as I could, past the short eaves so that sunlight could dance on my fingers. Hot air crept over the windowsill and into my room. Again I thought of Lo's wish.

Retracting my hand, I turned back to my room and spied my saddlebags at the edge of my bed, packed and ready for the trip to Euwan. I knelt beside them and searched their contents until I found the last book Lo had given me: *Garen's Wish*. I opened its worn spine and turned its aged pages, then read through the story again, lingering once more on the passage Lo had highlighted.

Garen had wanted to know the wish of his heart so badly he'd asked the genie for the answer, knowing very well it could be something unobtainable. He had risked everything for the chance of happiness.

Lo had given up so much for me. Could I not take this one chance—this one risk—for him?

After shutting the book, I changed into my mauve dress and brushed my hair, not bothering with the head scarf. I looked at myself in the small mirror over the empty dresser. I looked tired but healthy, peach colored and golden haired, green eyes free of violet bags, pink lips instead of blue. I looked at myself and committed the image to memory, for I knew it might be the last time I saw myself this way. I planned to do one last, selfish thing, even if it cost me everything else.

This, I did for me.

I walked through the hallways, my steps in beat with my pounding heart. I stopped a young serving boy once to ask where the captain of the guard was, but he did not know. Still, he gave me directions to Lo's quarters, and after some searching I found them in the basement of the palace, about as far from my own room as one could get without stepping outside.

Narrow windows close to the ceiling illuminated the long hallway carpeted in red, doors lining either side of it. I passed one guard whom I recognized and nodded to him briefly, then began counting doors.

Seven, eight, nine. Lo's room.

I lifted my hand to knock, but bit my lip, hesitant. How to say what I felt inside? How did one put the fear of winter and the hope of music into words? How could I possibly explain the torrent of desperation and love eddying in my soul? The absolute adoration that blinded me?

I twisted the doorknob slowly, pushed the door open, and peered into the room.

Like the hallway, the room was dark save for the evening sunlight that filtered through narrow windows against the ceiling, these ones silhouetted by the plants that lined the palace's base. For a moment I thought the room unoccupied, but my eyes made out the form sleeping on the bed on top of the covers. I recognized Lo's earrings.

After shutting the door behind me, I tiptoed to his bedside. He didn't wear a shirt, and in the dim lighting I found the long scar on his ribs he had described to me. It certainly didn't look like a shallow cut. He had others as well—a faint line to the right of his navel, puckered tissue almost hidden by an arm that looked like a poorly treated arrow wound. There were other, smaller marks almost too faint to see, criss-crossing this way and that like cat scratches.

I sat on the edge of his mattress, soft and slow, but Lo was a trained soldier and captain of the guard, and he awoke easily. Startled, because he shot upright and almost knocked heads with me.

He blinked several times. "Misa?"

I pursed my lips, but the smile came anyway. Hesitantly I reached toward him and touched his shoulder, the skin smooth and warm. I ran three fingertips down his arm, over firm muscle and into the crook of his elbow.

My pulse pounded in my head. I shivered.

He watched me, wordless.

"There were so many times," I whispered, tracing my way back to his shoulder, "that I wished I could touch you, even if only in thanks or play." My fingers crawled up his neck, grazed the short, dark hair on his jaw, caressed smooth, full lips. I felt ready to burst, as though my very spirit pushed against my skin.

He lifted his hand and clasped mine, then kissed each fingertip. His hands were rough and calloused, but so very warm.

I gently pulled from his grasp, touched either side of his face, and pushed my fingers into the thick ringlets of his hair. Smelled the sweet sandalwood that lingered on his skin. My heart settled and for once beat steady.

"I love you," I whispered, leaning until our noses touched. Tilting my head, I carefully brushed my lips against his.

His hands found my shoulders and pulled me into him, pressing his mouth against mine, the smell of cardamom and sandalwood flooding my senses. I kissed him, knotting my hands into his soft hair.

I kissed him, and I stayed warm.

CHAPTER 29

Three Months Later

The ride back to Euwan is longer than I remember it being; perhaps because Lo and I do not ride at an army's pace, or because I fear too much time in a saddle may harm the small life growing inside me. Maybe we move slowly because I tend to linger at the places I recognize, remembering the time I spent there and telling Lo stories of my first three years in the cold. Tales that, for some reason, I look upon with a strange sense of fondness.

I can't believe how nervous I am when Heaven's Tear Lake finally surfaces on the horizon. Soon I can make out Euwan in the distance, the village of my childhood. A place I have not seen for four and a half years. My hands sweat where they hold my dun mare's reins.

"Are you ready?" Lo asks me, slowing his black gelding.

I nod and tuck a stray piece of hair behind my ear, fallen out from its short tail at the nape of my neck. "I'm ready. Are you?"

Lo doesn't answer, and I laugh at him. "The children's stories of Southlander mercenaries are not too severe; the worst anyone will do is hide from you."

He smirks at me and whips his reins, trotting his horse over the rocky road. I guide my mare after him, and it's all I can do to restrain myself from galloping.

We reach the west edge of Euwan, where Cuper Tode's mercantile lies. Lo dismounts and helps me do the same, his hands on my waist. Together we walk our horses down the packed dirt road.

"It's all the same," I say, scanning the town. "But it looks so much smaller."

Maddie Jesron steps out of the mercantile and stares at Lo with wide eyes, looking ready to faint. I do not think she recognizes me, but I wave regardless.

Jacks Wineer—Ashlen's father—comes up the road on a new horse, looking very much the same save for a mustache and a few gray hairs around his temples. He stops at the sight of Lo, then squints at me. He nearly falls off his horse when I smile at him.

"Hello, Mr. Wineer," I say, grinning.

He doesn't respond for a moment, but after we've passed I hear him say, "S-Smitha! Smitha . . . Maddie, is that Smitha Ronson?"

Lo chuckles under his breath.

"Is this funny?" I ask, smiling. We pass Coltin Drayes—how big he's gotten!—on his front porch, and he stares at us long and hard.

"They are very forward with their emotions, Northlanders," Lo says. "You are a ghost to them."

"Smitha?"

I slow and turn to face the person who called out to me. Ashlen stands there, at the fork in the road, a little rounder in face and very much pregnant, her long hair pulled back into a bun. She looks like she's seen a specter, and I nearly cry at the sight of her.

"Ashlen!" I shout, dropping my horse's reins and running to her. She hesitates at first, but then she waddles to meet me, her arms open wide. We embrace, and she squeezes me so hard I cough.

"It *is* you!" she exclaims, tears in her eyes. "Smitha, look at you! You're not . . . You're . . ."

"It's broken, Ashlen," I say, holding her shoulders. "Oh, Ashlen, I've thought so much of you. I'm so sorry for everything. Your brother, is he well?"

"Sorry for *what?*" she laughs, hugging me once more. "I never thought I'd see you again! Oh, Smitha, Smitha! He's fine. We're all fine."

A couple passing by—the Magalies—pause nearby and stare. Mrs. Magalie leaps a foot into the air and runs back up the road, shouting something I cannot hear. I laugh and pull away from Ashlen.

"You're pregnant!" I say. "Ashlen, look at you!"

"Alvin Modder!" she says. "And it's our second one!"

"When did you get married?"

"Two years ago last week," she says, grabbing my hands and squeezing them. Glancing past my shoulder, she sobers.

I turn and spy Lo, who is now holding my horse's reins along with his.

Gripping Ashlen's hands, I pull her down the road to him. "Ashlen, this is my husband, Lo. Lo, this is Ashlen, my best friend growing up."

"The one with the handtalk," Lo says, nodding.

Ashlen's eyes bug. Leaning toward me, she whispers, "He speaks Northlander?"

I laugh. "Better than most Northlanders," I say, twining my fingers through Lo's. "I best hurry, or word of my arrival will reach my home before I do. Do they . . . Does my family still live there?"

Ashlen nods, eyes sparkling.

I squeeze her hand once more before releasing it. "We'll talk soon. I have so many stories to tell you." And so little time to share them before we return to the Southlands.

"I know you do," she says, regarding Lo with wide eyes. "Get on, then! Not much farther!"

She hugs me one more time before I take the reins from Lo and lead him down the road and around the hill I so often climbed as a shortcut to the Wineers'. It's early evening, about dinnertime, so most people are inside their homes. I'm grateful for it—I don't think either Lo or I could handle a mob of questioning people, no matter how badly I want to see them.

I spy my barn, and my old home tucked behind it, the willow-wacks tucked off to the side. "There it is," I say, pointing. "My old home."

"Misa."

"I'm okay." I squeeze his fingers.

I tie my mare to the post outside the barn, and Lo does the same. We walk to the front door. The smell of chicken and garlic wafts from the windows, and I can hear soft chatter inside.

Lo kisses the top of my head. I open the door without knocking.

They sit there as if I never left: Father at the head of the table, Mother at the end, Marrine with her back to me. All three of them turn at the sound of the door.

"Papa, Mom, Marrine," I say, taking my first step into the house, "I'm home."

ACKNOWLEDGMENTS

I have many heartfelt thanks to offer for those who have helped with this book. This tale has been my favorite to write so far, but it wouldn't have gotten where it is without the aid of some amazing people!

I want to first thank all three of my sisters—Danny, Andy, and Alex—for reading and helping me with this story. This is the only book I've written that all of my siblings read!

Of course a big thanks to my beta readers Lindsey, Hayley, Juliana, Whitney, Andrew, and Jennifer. They critiqued this book for me three years before it ever got published.

Thank you to my agent, Marlene. She rejected this manuscript a couple years before signing me, but she represented it anyway! And thank you to Jason Kirk, Angela Polidoro, and the 47North team for shaping this manuscript into something publishable. (And thank you to Matt, my copyeditor. Copyeditors don't get enough thanks nowadays.)

Much love and appreciation to my (smoking-hot) husband for all his support.

And, as always, my utmost thanks to my Heavenly Father for blessing me with such an awesome career!

ABOUT THE AUTHOR

Born in Salt Lake City, Charlie N. Holmberg was raised a Trekkie alongside three sisters who also have boy names. She graduated from BYU, plays the ukulele, owns too many pairs of glasses, and hopes to one day own a dog.